# LEAVING
## LOSAPAS

# LEAVING
# LOSAPAS

*Roland Merullo*

HOUGHTON MIFFLIN COMPANY   BOSTON   1991

For information about permission to reproduce selections from
this book, write to Permissions, Houghton Mifflin Company,
2 Park Street, Boston, Massachusetts 02108.

Library of Congress Cataloging-in-Publication Data

Merullo, Roland.
    Leaving Losapas / Roland Merullo
       p.     cm.
    ISBN 0-395-53377-5
    I. Title.
  PS3563.E748L4   1991   90-42880
  813'.54—dc20  CIP

Printed in the United States of America

BP 10 9 8 7 6 5 4 3 2 1

ACKNOWLEDGMENTS

First thanks to Amanda for her love, understanding, and patience.

Special thanks to Michael Miller for his
tireless encouragement and wise counsel.

I am grateful also to those friends who
read the manuscript and offered sugges-
tions, especially: Dean Crawford, Peter
Grudin, Donald Nitchie, Bill Ryan, Gerard
Sikorski, and Brent Filson.

Thanks to Sergeant Raymond Maya for
his hospitality, to the Edna St. Vincent
Millay Colony for a month of perfect working conditions, and to Anthony Pierni for
helping a young boy see the world.

*For Roland, Eileen, and Amanda*

I had the good fortune to grow up in Revere, Massachusetts, and to spend some time in the islands of Micronesia, two places where love and generosity still flourish. Though there may be some superficial resemblance, the locations and characters described in this book should not be mistaken for real places and real people. I have taken great liberties with the facts. Averill Beach and Losapas do not exist beyond these pages and beyond the realm of the imagination. The Losapan language used here has something in common with a certain Trukese dialect, but whole words and phrases are pure invention.

It occurs to me that the hope of persisting, even after fate would seem to have led us back into a state of nonexistence, is the noblest of our sentiments.

— *Johann Goethe*

Cures take strange shapes.

— *Losapan proverb*

# Prologue

MARKIN WONDERED if he
was running out of places to escape to, if the world was backing
him into a corner. The place he was headed for now was nothing
more than a dot on even the best world maps, a few acres of sand
and green in a gigantic sea. A supply ship stopped there once a
month. Every few years, when a particularly strong typhoon
tore across the central Pacific on its way to Guam or Indonesia or
the Philippines, this place — Losapas — would capture a line or
two of coverage in the world news, then disappear again, slip
back into the shadow of undevelopment. Losapas promised
exactly the kind of life he was looking for —anonymous, plain,
far from anyone who knew. Still, it worried him: from such a
place he would have nowhere left to run. He was approaching
an end of one kind or another.

He walked on and thought about how things happened. Three years ago he had never been out of New England. A year ago he had never even heard of Micronesia. A month ago he had bumped into a muscular, brown-skinned spearfisherman on the stone dock in Sapuk, and here he was, running again, carrying his fifty-pound seabag down the middle of Owen Town's only paved road at four o'clock in the morning so the supply ship wouldn't leave without him, being drawn forward through the mystery of his life by another chance meeting, another casual remark, the same type of thing that had brought him to Micronesia in the first place.

It was a hot night in Owen Town, the air heavy and still. Soon the rain would start, not at all like rain started at home, with a few sprinkles of warning, but suddenly, violently, pouring from the first minute, tearing through banana leaves and palm fronds, and spawning small, brutal rivers in the dust, cutting ragged scars into the hillsides from Weichap to Monoluk, drumming on the corrugated iron roofs of clustered plywood shacks, filling the fifty-five-gallon drums people drank from, soaking the chickens and tethered pigs, washing all kinds of debris out into the open, then down to the sea.

Twenty minutes and it would be over. The trees would drip. Immediately the air would turn heavy again and warm, but now the dark harbor would be muddied with run-off, and the mosquitoes would be out again and Owen Town would be littered with cigarette wrappers and paper boxes, styrofoam cups, brown nut husks and palm fronds — all of its garbage flushed into view. A few stars would reappear, and the nation of dogs that roamed the alleys searching for scraps would set up a furious howling.

It was an odd place to have run to, he thought. He was an odd person, a white among browns, the perpetual outsider. He was reminded of Averill Beach, a place he believed he would never see again. His father had told him once that you loved or hated a place because you loved or hated yourself in that place.

That seemed true. It seemed to make sense that he was hoping to find on Losapas the self he loved, a better self, something long ago lost. That was the thin hope that drew him farther and farther from anywhere the modern world might know. That was what kept him running.

A Micronesian passed him in the darkness, barefoot, making no sound. The man said something Markin only half understood, a warning of rain, it sounded like. There was nothing but kindness in the voice but Markin took it as an omen. In the dusty air of the Shipping Company yard he encountered a strange memory, a piece of loose history: before the white man came, there had been no rats in Micronesia and no venereal disease.

He could see the ship now, the *Micro Dawn*, brightly lit and held to the dock with thick loops of braided rope. For some reason the sight of it brought him to the conclusion that — along with penicillin and canned food — the white man was probably always bringing something like rats and venereal disease, some new plague or vermin. On the big scale, at least, there seemed to be no such thing as progress, no ground gained and held, only changes of scenery. If that was the case on the smaller scale, within a person, then why go on?

But he went on. At the base of the gangplank that led from the dusty lot to the *Micro Dawn*'s lower deck, he looked up and saw a white-haired, stoop-shouldered old man, half of his face illuminated in the dock lights, staring down at him as if he were a rat-bringer, an infected one, the kind of son no father needed.

Markin stopped and put his seabag down and came that close to not going to Losapas at all.

# PART ONE

# 1

THE PATH was a shadow. As Markin stepped cautiously from stone to root, from root to patch of sand, from patch of sand into complete darkness, his mind was occupied by a single thought, the distillation of an idea that had haunted him for nearly a decade: it occurred to him that, at some point in the unfolding of history, humanity had separated into two distinct halves, two worlds — those who could see in the dark and those who could not.

Ahead of him walked Mahalis, one of the sighted ones. Crouching, holding his club upright so that its tip hovered next to his ear, Mahalis moved fluently through the darkness without tripping over the mangrove roots or stubbing his toes on the coral stones or bumping his head against the thick breadfruit limbs. From time to time he would glance over his shoulder and give furtive hand signals. Then his lithe body would return to its crouch, his eyes would sweep the tree roots, the club would float along beside him, dipping and swaying to avoid Ayao's dark wooden arms. Markin followed like an apprentice, a civilized hunter, too white and tall and pensive to be of much use in the jungle night.

Ayao, the food island, was separated from Losapas, the people island, by a shallow inlet. From a boat at sea they appeared to be joined, to form a solitary, dark green hedge. As one moved closer, a shelf of white beach rose into view beneath the hedge and the monochroic green speckled: some of the palm fronds showed lighter, lime-colored; banana plants drooped along the lower tier. But it was only after a visitor passed through the cut in the reef and sailed well into the lagoon that the mouth of the inlet became visible. There was not one island here, but a matching pair — tiny, ellipsoidal pieces of land that had coagulated on a crescent of reef framed by empty horizons. Losapas bore a woman's scent, a mixture of ripe fruit, woodsmoke, and human waste, the rich odor of fish and sweat and topsoil. Ayao was acrid; it could be tasted at the back of the mouth. At night especially the soil there emitted a bitter, sulphurous smell. Markin imagined it was the sexual lure of robber crabs visiting each other, perfumed, in the darkness that was their light, clacking and clattering from tunnel to tunnel, courting beneath a deadly surface.

Mahalis stopped and held up his left hand.

Markin stood still on the path and tried not to breathe.

In a moonlit path eight feet in front of him something pushed up through a hole in the ground. A crab emerged, unhinging its legs, squirming its shell out of the sand. It paused a moment, as if mistrustful of the moonlight, then clattered across the path toward another tunnel. Mahalis took a quick half step and brought his club down with a snap, crushing the shell and killing the crab before Markin was even sure he'd seen it. Markin held open the copra sack and Mahalis deposited the kill.

For two hours they crisscrossed Ayao this way — stalking, listening, striking — the burlap sack growing heavier. Sometimes Mahalis stopped, waited half a minute, then moved on with his club still poised. Once or twice his blows fell late, behind the crab's hind legs, and the prey disappeared down its chute. But a dozen other times the snap and thud echoed among the trees, the sack opened, Markin collected another meal.

When they had made their last pass across the island and were returning to the boat, Mahalis took the sack and let Markin lead, club up, feet feeling along the path. In the brighter moonlight of the beach he finally spotted a crab. He chased it madly across the sand, zigging and zagging behind his terrified prey, gaining on it too slowly as it made for its hole, at the last moment diving after it, arms outstretched. His chest thumped on soft ground. There was sand in his mouth. He jumped up and cursed and slammed the club against the entrance to the tunnel several times, but this little tantrum made no difference. The chase was over.

"*Esse lefil-ifil*," Mahalis said calmly from somewhere below Markin's shoulder. "Not importan'."

They loaded the clubs and copra sack into the outrigger canoe, shoved off, and drifted into the inlet without dipping their paddles. The water was perfectly flat; in the moonlight they saw a fin glide toward them, a blacktip. The shark patrolled the shoreline for a few minutes, then slipped beneath the canoe and meandered north toward the darkness of the open sea.

"It is time for you and Ninake to have children," Mahalis said, watching the fin blend into the night. They drifted onto a sandbar and the bow stuck. Neither of them made any effort to free it. "If you want, I will speak to Pwa, the father spirit, for you."

There was something not quite human about Mahalis' voice, Markin thought, listening to the soft Losapan syllables float away into the night. *Porausel Pwa emwal.* It was too sweet, too smooth, as if a great and mysterious power were being forced through a tube, steamlike, and some kind of sophisticated valve were turning the roar into a clear, steady note. Mahalis was small in a race of small men: he stood an inch or two over five feet, weighed less than a hundred and thirty pounds. His arms and legs were muscular; a modest collar of fat pressed out against his belt. Like all middle-aged Losapan men, he wore his hair short and shaved every other morning, holding the bare razor blade in his fingertips. The only features that distinguished him from the rest of the men on the island were this otherworldly voice and his lineage: Mahalis was a starman, son of a starman, grandson and great-grandson of starmen. On certain moonless nights, the Losapans believed, he could look into the sky and read the map of the future there, foresee typhoons and deaths and unexpected arrivals, have a word with one of the twelve spirits who governed the universe. Like his Micronesian ancestors, he could sail across hundreds of miles of ocean guided only by the constellations, and land on an island the size of a city block. Markin had seen him handle a boat on the open sea at night; there was no arguing that. He wasn't sure, one way or the other, about the twelve spirits.

"I don't think we're ready for Pwa just yet," he said, half turning on the wooden seat.

"Why not?"

With the tip of his paddle Markin pushed off from the sandbar and headed the canoe in the direction of Mahalis' beach. "Pwa is angry with me."

"Why?"

Markin took one hard stroke and kept silent. Not the right time to talk about it, he told himself, not the right place; though he had understood for years now that there was never going to be a right time or place. There wasn't a father spirit in the universe he hadn't offended.

"You are like a second father to Elias," Mahalis told him.

"Elias and I are friends."

"A second father," Mahalis corrected, then he paused in thought. "He wants to go to Owen Town again."

Markin made no reply.

"He wants to see trucks. That is the only thing he talks about. I don't have the money to take him."

"Next time I go I'll take him," Markin said, concentrating on the black water in front of him.

"When will you go?"

"Six months."

"Most people would go every month if they could. If they had as much money as you, Marr-keen, I think they would go almost every month."

This, Markin knew from other discussions on similar nights, was Mahalis' favorite method of interrogation. He took hold of an idea — tonight, for some reason, it was fatherhood — and squeezed it relentlessly, pressing his questions like an Oriental master until the truth was wrung out. A bad time for it, Markin thought, steering the canoe around a disturbance on the placid black surface. It was high tide; the tops of the coral knobs were all but invisible.

"Marr-keen."

"What."

"Why don't you like the District Center?"

It was like dealing with a chess master or a slick lawyer. Your attention would be diverted by predictable pawn moves or simple, apparently straightforward questions. You would begin to relax. He would pounce.

"You can get Merikan food in the District Center." A few seconds of silence. "You can shit in a toilet."

"Maybe I don't want to shit in a toilet, Mahalis. Why don't *you* go to the District Center? You sold a lot of copra last month. You're always telling me you like American food."

"Toilets worry me."

Markin stopped paddling and looked over his shoulder. "Bullshit artist," he said in English.

"*Ballshed ardis,*" Mahalis repeated happily. He took a deliberate stroke and let the canoe glide. "Those toilets are dangerous. I am afraid of being sucked in. A person could drown."

Markin knifed his paddle into the water and a fine spray arced toward the stern.

Mahalis ducked and grinned, a grin too large for his face. "I will tell you the truth," he said, holding up a hand in mock surrender, "if you will tell me the truth."

"You first."

"All right." Mahalis cleared his throat. "The District Center is a dirty place. The water is dirty, the air is dirty. Even the people — dirty. You can't fish there. You can't sleep. You can barely see the stars. It makes you feel you are not alive."

Markin nodded.

"Now you, Marr-keen."

Markin cleared his throat. "The women there cover their breasts."

Mahalis laughed quietly and shook his head. "Marr-keen is an eel," he said. "*Ballshed ardis.*"

Satisfied with a stalemate, Markin took up his paddle and turned forward again.

"Marr-keen."

"What."

"Are you going to stay here, on Losapas?"

The question caught him in mid-stroke. For one long moment he was too surprised to answer. "I've been here almost seven years, Mahalis. You still have to ask me that?"

"I have to ask you because if you're leaving I won't summon Pwa."

They could make out Mahalis' house now, a concrete box with a corrugated iron roof. In front of it stood the thatched shelter where the family ate and played cards. To the right beyond the water tank, at the edge of the trees, was Markin's "typhoon hut," similar to Mahalis' house but smaller and protected by a foot-thick concrete roof.

"The ship is coming tomorrow," Mahalis said, changing course without warning.

Markin brought the paddle in too close and pinched his knuckles against the gunwale.

"Belinda heard it on the radio."

"When?"

"Before we left."

They beached the canoe and dragged the bulging copra sack up the sandy slope.

"Why did you wait so long to tell me?"

Mahalis leaned the paddles against the thatched shelter and turned to face him. "Because if I told you earlier, you would have been no good hunting crabs."

"I was no good anyway."

"You would have stayed in your house sulking, getting ready to go spearfishing tomorrow off the deep beach. I know you, Marr-keen."

Markin felt something twist into a knot just below his navel, but he said nothing. Mahalis patted him on the arm. "Drink coconut milk before you go to sleep or the crab spirits will haunt you in your dreams."

Markin looked at him. "Mahalis."

"What."

"Fuck the crab spirits."

Mahalis shrugged his eyebrows twice and smiled.

Markin turned and walked toward the spring behind the hut.

One week after his arrival on Losapas, Markin had moved out of Mahalis' house and into the vacant typhoon hut. A day later, using saplings and twine and precious sheets of plastic, Mahalis had built him a bathing stall against the back of the hut. Markin protested: he wanted no special treatment. If he was going to stay on Losapas he would eat what the Losapans ate, do the work they did, bathe where they bathed — at the brackish mid-island wells. Mahalis demurred. Markin insisted. A pained expression came over the brown face, the eyes moved to one side and down, the mouth twisted. Something resembling the edge of a man's patience came briefly into view, then vanished. It was as close as they would ever come to arguing; Markin bathed in the new stall. He had deferred out of politeness, but gradually, over a period of years, he came to see the sense in it: if he was ever going to feel at home on Losapas, he would have to hold on to some of his separateness, his Americanness. Mahalis, of course, would never come out and say anything that directly. He preferred to communicate in a kind of code, to convey information through a complex system of suggestion, hint, facial expression, an occasional vague remark. It was the Losapan way. Sometimes Markin thought it would drive him mad.

He filled the plastic washbasin, carried it into the stall, and began to soap his feet and legs. This latest session of advice and interrogation puzzled him. Why bring up the subject of having children now, tonight, after six and a half childless years with Ninake? And what was this about leaving Losapas? They had never talked about that before, never even joked about it. It was not an option he needed to be reminded of.

A dog barked once in the distance. Markin stopped moving and listened, but the only sounds were the chirring of crickets and the faint rumble of surf on the back beach. As he returned to his washing, something disturbed the night again and the crickets hushed. Branches scuffed the walls of the hut. He pushed the plastic aside but saw only a textured darkness, palm trunks swaying in the rising breeze like thin, tousled-haired girls. The night was teasing him. He stripped off his shorts, lathered his torso, arms, and face, and began splashing away the sweat and dirt and smell of crab.

A hand reached through the curtain and touched bare skin. Markin's legs sprang reflexively, his head bumped concrete. Ninake's quiet laughter filled the stall. He swept the plastic aside and pulled her in beside him.

"*Le-pong al-lim,*" she said, looking him up and down.

He untied her skirt and hung it over his shorts on the sapling. Gently, like a man bathing something fragile and precious, he washed her feet, rinsed them, ran a soapy hand between her legs, then in small circles across her belly, breasts, and face. She shivered and turned so he could soap her back and the bolt of black hair that hung to her waist. When he'd finished he dumped the last of the water over her head and wrapped them both in the ragged towel.

They made love on the woven pandanus mat he slept on, making no sound that could be heard outside the small hut. Ninake kept her eyes open and locked on his, as she always did. If he tried to rest his face in the soft flesh of her neck she would lift his head and stare into him as steady as moonlight, greeting him across the small, unchangeable distance that always separated and linked them. Tonight she stared and stared and stared until neither of them could bear it any longer. Finally he saw her lips move apart and her eyes slowly close. She squeezed him around the ribs and lifted herself off the mat with him and the softest sound escaped her, and then him, and she seemed to fight against something once, then lie still, breathing hard, quiet, coated with sweat. They rested against each other for a time, then went out to the spring and rinsed each other off, a perfect silence between them, as if they were one person and had always been that way. Markin thought of places he had been and might now be and he offered up a wordless thanks.

Inside, the hut was cooling. They lay beneath a sheet, unable to take the final step into sleep, listening to Ulua's dogs baying at the ocean darkness, as though there were someone or something out there to hear them.

"I think you will be going home soon," Ninake said.

"I am home."

"I think you will be going back to Merika."

He ran the words through his mind several times, searching for a clue, a hint of feeling, but as always her tone was strictly factual. Usually this earnestness made him happy; tonight,

coming on the heels of the conversation with Mahalis, it unnerved him.

"Will you take me with you?"

"You wouldn't like America." He thought of Tommy Mario,
a neighbor in Averill Beach who'd taken home a bride from
the Korean War. Over the side fence on summer evenings
Mr. Mario would complain about all the ways his wife had
changed — gained weight, lost interest in sex, taken to buying things like electric can openers and electric toothbrushes,
gadgets he couldn't afford. "She's gone electric-crazy," he'd
say, squeezing the tops of the fence pickets and pursing his
lips.

"You'd go electric-crazy," Markin said, trying to make light of
it. "You'd turn into a different person."

It was a long time before Ninake spoke again, and he realized
she'd taken him literally.

"The ship is coming tomorrow."

"Mahalis told me."

She rolled onto her side, ran a fingertip down to his navel, and
began tracing long, sweeping patterns there, tattooing him with
underwater reeds, octopus arms, sea snakes. "If I ask you to stay
away from the back beach tomorrow, will you?"

"No."

"If I ask you to help me read the medicines?"

"Not tomorrow, Ninake."

"The waves have been smashing the reef all week."

Markin concentrated on her finger and imagined she was
redesigning his anatomy, reclaiming the swamp of bile and half-
digested food, planting tulip fields. His new interior would be
like the world of her mind, a place as neat and intricate and
definite as a petal, a world that could not be more different from
the one he knew.

His thoughts fluttered around the arrival of the supply ship
but could find no resting place, no sensible emotion to cling to.
Every month it was the same torture.

"You are selfish with your death," he heard her say before she fell asleep.

He dreamed of Averill Beach, of the brick funeral home on Atlantic Street with the big concrete urns on either side of the front entrance. He smelled the sweet air — flowers, a trace of formaldehyde, that vague tobacco and perspiration and cotton scent children associate with crowds of adults. Rows of folding chairs faced the casket. The room thrummed with conversation — quiet, respectful tones hovering near the body, a half-stifled laugh or exclamation lifting, like a reassertion of life, from the far corners. He felt his father's hand resting on his shoulder, guiding him across the carpet, through the stares, toward the open coffin. "We have to be strong now," his father said in a voice that had been broken apart. His aunt Amelia appeared in the aisle and clasped his face to her bosom, nearly suffocating him in powder and perfume. When she released him he was aware of faces all around — Angela, her eyes a wet, black-flecked blue; Stevie's squirrel cheeks; the stone-sculpture jaw of Carmine Panechieso. He floated past them, approached the coffin, and knelt next to his father. There she was! The necklace he and his father had given her had been arranged neatly around her throat and she was wearing her good blue dress and her hair was curled up over her shoulders just as always. If it hadn't been for the skin he could have made himself believe she was only sleeping. If it hadn't been for the skin it would not have been so bad, because at last he could see her again, almost lean over and kiss her. Next to him he could feel his father trembling, then sobbing. He, too, started to cry, but even the lens of tears could not make the skin right again. It was hard, like wax or plastic, and it would always be hard and the shoulder would always be crumpled like that, the lips pressed stiffly together. His eyes fled her face. They ran along the left arm, and as they reached the folded hands where someone had draped a string of rosary beads, a robber crab slipped out from the lower half of the casket. It crawled up over his mother's breast and throat and onto her face — which changed into his father's face — a handsome, defiant mask into which the creature disappeared.

Markin sat up abruptly and listened to his shout echo in the hut. Ninake stirred. He sank back onto the mat and lay there, considering the spirit world.

## 2

EARLY MORNING on Losapas was symphonic. At the first suggestion of dawn, roosters stepped out of the emerald underbrush, chortling and squawking and strutting about as if proclaiming the first day of creation. Their trumpeting woke the dogs, who woke the children, who spilled from cool houses like a naked army determined to conquer the solemn Pacific night, marching across the island, shrieking beneath the windows of sleeping adults, singing new numbers out loud and in unison.

On Ship Days it was even worse, a cacophony approaching chaos. An hour before dawn Markin was awakened by a four-year-old sergeant screaming orders from the sandy clearing in front of his house. *"Cahndy!"* the girl shouted. *"Marr-keen, Cahndy! Gumb!"*

He sat back against the concrete wall, listening to the hilarity outside, watching the room slowly fill with light. It was a Ship Day, the closest claim Losapas could make to a national holiday. In an hour the *Micro Dawn* would steam into the lagoon bearing the sweet fruit of the developed world: sugar, kerosene, coffee, boxes of fishing lures and candy and cloth, a case of batteries, enough bagged ice to ensure cold drinking water for almost a day. To the Losapans the ship was a drug, instant relief from the monotony and claustrophobia and unending heat. To Markin it was something else entirely.

He got up, pulled on a pair of shorts, and carried his spear, *kumi,* and a battered pair of running shoes out to the front step. Elias was kneeling in the clearing, building a wall around his latest sculpture, a miniature city he'd created from pieces of rusty metal, glass bottles, Pepsi-Cola cans, pebbles, and sand. He sensed Markin's appearance and waved his good arm without looking up. *"Kopwele feile ia, Marr-keen?"*

Markin had to smile. On an island less than half a mile square, a place that offered no more than a handful of possible destinations, this was the universal greeting: *Kopwele feile ia?* Where are you going? People said it to each other constantly. Where are you going? Where are you going? Where are you going? until he began to wonder if it wasn't some kind of psychological trick, the Losapans' way of making up for the fact that there was nowhere for them *to* go, that they were marooned on this spot of sand forever.

Ordinarily, by this hour, the adults would have breakfasted and gone off to work. The men would already be cutting copra or fishing the lagoon reef, the women hunting for octopus in Ayao's shallows or sitting by the meeting hut mending clothes. But today they lingered near their houses and along the beach, watching the southwestern horizon as though a second sun were about to appear there. Ulua, Markin's nearest neighbor, sat with her wide, bare back propped against a palm trunk and pretended to weave a mat. Every month since the beginning of regular supply service to the outer islands, Ulua had been the first to spot the ship. It was her patch in the quilt of island life, her source of reputation. As soon as the *Micro Dawn*'s bridge broke the horizon, her voice would boom out across the clearing: "There is the ship! Ship! Ship! Here it is!" and over the next few hours she would collect enough compliments to last her through another month. "You have eyes like a bird, Ulua," people would tell her. "You must be able to see right through water." She would struggle to contain a smile, and her fingers would fly across the pandanus strips.

Markin watched her for a few minutes, savoring the last of the coolness, reaching unsuccessfully for the half-remembered strands of his dream. The night had seemed quick, incomplete. He hadn't slept well and had awakened to find Ninake gone and the morning filmed with a vague, persistent apprehension. It was the same feeling that always came over him on Ship Days. There was no way around it, nothing to do but keep busy until nightfall. By then the ship would have sailed off toward the western atolls and his hut would fill with friends and neighbors, all of them tired from the excitement, some of them already beginning to exhibit that air of contented hopelessness he loved. Where else but in war could you find people who asked so little from life? A cup of coffee and an hour or two of talk was the Losapan idea of a celebration. After that, the women would start a song, and its sweet *a cappella* harmonies would float across Losapas, lulling the island into a sleep so peaceful and God-blessed that Markin would be able to forget for another month that any other reality existed.

His thoughts were interrupted by a familiar rhythm: sandals scuffing the path, rubber slapping up against the soles of a friend's feet. Mahalis appeared, checked the horizon, and sat next to him on the step. "What are you doing?" he said, sneaking a suspicious glance at the salt-eaten running shoes.

"Watching Elias. What are you doing?"

Mahalis shrugged. There was only one thing he could be doing. "Waiting for the ship."

The sun rose over the palm trees behind them and the clearing's thin coat of moisture dried instantly. Without delay or mercy the real heat began to build, pressing down on them, siphoning a film of perspiration from their pores, as if to compensate for the evaporated dew. Ulua's mongrels raised themselves on wobbly legs and slunk into the shade behind her house.

Mahalis started to fidget. He made a hole in the sand with his heel, filled it in, scooped it out again; he tossed coral pebbles at a pile of fish bones; he scratched at a callus on his leathery palm. Finally he spat into the dust between his feet and unburdened himself. "Marr-keen."

"What."

"Let's swim out to the drowned boat and spearfish there before the ship comes."

"You know where I fish on Ship Days, Mahalis."

Mahalis shook his head sternly. "It is a bad time for that place. Listen."

They sat perfectly still for a moment and listened to the song of the back beach, a continuous rumble, one enormous wave breaking ceaselessly on the shore.

"I was walking on the back beach now. The shells are bouncing."

"That's a new one."

Mahalis let out a sigh and fixed his gaze on the lagoon. "When you first came to live here you used to run along the beach until you were so out of breath you could hardly stand. Everyone thought you were strange. I told them no, he's not strange, that's just what they do on his island . . . Then you used to walk up to Ulua's dogs — before we ever cooked a dog for you — and scratch their bellies. Everyone thought you were foolish. But I said no, he's not foolish, that's just what they do on his island. They probably don't eat that kind of dog in America . . . When you first knew Ninake you used to try to kiss her when other people were watching — do you remember? Everyone thought you were rude, but I told them no, he's not rude, that's just the way men and women behave on his island." Mahalis found a twig in the sand and began cleaning his teeth with it. "Now, whenever the ship comes, you go fishing off the deep beach alone, something even Losapan men don't do — especially on a day when you can hear the waves all the way from Lawrence's house. People say you are wild, that you are trying to kill yourself. I don't know what to tell them."

"Tell them I'm a Marine. We have manhood problems."

Mahalis looked at him as if he had never heard of manhood problems, as if he could not even begin to imagine what a manhood problem might be. He opened his mouth to say something, but Markin had already pulled the mask down over his forehead and was adjusting the snorkel and strap. Mahalis nudged him with an elbow and lifted his chin at the horizon.

A second passed, and Ulua bellowed, "Sh-i-ip! Sh-i-ip! Sh-i-ip! Here it is! Sh-i-ip!"

Markin stood and started toward the path.

"Elias will watch you," Mahalis called after him, and immediately the boy abandoned his sand city and trotted across the clearing, the narrow stump of his left arm flailing in the hot light.

The path ran parallel to the inlet for a few hundred feet, then opened onto a swath of dead coral Markin thought of as "Moon Beach." He paused there to try and set his mind in order. To his left was Ayao's northern shore. Along that sickle of coast swept currents which, over millions of years, had deposited enough silt and sand against the reef to form the twin islands. Markin had learned to spearfish there, learned how to use the currents — when to fight and when to give in and float around the far side of Ayao and into the still lagoon. For most of his first year on Losapas he had spent every morning there, testing the limits of the ocean's patience, diving until his ears ached, swimming out until he felt the subtle, persistent tug of the open sea, fitting the notched end of his spear like an arrow against the loop of surgical tubing — the *kumi* — a hundred times a day until after a week he brought back his first fish — a hand-size, inedible *la* — and after a month he was able to catch his own dinner.

Spearfishing became his profession. Ancha cut hair; Ulua watched for the ship; Lawrence cut barbs into the tips of new spears. Others could have done these things almost as well, but a balance had to be maintained in the community. In order for the organism to survive, each organ had to play its part and receive its due. Sometime during his third year on the island the Losapans had stopped seeing him as *Re Won*, the pink-skinned giant, and begun thinking of him as *Chon Lekapir*, the fisherman.

It was only on Ship Days that he became distinct again, that his Americanness mattered. On Ship Days the kids decided he had a stash of chocolate he was keeping from them, and the adults suddenly had trouble with his accent, or they commented, in a friendly way, on his height, or his large feet, or his habit of bathing outdoors during rainstorms while they huddled in their houses wrapped in blankets. For some reason they seemed to think of the luxuries the ship brought as *his* luxuries, and their desire for what he had always taken for granted shamed them, erected around them a small line of defense, a skin of insecurity.

Markin's eyes followed the brow of reef as it broke with Ayao's shore and arced north and west — only inches below the surface in some places — past two turtle islands and as far as the jagged horizon. The Losapans' change in attitude on Ship Days was as subtle as the curve of the earth. It had taken him years to become aware of it. Even now, he wondered if it existed only in his imagination, a product of *his* insecurity, not theirs. He pushed the notion aside but it left a residue, a separateness, a feeling he'd come to think of as the Ship Day blues. He'd finally learned that the best cure was simply to immerse himself, to face the sea, to make himself small against it.

And on a day like today that was not difficult: the sea was massive, all-powerful; it made his problems seem petty. On the far side of the white mouth of the inlet, where he had learned to spearfish, the water was shallow and relatively calm. But to his right, east, on the Losapan side, where the larger fish lived, the reef fit itself tightly to shore, reducing the amount of shallow buffer, letting the ocean's power closer in. A hundred yards from the beach the water stood eighty feet deep. A hundred miles out, according to the islanders, there was no bottom at all, only the walls of the Costilan Trench dropping into what they referred to as the "womb of the ocean."

This morning he did not let himself think about the womb of the ocean. He crossed the point to get a better look at the waves, and felt something running lightly over his skin like the fingers of a lover. Elias came up beside him and clutched his arm. "*Naw mi wattei, Marr-keen!*" he shouted wide-eyed, his voice sounding tiny and shrill in the roar.

Markin tried to see over the breakers to get a sense of the spacing of the swells, but each wave that smashed on the coral sent up a ten-foot spray of white water that settled just in time to expose another rising, advancing blue-green wall. A single moth tested its wings in his belly; he managed a tight grin. *Chon Lekapir*, the fisherman, had been squeezed down into a frightened, powerless speck, a dot in the universe. It was a fine perspective.

Markin spit into his mask and spread the saliva with two fingers. Taking that as his cue, Elias took several steps backward and sat cross-legged on the sandy slope. A wave curled and boomed. Foam hissed back across the coral and was drawn up into the next curl. Another wave crashed and thundered. Markin forced himself forward and the water swirled and sucked around his sneakers and knees. Before he'd gone three yards the next wave was there standing over him. He took a breath, dove into the base of the wave, hugged bottom for a few strokes, and surfaced on the ocean side.

Automatically he cleared his snorkel, checked his shins and knees for scratches, and carefully slid the *kumi* down over his left forearm. It took a few seconds for his breathing to return to normal, less than a minute for him to see what he'd been too stubborn to see from the beach: the sea was not just rough; it was the kind of sea that ran before a typhoon. Swells were lifting and dropping him like a scrap of paper, each one ultimately moving him a few feet farther from shore. He looked up. Sliding in among the usual cumulus towers was a high, thin cirrus, the first sign of storm.

As the next wave lifted him, Markin turned and saw Elias standing now, worried, a hundred feet away. Markin flashed him the thumbs-up sign but realized, as he and his stomach were dropped separately into the next trough, that the gesture was a lie, a thin cirrus, panic's leading edge. For an instant then he saw his stubbornness in a clear light, saw where it came from and what would become of it. In time the world would hammer it out of him. Taking the shape now of a rough sea, or a woman, or a war, the world's mysterious workings would squeeze him clean, burn him pure. It was all God's gloved hand at work, somebody had said to him once. There was no vengeance in the process; it happened automatically, with absolute correctness and impersonalness. He no longer even thought of resisting. He only wondered — during this clear fraction of a second — what, if anything, would be left of him in the end.

He made himself swim into deeper water. There the tossing of the sea lessened somewhat. He tried to relax. Mahalis hadn't said anything about a typhoon; there hadn't been any warnings on the radio. Maybe it wasn't a typhoon after all, just one of the blowy, two-day rainstorms that surprised the island now and then, reminding him, with their cool salt air and low clouds, of Averill Beach. If he stayed out for an hour or so the worst seas might pass. Markin studied the white line of surf from the tops of the next two swells and saw that he had no choice. Going ashore now would be suicide, an aquatic Russian roulette. Even spearfishing seemed out of the question. His maximum diving depth was forty feet. In deeper water he wouldn't be able to retrieve the spear; in shallower water the surface motion would be too violent, the undertow too strong, visibility poor. He was left with two options: float around for a while on the slim chance the weather would soften, then make a desperate run at the beach; or risk the long swim west around Ayao, through currents that would be treacherous on a day like this, then finally, with tired legs and lungs, cross the reef at another, slightly safer point.

Markin swam back and forth in the troughs, buying time. Beneath him the water was over fifty feet deep but he could see the bottom clearly. Nothing survived there, no reeds, no shellfish, not so much as a sea cucumber. A moment of despair overtook him. He swam on.

After a few minutes he came upon a kind of plateau, an undersea altiplano sixty yards square, the high end covered by only fifteen feet of water. In all his hours spearfishing out here he never remembered seeing it. The bottom was split in three places by dark fissures that widened and deepened as they stretched away from the beach. He could see clusters of fish in the shadows. Occasionally a *sanisan* or *pula* would swim up into the light, nose around on the plateau, then drop back into the safety of its canyon.

Markin drew a breath and dove. Flattening himself against the gray coral, spear half cocked, he kicked and coasted along one edge of the cleft for a minute, then surfaced for air. He repeated this strategy down the length of the first crevasse until he was in thirty feet of water, then, breath by breath, worked his way back to the shallow end. On his sixth or seventh dive he saw a silver and blue *sanisan* swim up into the light directly in front of him. He speared it behind the gills, retrieved spear and fish from the bottom, then surfaced. He wanted to kill the fish immediately to avoid attracting sharks, but the surge was sweeping him in and out, the swells lifting and dropping him in close order, and the *sanisan*, barbed tail flailing, was slipping down the shaft toward his hand.

Finally, after several tries, Markin was able to hold the fish's head still and crush the slippery skull between his back teeth. As he strung the *sanisan* on the wire around his waist, a shadow appeared on the edge of the plateau. Barely affected by the undertow, a six-foot reef shark crossed the deep end of the crevasse. Markin was suddenly aware of the pulse thumping in his ears, of the salt, fish, and rubber taste of the mouthpiece, of his legs, fleshy and pale-skinned, dangling conspicuously beneath him. He put his hand on the *sanisan* — still as death — and floated motionlessly, breathing, staring. The shark ignored him and sidled off toward Ayao.

Slowly Markin pushed himself in the opposite direction. When he did not see the shark again he explored the other two crevasses, spearing another, smaller *sanisan*, coming to the surface for the last time only when he realized his dives were becoming shallower, his legs and arms heavy. He swam parallel to shore until he was abreast of the point where he'd entered the water, then turned in.

At first, as he started working with the swells again, Markin could see Elias on the beach, watching him. But as he got closer to shore — making a yard of headway, being swept out in the backlash, riding another swell, kicking hard, gaining another few exhausting feet — the breakers and white water rose between them. The waves had grown larger during the time he'd been fishing. Beginning a few yards beyond the place where he'd given the thumbs-up sign, the surge was now pulling him so powerfully out to sea that he had to frog-kick constantly just to keep from losing ground. His running shoes felt as heavy as boots. Without the rest period between swells he tired quickly, and the more tired he became, the more ground he lost after each swell. He thought of floating back out and signaling Elias for help, but even if he understood the message, Elias would have to run down to the landing beach, find Mahalis, Mahalis would have to run all the way back to the island's one motorboat, get the gas for it — if there was any gas left this late in the month — start it, take it through the cut in the reef and around the east side of Losapas before he could get to him. By that time he'd be floating in pieces somewhere south of the Marianas.

Markin put his head down and kicked hard and told himself he wouldn't look up until ten waves had broken on the beach. But when the eleventh swell rolled beneath him, he was only a few feet closer to shore. "You are selfish with your death," he heard Ninake say again, and the words brought together the memory of his dream and a momentary vision of his childhood in Averill Beach that was so clear and real he turned his eyes, half expecting to see his father or Angela there beside him. He shook his head and let his spear drop to the bottom.

Fifteen minutes later Markin was still the same distance from shore, fighting the sea for his life, for one more chance to change. All he saw was the bottom slipping back and forth beneath him, now lighter, closer to his mask, now slightly darker and farther away, his arms flailing there in front of him, part of someone else's body. All he heard was the wild rhythm of his heart and the desperate rasp of his breath in the rubber tube. That was everything left of him. As he tired, he sank slightly and took in more water. He was having to spit hard to clear the snorkel now, and each time he sucked in a watery breath and spit it out, he felt as though he were spitting out everything he didn't need, whittling his attention down to the pure and un-decorated fact of his existence. Every cough and gasp was a lesson. He was sure he understood it. He was ready to change. He could see his life now, a frail line of errors and moments, small bubbles.

A clot of noise moved through the snorkel, an odd laugh. Markin kicked furiously, legs out of rhythm, and sank two feet. One sneaker struck something hard. He looked down. The bottom was right there — shifting silt and thin lines of rising bubbles — unmistakable. The backlash of a wave caught him and dragged him out. Immediately the first curling of another wave flipped him over and he took a breath that was only water and fought to the surface choking and gasping, then coughing and choking again until he was sure all the blood vessels in his head were about to burst. He made a fist with his right hand and struck at the water. The sea dragged him out again. He rode the next swell partway in, then stopped paddling and veered off as it broke. He looked up. Elias was standing ten yards in front of him, ankle-deep in white water, swinging his good arm like a windmill.

Markin could not get his breathing under control. There was one long, empty second of panic before he felt a giant wave lifting him — feet, hips, chest — and he was perched on the crest of the curl, held there like a wrestler about to be slammed to the mat, his nose and eyes filled with salt water, his head spinning. He saw a brown blur at the top left of his vision and struggled to get his legs down, out of the clutch of the curl, to get his hands forward, to keep his head from being smashed like an egg on the reef. At the last possible instant the wave let go of him. His feet struck the sharp reef first, then hands, elbows, chest. He was drowning. When the spray settled and rushed out, he slid backward, unable to get a grip on the coral. Elias was close to him now, thigh-deep, screaming, "Get in, Marr-keen! Get in! *Get in!*" A wave knocked the boy down. He got up, encircled Markin's left shoulder, and started dragging him on his knees, inch by inch, across the top of the reef. Markin stumbled halfway to his feet before the next wave hit, knocking both of them forward, face-down in a foot of water.

They sat together on the sand, examining their wounds, skin already dry and tingling with salt, chests heaving, an unspoken exhilaration building between them.

"Marr-keen!" Elias gasped, unable to contain it. "You speared two *sanisan!*" He reached for the wire around Markin's waist, separated the fish, and turned them this way and that, pushing a finger into the small round holes behind their gills. "Even Lawrence and my father couldn't have speared fish out here today."

"Lawrence and your father are too smart to fish out here today," Markin said, but he was grinning, glad to be alive. His breath felt like silk.

Elias' brown-black eyes went to Markin's ribs. "You're bleeding."

"You too."

"Our blood is exactly the same color. Look!"

Markin thought of his first weeks on the island when the children would crowd around him, pressing their fingers into his forearms and thighs, fascinated by the way the skin turned white, then gradually back to pink. In those days he'd imagined it would take him a couple of months to learn to fish and feed himself, and that after his short training period, he would blend into Losapan life as completely as if he'd been born here. But seven years had passed and he was still the same person. His skin still turned white when the children pressed it; his stubbornness was still intact; his past still followed him, clung to him, unchanged.

Elias rested the stump of his arm on Markin's knee. "When will you take *me* spearfishing, Marr-keen?"

Markin looked into the happy face and kept his eyes away from the arm. How much of yourself could you change by sheer will? At what point did you have to say *this* is an unchangeable thing, this is me, and just go on?

A breeze brushed their backs and rustled the palms, surprising them so much in the middle of the morning that, with identical movements, they lifted their faces skyward.

"It is good the ship is here and not at sea," Elias said, assessing the new clouds. "After it is unloaded the captain can take it out deeper in the lagoon and keep it pointed into the wind."

"Are you in a hurry to get to the landing beach?"

The boy shrugged.

"Marcellina will be there."

Elias shrugged again and busied himself with a scratch on his knee. "I will have to put lime juice on this to kill the coral," he said manfully.

A wave broke, showering them. Elias would not meet Markin's eyes.

"I saw you two talking yesterday," Markin said.

"I was telling her about trucks. In the District Center."

"Was she interested?"

"Uh-huh."

"She's a nice girl. Pretty."

Elias shook his head and flung a shell into the surf.

"Her mother is my girlfriend, you know."

"Everybody knows," Elias said. "She sleeps with you. Except on the day the ship comes."

Markin laughed and lay back in the sand, suddenly exhausted.

Elias gave him a sly smile. "When the ship comes she doesn't like you."

"What am I doing wrong?"

"You don't meet the ship. That is where Ninake goes. That is where everybody goes — everybody but Marr-keen."

Markin closed his eyes and nearly fell asleep. He could feel the sand trembling beneath his back — it almost seemed as though the shells were bouncing. And there was something in the air, a tension that reminded him of Averill Beach in September, hurricane season, when he felt that the universe was coming to pay a visit and no one was ready.

Elias checked the clouds again. "Typhoon!" he said excitedly. They stood and started down the path toward the point.

Markin took the wire from around his waist and handed the fish to Elias to give to his grandmother. "Marcellina brings me my mail on Ship Days. Why don't you stop by later and talk with her?"

"I can't."

"Why not?"

"Because I'm shy."

"Then when I see her I'll tell her you saved my life."

Elias scrutinized Markin's face for a few seconds, then turned forward again and began swinging the fish back and forth and clucking his tongue. They turned the corner, crossed Moon Beach, and started onto the path, squeezing close to each other so they could walk side by side.

"What are you going to do now, Marr-keen?"

"Take a nap."

"But there will be a storm."

"Not right away."

Elias laughed. "Marr-keen is lay-zee, lay-zee," he sang delightedly.

When they reached Mahalis' thatched shelter Elias broke into an awkward trot and went to join his people. Markin stepped into his hut and stretched out on the pandanus mat. A pleasant exhaustion held him in place. For a while he studied the patterns of shadow and light on the pocked ceiling, the thin, irregular ridges where wet concrete had seeped between planks, a mute gecko clinging there. When his eyes closed he noticed the quiet and imagined the scene at the landing beach: Ninake kneeling next to an open carton, checking to see which medicines had been forgotten this month; her eleven-year-old girl, Marcellina, squirming through a maze of bodies in search of the mail from America; wrinkled old men and women squatting in the shade; Mahalis, Lawrence, and Ancha, waist-deep in water, passing boxes toward the beach. As always, the Japanese launch driver would be presiding over it all, sitting dry and aloof on the gunwale, studying the people on shore as if, after all these months, they were still just museum pieces to him, a bizarre, half-naked race clutching at the scraps of civilization.

Markin forced his eyes open. The scene had some special power over him. Today he'd nearly drowned himself, running from it. He did not want that kind of life.

## 3

MARCELLINA STEPPED into the inner room of Markin's hut and found the *Re Merika* lying on his pandanus mat being tormented by Leipwen, the spirit of dreams. His arms and legs twitched like a sleeping dog's; his lips moved apart and came together — he was talking to someone. The girl's eyes followed a trail of dried blood along his chest, both hands, and one knee, then jumped to the white shoes he wore for spearfishing, which had been kicked into a corner, soaking wet. For a minute or so, a mixture of revulsion and curiosity on her face, Marcellina squatted beside the pale creature and watched his pink belly rise and fall. She made magic signs over the shoulders. She reached out and touched the nose, tickling the tiny hairs there. After a few seconds of this, she lightly touched the lips and Markin's whole body jerked as though it had been struck. The eyelids fluttered open, then shut.

Impatiently she raised the heavy envelope over his chest and let it drop. Markin stirred, stretched, rolled his head once from side to side, opened his eyes, and stared up at her. "Marcellina," he said after a moment. She nodded.

When he sat up she reached into the pocket of her skirt and handed over the *ponam* her mother had cooked. He broke the cold pancake in two, handed her the smaller piece, and they sat chewing and looking at each other until he was fully awake.

"Where's your mother, Marcellina?"

She looked at him as if the question were foolish beyond response. "At the ship."

"Many people on the ship?"

"Some," she said, tilting her head to the side exactly the way Ninake did and pulling the black ponytail over one shoulder. "A *Re Merika.*"

"A *Re Merika?* Are you sure?"

"Mahalis says so."

Markin slit open the envelope and watched her face. Already, at age eleven, Marcellina had earned herself a reputation for inventiveness. She would tell her neighbors that the Japanese lobster boat was sailing into the lagoon, and they would hurry to the landing beach only to find themselves staring at an expanse of empty ocean. She'd terrify her friends with stories of eels crawling up onto the back beach — ugly, monstrous creatures with big painted ears and red teeth. She'd have Elias believing an old man lived alone in the middle of Ayao, hiding from people, talking to animals, living on fruit, coconuts, and robber crabs.

But, Markin thought, this time there was a slight chance she was telling the truth. It was not unheard-of for an American to book passage on the *Micro Dawn*. He'd seen it himself when he lived in the District Center. The tourist, sweating and restless in paradise, would reserve a deluxe cabin and spend a week or two cruising the northern or southern or western atolls, using up rolls and rolls of film on the bright lagoons and bare-chested women, finding, Markin suspected, nothing but more boredom and frustration in the *Micro Dawn*'s slow, uneventful voyage, in the sunny monotony of the islands. If the ship happened to be traveling to the northern atolls, and if the tourist learned there was an American living on Losapas, he would come ashore and stand on the landing beach in the beating sun, pointing to himself then into the trees, speaking English loudly, trying French or a few words of German. Markin had asked Mahalis to keep these uninvited visitors away from the hut. Over the years, the starman had developed an ingenious system: pretending to understand what the tourist wanted, Mahalis would lead him into the trees, tearing off a few pieces of banana leaf as he went. Gesticulating and speaking loudly in Losapan, he'd make it known that the banana leaves were to be used as toilet paper, then impatiently turn his back. It always worked. In all the time he'd been living on Losapas, Markin had never had to entertain a representative from his past.

He gave Marcellina a significant look before examining the contents of the envelope.

For eighty months he'd been sending his signed disability checks into the District Center ($66 a month for some hearing loss and the weakness in his left hand; it seemed a fair deal), and for eighty months two thirds of it had been deposited in the bank in Owen Town, and the rest — twenty-two one-dollar bills — sent back, with another check to be signed, on the next ship. He gave Mahalis and Miako fifteen dollars a month for rent, tipped Marcellina for her courier service, and carried the balance around with him for no logical reason. There was a very small cooperative store in mid-island, nothing but a one-room shack a Peace Corps volunteer had built in the mid-sixties. Markin would sometimes buy fishing lures there or a few pieces of candy for the children. But more often the money just accumulated in his sandy pockets like some kind of fetish. Once a year, when he went into the District Center to buy clothes and supplies, he'd stop in at the bank to check his balance, mail ten percent of it back to Averill Beach, then try to forget the money existed.

He endorsed the check, handed it and a new dollar to Marcellina, and watched her run out of the room holding the bill over her head like a trophy. He stood, poured himself a glass of tepid water, and leaned against the concrete, feeling himself falling back into the grasp of the Ship Day blues. It happened every month, every time Marcellina brought the envelope. Micronesia was governed by a United Nations trusteeship, administered by the United States, and all six districts used the American postal system and American currency. Seeing the new dollars, stiff and clean in the white envelope, inevitably brought on a wave of what could only be called homesickness, a deep melancholy Markin could not rise above. He always hoped time would erode the feeling, but the mood was strong, predictable as the tides. He was almost used to it.

His eyes went to the opposite wall. According to the map he'd purchased in Owen Town years before, there was nothing between Losapas and America but five thousand miles of water, two square feet of blue marked only by a freckling of small islands. At some point in his first year on Losapas he had tried to describe to Mahalis the various places he'd seen; he'd drawn pencil lines connecting Boston, Da Nang, Agana, and Owen Town. In broken Losapan he'd struggled to explain that the map's odd-shaped, multicolored blocks represented continents, huge expanses of land across which a man could not walk. But Mahalis had been unable to translate the diagrams into real space. To him, the world consisted of a handful of islands flung over an ocean so enormous that nothing, not even the sky, could possibly be larger. A map, to him, was a grid of sticks and shells lashed together with coconut twine, showing not only land and water but currents and stars as well. There was no word for "continent" in Losapan; the concept did not exist. America was a group of islands just beyond the reach of the sailing canoes, a magical place of airplanes and PT boats, canned food, and light-skinned, peculiar men who were all overgrown and thin.

Now, staring at the map, Markin realized that he, too, was having some trouble imagining the place. Counting the time in Southeast Asia and the six bad months on Guam, he'd been away more than eight years, almost a quarter of his life. He tried to picture Averill Beach and was able to conjure up the two-mile strip of amusements and hamburger stands where his father had taken him on Saturday afternoons and where, years later, he would spend summer nights with Angela and their high school friends. In those days it was a society held together by great, interlocking webs of family: parents who'd grown up within shouting distance of each other in the brick tenements of Boston's North End; aunts, uncles, and cousins enough for a column in the phone book; musical names that echoed from all corners of the city through two or three generations, so that when you entered a new grade the teacher would connect you right away with other Luongos or Santosuossos or Vitales or Ortolanis, clans with a common history. He'd always felt on the fringes of it. The name he carried with him was Russian, not Italian. He was a half-breed in a town of purebreds, an only child with no mother and a kind but taciturn father in a place where families were large and full of noise. In moods like this it seemed to him that his life had been an exercise in being different without wanting to be. The only time he'd ever felt completely a part of anything was in the Marines, and even that small sense of belonging had eventually soured and faded.

From a paperback Bible on the table he took an old snapshot, a black-and-white picture of Anton Markin standing next to his son just after the graduation ceremony at Parris Island. His father wore a pressed shirt open at the neck; a cigar tilted out of one corner of his mouth; his thick head of hair had already turned white. He looked trim, proud, invulnerable. But that was almost ten years ago. Markin let himself imagine what his father looked like now, why he never sent any pictures with his letters, what kind of life he lived in the big house on Wilson Street, surrounded by his own stubborn loneliness, his memories, and, farther out, a ring of old friends. Beyond the friends, light years away, one equally stubborn son orbited in the unimaginable distance.

Voices, then a certain laughter sounded in the clearing. Markin slid the photo of his father back between the pages of the Bible. After a few seconds Mahalis rapped on the doorjamb — something he hadn't done in years — and stuck his oversized grin into the room. *"Moren parous,"* he said — I want to talk — and immediately Markin noticed something different in the voice and in Mahalis' manner. For a few seconds his neighbor would not even make eye contact.

"Marr-keen."

"What, Mahalis."

"We should sit down on the floor together. I want to ask you something. An important question."

On the island, weighty matters were settled by a council of men who squatted or sat in a circle, facing each other. It was considered improper to discuss such things in a standing position, where the head and eyes of a younger man might be higher than the head and eyes of his elders. Markin was used to being asked to sit down; still, he watched Mahalis carefully. Something in the starman's manner made him wary.

Mahalis squatted with his feet flat on the floor and let his eyes wander around the room for a moment. He rubbed his throat. He scratched the bridge of his nose. Markin offered him a drink from the water glass but Mahalis refused. "Don't you think," he began at last, "that, sometimes, it is good to do something you haven't done before?"

*"Ewer,"* Markin said. Sure. Mahalis was fidgeting and Markin couldn't be certain whether it was because of nervousness or excitement or fear. He wanted to say something to calm him. He wanted to tell him what had happened on the back beach that morning, how he'd finally learned his lesson. But Mahalis didn't give him a chance.

"Even though you have done something a certain way for

many years, don't you think it makes sense to try doing it differently sometimes?"

"Sometimes, sure."

Mahalis smiled and squeezed his hands together, as if he and Markin had come to an important agreement. His nervousness disappeared instantly. He stood, took Markin by the arm, led him to the front window, and pointed toward the clearing. Standing there, looking perfectly relaxed and completely out of place, was a balding, heavyset, unmistakably American man. For just a moment Markin was not sure if he was seeing visions again — an affliction he hadn't suffered from since Guam. He stared at the man, then into Mahalis' smiling face. Mahalis shrugged, raised his eyebrows, said, "Your uncle," and hurried out into the clearing. Markin watched him talking to the stranger, gesticulating, pointing toward the window, smiling and nodding. He heard scraps of broken English — "very good . . . Merikan . . . fishing" — saw the two men start toward the hut, and then it was too late. There was nothing he could do. The vision was standing in his doorway, holding out a hand, speaking: "Gene Woodrow."

The visitor was wearing white chinos, running shoes, and a blue striped jersey, and at first he reminded Markin of the American tourists he had just been thinking of, the kind who could occasionally be found wandering Owen Town's streets: pale, late-middle-aged men with an air of money and confidence about them, a small frown on their faces — as if the District Center had let them down. Seeing another white person, these tourists would always affect an air of instant camaraderie, a conspiracy of superiority. He avoided them like a virus.

But it required only a second or two to realize that this man did not fit the stereotype. There was no offer of camaraderie, no smugness, no air of wealth. Beneath the thinning brown and gray hair, Woodrow's face was weathered and open; the blue eyes seemed alert, neither cold nor especially friendly. His shoulders, chest, and arms were a size too large for the rest of his body, but in some way Markin could not pinpoint, the man looked ill, or as though he had been or would soon be ill. Markin's first thought was that Mahalis had introduced him to an All-American ghost. "Do I know you?" was the only thing he could find to say, and the words did not come out kindly. Startled at the tone, Mahalis searched Markin's face, saw that he was truly angry, started to offer his defense, then closed his mouth and abruptly left the hut.

Woodrow shook his head and almost smiled. "Not really." He paused and held eye contact a moment longer than was comfortable. "I'm a friend of Steve Palermo, though. I believe you might know him."

The water glass slipped in Markin's fingers and nearly fell. He could feel the muscles at the back of his neck clench and release in tiny, frantic spasms. A horrible thought crossed his mind. "Is he all right?"

"He asked me to find out if *you* were all right." Woodrow took a handkerchief from his back pocket and wiped it across his forehead and eyes. Markin handed him the glass and watched him drain it in two gulps. "We have an arrangement. We've called each other every Memorial Day for the past thirty years. This year he asked me to look you up." The visitor paused again and appeared to be making a mental note of Markin's expression before going on. "He said to tell you he loves you."

Markin stood as if frozen, checking again and again to see if he was awake. There seemed to be an American in his hut, sweating rivers. They seemed to be conversing in English (the language felt heavy on his tongue). It seemed he'd just received a message from his godfather, a man who lived on the other side of the world, one of only three people there he'd never been able to stop thinking about. But something did not make sense. How could Stevie have had such a regular friend all these years and never mentioned him? Why would Mahalis suddenly decide to let someone through his defense system? What was going on?

He looked at Woodrow suspiciously. Perhaps, Markin

thought, it *was* just a dream, an illusion, one of Mahalis' tricks. Perhaps he had banged his head badly in the surf.

"We were in the service together before the war started, and then for a while in the Pacific," the visitor said. "We boxed some at Camp Lejeune. He was out of my league, of course."

Markin was jerked out of his disbelief — it was the way Woodrow squared his shoulders — by the most intense sensation of déjà vu he had ever experienced. Staring at the burly man framed in the doorway, he was suddenly convinced he had seen him a few weeks before in a strange and unforgettable dream. The man had been following him across the circumference of an empty, littered lot and had finally caught up with him, and was looking at him just the way Woodrow was looking at him now, expecting something, a politeness he felt incapable of.

"You came all the way out here just to deliver a message from Stevie?"

Woodrow shook his head. "I was visiting my boy in Tokyo. He married —"

"I meant all the way out here from Owen Town. It's a six-day boat ride, round-trip."

"I had no way of knowing that." Woodrow made a small movement with his lips and eyebrows, as though disguising a spasm of pain. "The address Steve gave me was a post office box."

Any ordinary person, Markin wanted to say, would have left a note in the post office box, waited around a day or two for a call, then gotten back on the plane and gone home. But Stevie wasn't an ordinary person; it made sense that his friends wouldn't be either, that they would do this for him — go hundreds of miles out of their way to fulfill a request.

"Nice voyage. I slept out on deck. Economy class."

Other than himself, Markin had never heard of an American willing to forgo the soft bed of a cabin for the crowded, noisy deck. Deck passengers weren't served meals. What had Woodrow done for food? Begged taro from the families sprawled on mats beside him? Fasted?

The wind had risen while Markin slept and was stirring the palm fronds steadily now. Above the noise, in the distance, he could hear children's voices; people were drifting away from the landing beach for lunch. "Rough trip?"

"Only last night and today. There's supposed to be a big storm to the southwest."

"Typhoon?"

"They didn't say. Or if they did I didn't understand it." Woodrow stepped across the room to the map. "I was wounded not too far from here during the war. That's another reason I decided to make this little side trip."

"Where?"

"Peleliu. First Marines."

Of course, Markin thought. The First Marines was the source of all his ghostly visits.

Woodrow ran his index finger lightly across the bubbled paper of the map. "How do you spell the name of this place?"

"It's too small to be on there."

Markin waited, weighing his options, trying to ascertain what exactly he was angry at, then what he was afraid of. In the end, as always, it didn't matter. The fear itself made him speak, just as, perversely, it had been the fear that had made him dive into the water that morning instead of walking away, fear that had sent him into the Marines in the first place. It ruled him whichever way he turned. "I can give you a tour," he said, each word spoken separately, the whole sentence heavy with implications he alone understood.

Woodrow looked up. "If it's no trouble," he said. "I'd like that."

They crossed the clearing, cut behind Ulua's house, and went along a shaded stretch of path where banana leaves brushed their shoulders and small, pearl-colored butterflies fluttered at waist height. After several minutes of silent walking, Markin leading the way, they came upon a small village, eight plywood houses and a store, each with cut-out squares for windows, corrugated iron roofs, unfenced front yards busy with chickens and cluttered with coconut husks and rusting cans. Through the trees on their right they caught glimpses of the lagoon, its waves plucked into white tufts by the wind, the *Micro Dawn* tethered there like a nervous gelding. A few steps farther east and the path opened to another clearing, this one bounded on their left by a whitewashed concrete church and on their right by the landing beach. Half a dozen people lingered there. The adults raised their chins in greeting. Three naked boys, penises bobbing, ran toward Markin singing the familiar chorus: "Where are you going? Where are you going? *Kopwele feile ia, Marr-keen? Kopwele feile ia, eh? Kopwele feile ia, Re Merika? Allo, Re Merika. Allo!*"

Woodrow returned their hellos and let the boys press their fingers into the flesh of his forearms. "They seem to like Americans well enough," he said over his shoulder. "You don't find that in so many places now."

It seemed to Markin a peculiar observation. "It's from the war," he said distractedly. "When the Japanese were here they'd shoot you just for cutting down a coconut."

"We did a service, then, clearing the bastards out."

Markin didn't answer. He was trying to picture himself in Da Nang in thirty years, surrounded by laughing Vietnamese children who wanted to touch him.

They freed themselves from the boys' attention, rounded the island's eastern tip, and started along the back beach. Losapas had taken on a surreal aspect in the tremulous air; the sunlight had changed from its usual white to muted gold. Woodrow stopped and shielded his eyes, admiring the leaping ocean, the curving stretch of sand and coral, dark palm crowns tossing in the wind. "Christ," he said. "I can see why you live here."

Again Markin said nothing. Something very strange was happening to him: he was beginning to look upon the island as an outsider. From the moment he and Woodrow had left the hut he'd started to see not *why* he lived here, but *that* he lived here,

what an odd thing it really was. The fact that Woodrow knew
Stevie somehow made it worse. He felt exposed, a foreigner.
The feeling infuriated him.

They walked the length of the beach without saying anything
else. The surf was still heavy. Whole continents of gray clouds
were sliding in now, and when the two men crossed the point to
Moon Beach a wall of cool wind pressed against them, stinging
their faces and arms with particles of sand. Markin thought of
hurricane Donna tearing at the Massachusetts coast in 1960. He
saw his father out in the early part of the storm, tying the big
willow in their front yard to a telephone pole on the sidewalk.
Even at age ten he'd had the feeling it was a futile tactic, suspected his father knew it, too, but just wanted to be out there,
hatless in the wind and rain, making one heroic effort to escape
the suffocating safety of his existence. It occurred to Markin that
Woodrow might have made this trip, sleeping out on deck, for
similar reasons. He sneaked a glance at the man.

"Gettin' bad," Woodrow hollered above the noise, but soon
they were in the lee again, sheltered by Ayao's low bulk.

By the time they reached the clearing the thatched shelter was
rattling in the wind, looking as if it were about to lift off and
smash itself to pieces against the house. Mahalis and his family
were huddled on a mat beneath it, and when Markin looked
closely he recognized the flicker of excitement in their faces. It is
out of our hands now, the expressions seemed to be saying. We
will stay close together, we will eat lunch, we will see what the
spirits have in store for us.

Markin felt the same way.

# 4

IT WAS, Markin thought, a strange group. To his right sat Olapwuch, one of the island elders, breasts resting like wrinkled leather pouches against her ribs, hands cupped around an American cigarette. Olapwuch was a repository of the ancient skills: she could weave strong rope from coconut husk fibers, catch fish in weather that kept her sons and grandsons on shore; it took her only a few seconds to get a fire going, even in wind like this.

Beside her was a man in Korean running shoes and a gold wristwatch, a gray-haired, pale-skinned foreigner who had just flown halfway around the planet. Woodrow was making a game effort to eat everything the women put in front of him — octopus, robber crab, breadfruit, salt fish, even the potent, sugary Ship Day coffee. Ants paraded up and down his lower legs, and the air near the shelter was ripe with the smell of dog feces, yet he seemed at ease, curious but not intrusive, polite without being condescending.

Opposite him, Mahalis and his wife, Miako, squatted in the Micronesian manner, with feet flat and arms wrapped loosely around their knees. They could not stop staring at Woodrow. Mahalis was sure that the two Americans were blood relatives; nothing anyone said could change his mind. "Gene," he asked politely, almost formally, "are you and your nephew from the same island?"

Markin was pressed into the role of interpreter.

"My island is Minnesota," Woodrow said. "His island is Massachusetts."

"Is the fishing good near *Mahnehsohtah?*"

"Excellent."

"Did you bring your spear?"

The lagoon had turned angry now and swollen so much it appeared to be just below eye level, but only Markin noticed. The others were bewitched by Woodrow's unusual clothing, the sound of his words, the way he covered his coffee cup with a plate to keep the sand from blowing into it.

"We don't use spears on our island. We use poles. Rod and reel." He pantomimed a fisherman reeling in his catch and drew puzzled laughter.

Olapwuch took a deep drag from her cigarette and eyed the ring on Woodrow's hand. "Why didn't you bring your woman? She could have helped us cook. We would have taken her net fishing with us."

"She died a year and a half ago. She would have loved to come."

A murmur of condolence passed around the small circle.

"Were you married many years?"

"Thirty-two years."

"Do you have many children?"

"A son and two daughters."

The women tilted their heads sympathetically. Mahalis started to say something, then closed his mouth and looked out at the water. Markin had the feeling he'd been about to divulge a starman's secret — tell Woodrow what had become of his wife's spirit perhaps — but had thought better of it and was now immersing himself in his own thoughts, sinking back into a place inaccessible to the rest of them. In the past Mahalis had always been extremely reserved, almost aloof, around strangers, but he seemed to have made an immediate connection with Woodrow. Before the meal he had taken Markin aside and told him, "Your uncle should not stay on the ship tonight, Marr-keen. It is too cold. He should stay with you." Markin had hemmed and hawed. Mahalis had pushed. It was the usual state of affairs — except that today, on this day of strange and exhausting events, Markin had been too tired to push back.

"There would have been more fish but for the wind," Miako apologized, and as Markin was translating and explaining her remark, Elias trotted over from his sand city, flopped down beside Olapwuch, and wrapped his arm around her shoulders. "*Now* it's a typhoon," he said happily. Everyone looked up. Clouds moved in wide arcs above them, dissolving and reforming and merging again into low, dark banks. Half a mile south they could see two diagonal bands of rain.

"Where do you go when there's a typhoon?" Woodrow asked Miako.

"We visit Marr-keen. He has the concrete roof. We wait there until the rain stops."

"Sometimes it takes three days," Elias added.

"Once, water covered the whole island. This deep." Miako held her hand two feet above the ground. "All the small trees were washed away. When the rain ended, we went outside to clean up and there was no shade. We turned black as flies."

"What did you eat?"

"Fish," she said, smiling. "Fish, fish, fish. The airplane came and dropped food for us, but the packages dove into the water and everything was ruined."

"Except the seeds," Olapwuch said.

Miako made a face. "Pumpkin seeds. We planted the pumpkins, and when the next ship came it brought coconut trees from Ponape and banana trees from Yap. In a year Losapas was green again."

"Was anyone killed?"

"No. The spirit protected us."

"Which spirit?"

Olapwuch laughed. Miako looked carefully at Woodrow, then at Markin to see if this was a joke. "Alali," she said when she saw that it wasn't, "the wind spirit."

Almost as soon as Miako had finished speaking, a gust crossed their little clearing, dusting the food with sand and moving the loose objects — plastic bucket, cardboard box, a small sheaf of cut flowers — a few feet closer to Ulua's house. Patiently, Olapwuch brushed the sand grains from the last fillet on the dish and handed it to Woodrow. "We might not have a typhoon this time," she said reassuringly. "The radio said the typhoon, *El-len*, is between here and Yap, deciding which way she will go."

"We will send the Yapese banana plants now!" Elias said, turning to his father. But Mahalis had stopped paying attention to the conversation. His eyes were combing the cloud layers, sweeping from horizon to gray horizon. He checked the tide and the yellowish light, turned to his left to see which way Ayao's palms were bending. Markin even thought he saw him wrinkle his nose at the air, sniffing out the eye of the storm.

"Tomorrow we will see the sun," Mahalis announced. "We will go spearfishing tomorrow, Gene. You, me, and the wild man, Marr-keen."

Out of the corner of his eye Markin watched Elias stop eating and turn his face away. Woodrow was nodding politely, stripping fish bones and tossing them over his shoulder like a tribal chief. Markin hesitated a moment and felt Mahalis staring at him, silently urging him on. "You're being invited to go spearfishing," he told Woodrow.

"In this weather?"

"Mahalis says it'll clear tomorrow."

"I won't be in the neighborhood tomorrow."

"You might. If the storm heads west, the ship will stay here another day or so."

Woodrow contemplated the lagoon for a moment, then looked into the expectant faces around him. Markin watched the distant blue eyes move from no to undecided to yes. "Sign me on then."

Markin relayed the message. Four brown faces lit up.

"But these are the only clothes I brought ashore."

"*Esse lefil-ifil,*" Mahalis said. "Not importan'." He bounced to his feet and headed off toward mid-island.

"You made him happy," Miako said, and Woodrow nodded as though he knew it.

When Mahalis returned he was holding an enormous pair of khaki shorts he'd borrowed from Miako's three-hundred-pound cousin, Hermon, the biggest man in the district. Woodrow got a laugh by wrapping the material three quarters of the way around his hips and puffing out his cheeks, but the merriment was cut short by the crack and thud of an old coconut palm toppling onto the beach. Markin glanced at Mahalis and Miako. There was no fear in their expressions, no surprise. He guessed Woodrow would interpret the only reaction, Olapwuch's quick laugh, as a symptom of a childlike view of things, and for one brief moment he found himself wishing the typhoon would make a sudden turn east.

But for the remainder of the long afternoon Ellen barely moved. The clouds pressed lower, the palm trunks bent beneath the weight of the wind, but no heavy rain or high seas reached Losapas. After two hours of conversation Miako brought out blankets and long-sleeved shirts from storage and everyone bundled up and watched the lagoon creep up the flat beach. From time to time a short burst of rain would slap the thatched roof or a roll of muted thunder sound to the southwest. But by mid-afternoon when the women left the circle to assemble kettles and driftwood for cooking, the air was still stretched taut, Ellen's course uncertain. Elias went off to check on his sand city. Woodrow leaned back against a post of the thatched shelter and watched with drooping eyelids. Markin thought he looked like a corpse. Asking him to spend the night on the boat was out of the question. Still, it took him a minute or so to get the words out: "Why don't you go into the hut and rest for a while?"

"I don't want to inconvenience you more than I already have."

"No inconveniences on Losapas," Mahalis said after demanding the translation. "You go in and sleep now, Gene. You spend the night, too."

When Woodrow was gone, Mahalis produced a deck of cards and dealt two hands. "Don't be angry," he told Markin. "Your uncle has traveled a long way to see you."

"Gene is not my uncle, Mahalis."

"Maybe he is and you don't know it. Elias thinks he's come to take you back to Merika."

"And he's *not* going to take me back to America. What is it with you? That's all you talk about lately."

Mahalis shrugged and fixed Markin with a starman's look, a patient, bemused expression, utterly free of doubt.

Markin remembered his battle on the back beach a few hours before. On this island, he thought, no matter how he tried, he would always be surrounded by people wiser than himself. "I know this, at least," he told Mahalis. "The reason Elias is unhappy is because he never gets to do things with the men, the way the other boys do."

"He's not like the other boys."

Over the tops of his cards Markin could see Elias carefully smoothing a palm-frond runway and straightening a tower of Pepsi cans. He was the last of Mahalis and Miako's seven children, the only one still living on Losapas. Two sons were working on Guam and had not been home in years. The only daughter had died at the age of eleven after stepping on a stonefish near the landing beach. The other three boys had married and spread out among the southern atolls to live with their wives' parents and inherit their in-laws' trees and land. "I do not understand why my sons do not like Losapan women," Mahalis had told Markin once, but it was no great mystery. Mahalis himself had left the island of his birth to marry. Leaving home was a common theme among the children of starmen. It had more to do with the expectations of the other islanders, the impossibility of living up to their fathers' reputations, than anything else. The youngest son was supposed to inherit his father's physical strength and extrasensory powers, but Elias had been born without a left hand or forearm (Miako said her milk had been poisoned by the smoke from Japanese gunships). Instead of becoming a starman, he became a watchman. When the two-handed children sailed coconut husks in the inlet, Elias watched for sharks; when the men dove for lobsters off the back beach, he stood on the sand and warned them of approaching waves. Mornings, when the other children sat in the concrete-block schoolhouse learning to multiply and write, he hid stubbornly in his father's taro patch or waded off to Ayao. Markin had made several attempts to teach Elias to read. They sat side by side on the floor, leafing through a picture Bible left by Catholic missionaries, Markin pointing out a word and the boy glaring at it momentarily, making a halfhearted effort, then shaking his head and stalking out of the room.

But Elias had learned to climb coconut trees, and he taught Markin. He had cajoled his father into teaching him the constellations — he knew dozens of them and the stories that went with them — and he shared them with his American friend. He knew the proper way to bait a hook, how to start the fifty-five-horsepower Johnson outboard, where on Ayao to find the best mangoes and papayas, which shellfish were edible and which toxic, which plants could be boiled to make a poultice for skin infections. Markin agreed: Elias was not like the other boys. He would come of age and discover that an invisible wall existed between him and the rest of the island. Eventually, after fight-

ing it for as long as he could, he'd leave Losapas and make a life
for himself somewhere else. But the island — these faces and
voices — would haunt him for as long as he lived.

"It would make him feel better if you took him to the District
Center on this ship," Mahalis said, scanning his cards.

"After what you said about the District Center last night?"

"What did I say?"

"That being there was not even like living."

Mahalis glanced over his shoulder and rubbed the palm of
one hand across his chin. His eyes settled on the cards again.
"Soon we will all live that way. You see how many children there
are on Losapas. When they grow up and have their own children there will not be any trees on Ayao to feed them. Fathers
will fight over taro bogs. Boys will forget how to spearfish. There
will not be any water to drink, any space."

Markin had never heard Mahalis talk this way and he was not
sure how seriously to take him. He decided to play the middle
ground. "The Peace Corps volunteer showed you birth control."

"*Birt contro*," Mahalis scoffed. "*Birt contro* is a sin." He snapped
down a card and curbed a smile, attacking on all fronts. "*You* use
*birt contro*, Mister."

"Never," Markin said. "We're *plono*. Virgins."

Mahalis' poker face dissolved. He closed his eyes and pressed
his lips together, two serpentine veins in his forehead bulging
with the effort. He sneaked a glance over his shoulder at the
women before the laughter leaked out of him, as smooth and
sweet as his voice. When he recovered he told Markin, "When
you get old you don't need *birt contro*. Old people don't need it.
Priests don't. Missionaries don't. Fish don't." He paused for
emphasis. "Young people need it."

"Elias will need it soon."

"With Marcellina. Two more years."

"Maybe one more year."

Mahalis considered this, then looked up from his cards as if he
had just thought of something wonderful. "When you marry

Ninake and Elias marries Marcellina, then you will be Elias' *mwa linal*," he said, and Markin watched the mischievous smile reappear.

"Father-in-law."

The smile stretched. "Pwa will have his way with you then. He will send Nengin the mother spirit to seduce you. You will be a father."

"I've always liked being seduced."

"I'll tell her that," Mahalis managed to say before the idea of Markin being made love to by a spirit got the best of him, and he lay back in the sand, shaking, cards face-down on his shirted chest, the Pacific's fury whirling around him.

"What is it, Mahalis?" Miako called from her place by the fire. "Tell us Marr-keen's joke."

# 5

WHEN MARKIN went into the hut to rouse Woodrow for the evening meal he found him leaning against the front windowsill in his underwear, staring west.

"Any news?"

"It's warmed up a little. Still nothing definite on the radio."

By Losapan standards the view from Markin's window was unexceptional. The left side was framed by the weathered plywood and rusting iron roof of Ulua's house, a few palm trees; on the right stood the water tank and Mahalis' thatched shelter, around which the family's assembled detritus — bundles of kindling, buckets, the beached canoe, hoes, mats, rope, flowers, green coconuts — clung like froth against a dock. Directly in front was a sandy clearing, then water. On good days astounding blues and greens danced there in the chop of the lagoon's surface; today the colors were muted and mixed in a roiling palette of browns, purples, and dirty whites. The sky was sullen.

"All that time I spent in these islands during the war," Woodrow said over his shoulder, "and I never took ten minutes to just sit back and look. What you have here is one of the only unspoiled places left on earth." He leaned closer to the window and went on. "But the restaurant where I ate breakfast in Owen Town had a toilet that flushed right into the harbor. You could see the pipe from my table. And some kids were fishing a few yards down the bank."

"I try not to think about it."

"That's one approach." Woodrow turned from the window to appraise his host. "I want to ask you something," he said, "and I want a straight answer, no bullshit."

"All right."

"Is it a problem for you, my spending the night here?"

Markin started pulling the laces out of his wet running shoes. "It's not going to be too nice sleeping out on deck if the rain comes." He draped the laces over a short clothesline in one corner and leaned his shoes against the windowframe.

"A bullshit answer," Woodrow said, smiling the same smile Markin had seen earlier in the afternoon, the smile of a person who could not be offended. "I just thought you might have someone sleeping over."

"She doesn't sleep over on the night the ship comes."

Woodrow turned and stared out the window again. From behind, Markin thought, he looked like a linebacker. It was only the shadowed face that gave him away. The man was dying.

"I've met you before, you know," Woodrow said. "One summer just before my boy started elementary school, we took a family trip out east — Cape Cod, the White Mountains, Niagara Falls. On the way through Massachusetts we stopped off in Averill Beach for an afternoon and had lunch with Steve at his bar. After lunch we went swimming at the beach across the street. He had a little boy with him, a three- or four-year-old, his godson, he said. I just made the connection."

"I don't remember it."

Ulua came out of her house and put a pan of food on the ground for her dogs. The palm crowns were making uneasy circles in the wind and bits of leaf blew horizontally across the clearing. "In boot camp," Woodrow said, "Steve used to talk about Averill Beach constantly. I'd always wanted to see it. I was sorry we could only spend part of a day there."

Markin poured water into his kettle.

"He made it sound like paradise. The shoreline, the people, the customs."

"At Parris Island every hometown seems like paradise."

"That's true." Woodrow waved to Ulua through the window. "Hungry?"

"A little. I think that octopus we had for lunch is trying to reassemble itself in my belly."

"I'll tell Miako we're going to have dinner here, just the two Americans."

While Woodrow dressed and washed up, Markin arranged a circle of coral stones in front of the hut and, after several tries, managed to get a fire going. On a makeshift grill of submarine wire — the same material his fishing spears were cut from — he started two *sanisan* fillets cooking in some oil, and set beside them a second skillet with leftover taro and rice. As he'd done every afternoon for the past several years, Elias had cut four green coconuts and left them in the doorway. Markin lopped off their ends and Woodrow joined him on the front step.

They sat without talking for a while, chasing small bites of fish with gulps of coconut milk, watching for changes in the wind. Just before six o'clock the clouds parted briefly, offering a flash of sunset — a rupture of scarlet and yellow that faded quickly into a threatening tropical twilight. A rooster crowed. Woodrow belched and sighed. "I saw those pencil lines on your map in there," he said as darkness separated him from Markin. "You fought in Vietnam."

Markin felt something freeze solid inside him. He wondered if it had, in fact, been the pencil lines on the map or if Stevie had spoken to Woodrow about him. He imagined Woodrow studying him in the darkness, compiling a dossier for Stevie on the mental and physical health of his godson.

"Still think about it?"

Markin slid his eyes left, not quite as far as Woodrow's shoulder. The *Micro Dawn*'s lights had been switched on, and they winked at him through the trees, transmitting a message in some mysterious code. What you should do now, the lights seemed to be telling him, is stand, go into the hut, start the stove for coffee. That will kill the conversation. Woodrow will give you space, make small talk for the rest of the night, leave tomorrow morning with a handshake and the promise of a letter. Just stand, stretch your legs, break the mood.

But somewhere between brain and feet the message was lost. Markin turned his face away, toward the far edge of the clearing, where a child's shadow stretched and jumped in the firelight. The word "Pwa" came into his mind. Woodrow would probably find the idea amusing, but it meant something important to the Losapans and, Markin decided, to him, too. Pwa was more than just a kind god who arranged for children to be brought to earth. He was the father spirit, the part of a man, or a woman, that had some authority in the world — over his or her own life if nothing else. When Mahalis offered to speak to Pwa for him it meant not only that he'd ask for Ninake to bear children but also for Markin to conquer a certain heaviness of spirit that separated him from the Losapans, to take his problems toward a solution instead of wallowing in them. Mahalis had been subtle, as always, but the message was clear enough. Markin's past was not so well wrapped after all.

The thought made him feel naked. He tried to think of something clever to say, some garment of words with which to camouflage himself, some small joke or verbal sleight of hand. But Woodrow's solid, patient silence would not allow it. "I murdered a little girl over there," Markin said suddenly, without knowing he was even thinking about it. He was immediately sorry. Now Woodrow would think the reason he lived on Losapas was to keep from hearing mortars at night and seeing burned bodies in his dreams. There was so much more to it than that, so many other subtle layers of feeling and history, so many better reasons to stay here. He couldn't stand the idea of being lumped together with everyone else who had ever set foot in Vietnam. He had a separate life.

Markin could feel the eyes leave him, could feel Woodrow shrinking away in the darkness and the huge, trembling, unsympathetic night moving in. Ulua's mongrels began their evening serenade, filling the air with drawn-out, woeful howls that floated off toward Ayao. He lobbed an empty coconut shell in their direction and the racket stopped, leaving only the low whine of wind.

Woodrow coughed. "My boy, Gary, was there," he said in a strained voice. " 'Sixty-six, 'sixty-seven. Lost his right foot. Won't say so much as a sentence about it." He paused. "I had an operation a month ago and he paid my way out to Tokyo to recuperate. I thought we might talk about it, finally. I even suggested we take a trip out to Peleliu together. No dice."

Markin sifted through a series of replies and found that none of them fit. The fact that Woodrow's son remained mute on the subject year after year, with his own father, probably even with his own wife, made perfect sense. War had that power over words: it shriveled them on the tongue, made them seem like so many silly vibrations, puffs of air. The problem was, though, that even a disciplined silence changed nothing. You could talk or not talk; either way it was still there.

They sat for a few minutes, wrestling with an awkward silence, Markin frozen in a dark terror he associated with a hospital room on Guam, Woodrow beside him, perched on the edge of the sandy step like a man listening for a certain sound. Markin heard a raindrop tap on Ulua's metal roof, then all of the wet, black sky seemed to fall on them at once.

Mahalis, Miako, Olapwuch, Ninake, Elias, and Marcellina scraped their feet and dropped their sandals on the front step and crowded into the hut. They sat on the floor in a tight circle, legs crossed, wet faces and hair lit by the kerosene lamp, and watched as Markin poured out eight mugs of coffee. Mahalis was in charge of the sweetening. He'd told Markin once that he considered sugar to be a kind of American folk medicine — food of the light-skinned gods — and on nights when he felt the need he'd add as much as six teaspoons to a mug of coffee. Markin had even seen him sweetening glasses of rainwater, his face creased by the perfect, white-toothed grin. Tonight the excitement of the ship, the unexpected guest, and the violent weather added another dimension to Mahalis' usual cheeriness and he spooned through his duties with great dignity. Markin watched the performance and tried to forget about the conversation on the step. A day, at most, and Woodrow would be gone.

Ninake had brought a bowl of lime juice and a washcloth, and when the coffee had been sweetened and served, she leaned close to Markin and began the treatment he'd been avoiding all day: pressing the saturated cloth against his scratches so that any live coral embedded there would not continue to grow.

"You should have done that as soon as you got out of the water," Olapwuch scolded. "Before the blood dried."

Markin nodded, then winced in such an exaggerated way that the others laughed. He knew he could have saved himself some pain by killing the coral when the wounds were fresh, but there was something right about doing it this way. It seemed like a proper penance.

"How did you get all scratched up like that?" Miako teased.

"I was wrestling with a dog," Markin said.

"You were not," Marcellina said, looking at him with something akin to hatred in her eyes. It did not surprise him anymore. Marcellina had been looking at him that way for years. It went far beyond jealousy. She saw into his heart; she accused him in dreams.

"He was not, Mama," the girl repeated, turning a petulant face toward Ninake. "He went spearfishing off the deep beach. Alone. Elias saved him from being washed away."

"Is that true, Elias?"

"The waves were so big —" the boy began proudly, but he was interrupted by more scraping and sandal slapping at the front step. Lawrence, Mahalis' oldest friend, and Ancha, Miako's brother, came in and sat down. Markin winked at Elias and poured two more cups of coffee.

"The typhoon has turned," Ancha announced when he and Lawrence had settled in and wiped the rain from their faces. "Ulua just heard it on the radio. She's going from house to house like a wet chicken, telling everyone."

"The storm is headed for Yap," Lawrence added.

Woodrow was given the good news. Miako suggested a moment of prayer for the Yapese, and the family sat quietly for a few seconds, eyes closed, as a heavy rain drummed on the windows and door. Mahalis dimmed the lamp momentarily in the traditional gesture of commiseration.

"They had a tiger shark near Ruo," Ancha said when the lamp was bright again. "The driver tried to spear it from his launch. He says next month he's going to bring his rifle and shoot it."

"If he ever sees it again," said Mahalis.

"He says he knows where it lives."

"He is an even bigger fool than we thought," Olapwuch muttered. "A Japanese fool."

Ninake finished working on Markin's knees and hands and moved the cloth up to his side, where a scab the size of a silver dollar had formed. Expertly, pausing from time to time to let the pain subside, she loosened the dried blood and soaked the wound in citrus. There was a lull in the conversation. Instead of the crickets' undulating song and the growl of surf from the back beach, all they could hear was the drip and splash of rain.

"We should sing for Gene," Ninake said as she completed her work. She turned toward their visitor and smiled. Woodrow was sitting with his back propped against the wall, coffee mug held in both hands, lost in thought. He smiled back at her tiredly. Markin poured him another round.

"No, a story," Elias said. "Papa always has a story on Ship Days."

"A story first," Lawrence proposed. "Then we'll sing. And then we'll go to bed. Markin is yawning like a fish."

Mahalis cleared his throat and assumed his storytelling posture, head bowed, eyes steady.

"The baby Jatsos," Elias suggested.

"Shush, Elias," Marcellina said. "It's not Christmas."

"I *know*. But there was almost a typhoon, and I like to hear my father tell it. Will you, Papa?"

"I will tell it slowly," Mahalis said without looking up. "So Marr-keen can tell Gene." He cleared his throat again. "Near an island far away," he began, pausing so Markin could translate. "So far away that the oldest fish in our sea had never swum there and the oldest bird in our sky had never flown there, an island so far away that no one from Losapas could ever sail there, a man and his wife were going along in a sailing canoe. The woman had a baby swimming and kicking in her belly, and her husband, who was an old man, older than me, older than Olapwuch, was worried they would not reach land before the baby was born.

"After sailing three days and three nights, they came to an island that had no name, an island no one knew about. There were many houses on the island, and leaving his wife under a breadfruit tree near the beach, the man went from house to house, saying, 'Can we stay here tonight? My baby is about to be born.' But the people did not know his name or the name of his island, and no one had any room in their house for his wife. The man went on this way from house to house until he came to the last house on the island, a small hut with a dirt floor, and he said to the woman who lived alone there, 'Woman, my wife is about to set our baby free from her. Can we stay in your house tonight? We have been at sea and the wind is blowing us a typhoon.'

"The woman let them stay, and the baby was born in the middle of the night on a mat on the dirt floor. Just as he was crying for the first time, the typhoon struck the island. They stayed inside for three days and three nights, and for three days and three nights rain fell and the trees bent and the wind tried to knock down the walls. All they had to eat was salt fish and a few coconuts.

"On the second night the roof blew away. They stood up to their ankles in sea water, shaking like old people, drinking rain. And all that time the baby cried out over the noise of the wind. So they named him Jatsos, the Loud One.

"When the typhoon passed, the man went outside to get food, and when he came to the beach he saw that the sailing canoe was not there. All kinds of fish covered the sand — *risal, mon, sanisan, la, pula* — some living, some dead. He put the dead ones into his basket and returned the living ones to the sea, then went back to weave the old woman a roof.

"Late that night, when the sky cleared, the starmen on the other islands noticed a new star above them. They got into their boats and followed the new star and it led them to this island, and they brought gifts to the father and mother of Jatsos. One brought a sail, one brought coconut rope, one brought a breadfruit log so Jatsos' father could make them a new boat.

"Many years passed. Jatsos and his mother and father stayed on this island, and for a long time Jatsos worked with his father, digging taro and learning to fish and climb coconut trees. But he was not like the other boys on the island. All of the other boys wanted to get married and have children of their own, but Jatsos did not want those things. When he had learned to sail he went out one night while his mother and father were sleeping. He took their boat and sailed away, leaving his parents and his home behind because he had important work to do. He sailed through the darkest part of the ocean, where there was no moon and no stars and no fish. He sailed on and came to these islands — Ruo, Losapas, Afanu, Mulo, Namulo, and the District Center islands. There were no people on these islands then and no light. The coconut and breadfruit trees grew in darkness. The fish swam always in darkness. Octopus and eels crawled over the land, but this was the place he had come to do his work. Jatsos stepped out of his boat on Ruo and the octopus and eels went into the sea. And the same on Losapas, Afanu, Mulo, Namulo, and the District Center islands. On every island the same; he stepped out, then back into his boat.

"Then Jatsos began to sail back, through the darkest part of the sea, as if he were going home. But in the middle of the darkest part of the sea, he rose up into the sky and his body dissolved into all the stars we know. When his father and mother saw the boat drift up to their island without Jatsos, they were so sad they died. When the father died he became the sun that shines on our islands. When the mother died she became our moon. Jatsos' footprints grew men and women and boys and girls on these islands the way the mud grows taro. And whenever all these men and women and boys and girls on all these islands look up at the stars, they remember Jatsos and how they came to live on Ruo, Losapas, Afanu, Mulo, Namulo, and the District Center islands. And as long as there is a night and stars and sun and moon they will remember him."

When the last words had been translated everyone sat quietly for several minutes, absorbed in their own thoughts. Markin could feel Woodrow's eyes on him. It seemed like an hour before Olapwuch coughed and ground her cigarette out against the side of her coffee mug and Miako started to sing: "*Re Losapas.*"

"*Re Lo-sa-pas,*" Marcellina echoed, holding the soprano line as the others joined in.

"*Mo-ren pwe Jatsos che-che-menni.*
*Pwe Jatsos a mu sah-lah.*

*Ai tipeis meineisin, ai tipeis meineisin.*
*Ren om tom,*
*Ren om,*
*Kir e-kie, kir ekie."*

Had he been translating, Markin would have been telling
Woodrow that the small circle of people sitting in this room —
men and women who lived so gently with the earth and with
each other that to speak of sin among them was almost to invent
the concept — were singing a hymn the missionaries had taught
them, confessing their impurity, offering as an excuse the difficulty of life on earth, appealing to Jatsos' great mercy to save
them. But Markin would not spoil this with a translation. He
closed his eyes, leaned back against the cool concrete, and let the
sound sink into him. Every time he heard this hymn with its
beautiful, plaintive harmony, he became convinced, for a little
while, that there was no need to ask forgiveness. From a God
who created music like this, people like these, forgiveness would
be automatic.

The hymn rose and fell and twisted back on itself, Lawrence's
vibrating bass and Marcellina's soprano winding like bright
threads in the fabric of Mahalis' and Ancha's tenor, Ninake and
Elias and Miako harmonizing when the phrases repeated, Olapwuch sitting meditatively through all four verses. Then the four
verses were sung again until the concrete room seemed to be
holding all of the notes at once, to be filled to bursting with
sound. At the end of the eighth verse everyone stopped
abruptly, and there was only the drumming of rain for a three
count before Marcellina added the final, high-pitched plea:
*"Emwan cheche menni-i."* Father, forgive us.

When these sweet, sad notes had settled, the guests sighed
over the end of their holiday, uncrossed their legs, stretched,
yawned, looked about as if hoping for something to prolong the
special evening. Mahalis examined the last of the coffee in his
cup and drank it down. Finally, one by one, they stood, bade
Markin and Woodrow good dreams, and went out into the rain.

Markin listened to them go, feeling the caffeine energy in his arms and legs giving way to a deep weariness.

Woodrow seemed to be under a spell. He said nothing as they collected the mugs and rinsed them in a bucket of well water. Markin located a clean sheet, unrolled a second mat, and made a makeshift pillow out of a sweatshirt stuffed with clothes.

"What do you do for a toilet around here?"

Markin took his flashlight and they walked down the slippery path and along the inlet as far as Moon Beach. "Go back into the bushes," he said, handing Woodrow the dripping light. "Don't worry about what you hear moving around in there."

Afterward they walked out past the point and stood beneath a pair of palm trees that grew close together, an imperfect natural umbrella. Sheets of rain tossed back and forth over the water in front of them, but Markin saw that the surf had diminished. The thought that he had nearly drowned himself there that morning was tearing him in two: half of him had to talk about it, the other half had to keep silent.

Woodrow was so still he seemed not to be present at all. The wind in the trees, the persistent rain, and the ocean buffeted them with sound, but between them the air was charged with a compacted silence. At last, in the strained and somber tone of voice he'd used on the front step, Woodrow broke it. "What keeps you from going back?"

Markin let his mind dwell on the question for almost a full second. For that brief moment he considered really asking it of himself, searching back across a string of decisions and conclusions he had long ago taken for granted. But it took him hardly any time — the duration of a thought — to find an easier route of escape, something close enough to the truth to seem believable. "I'm afraid if I go back for a visit I'll stay," he said.

It was, he thought, another bullshit answer.

"Would that be so terrible?"

"For someone else, no."

Woodrow paused. "But for you?"

"I've abandoned enough people in my life as it is." Markin tried to make the statement sound casual, half facetious, but even as he spoke he knew the words had an undisguisable weight to them. Woodrow knew it, too.

"There's more to it than that."

"Is there?"

"That's my guess."

Markin knew better than anyone that there was more to it than that, but he could not bring himself to go that deep. He'd crawled down into those depths before, a thousand times before, and found nothing but confusion and pain. At one time he had loved Averill Beach. He loved the fierce loyalties, the sense of offended dignity that seemed to bind the old immigrants together and that, even after two generations, kept them from ever really blending into the America that surrounded them. Even without his mother, who was his blood connection to that way of life, and even though he'd sometimes felt he did not truly belong there, he'd grown up feeling protected by it, nurtured. The food, smells, gestures, facial expressions, religion, the rituals of birth, marriage, and burial — they were in his blood; they conspired to create the illusion of perfect security. When had he turned away from that security? Why?

He was tempted to blame Vietnam, but that was too easy. Other people had been to Nam, seen and done what he'd seen and done — or worse — and they'd gone back home, settled down, started a family. The war provided a good excuse, but for him at least, there was much more to it than that.

"I wouldn't feel right going home now," he said lamely.

"Why not?"

"What difference does it make to you?"

For a moment Woodrow seemed taken aback. They'd both gotten quite wet on their walk, and now a steady drizzle was finding its way through the palm fronds, plastering Markin's hair to his forehead and soaking Woodrow to the skin. The silence was swelling between them again, and Markin wished more than anything that Woodrow would be offended enough just to turn and start walking toward the hut, take his ghostlike looks and his probing American curiosity and —

"So you don't even think about home?"

"Of course I do."

"You don't miss anyone there? No family? No girl?"

This was a page from Mahalis' book, this persistence. Markin turned his head and glared at Woodrow. Incredibly now, in the rain, in the darkness, Woodrow seemed to be smiling at him — not a real smile, not one of Mahalis' big grins, just a small change in the muscles around the mouth and eyes. A second passed and it vanished. Woodrow was just looking, expecting only the truth.

Beneath the weight of that gaze Markin could feel something breaking apart inside him. If he didn't speak now, the truth would be lost to him forever. There would be no other chances like this one.

"I miss Stevie," he said, trying out his voice. "I had a sort of fiancée, who I left cold, no explanation, no letters, nothing." He waited and knew Woodrow was waiting, too, still as a stone. "My father's there," he squeaked out before his mouth finally clamped shut and the world began its slow black spinning.

Woodrow nodded as though none of it surprised him. He turned his eyes out to sea.

Markin felt there was something else he had to say now, some defense he should offer, some logical argument he'd overlooked that explained everything. But he could not seem to arrange his thoughts. His mind was sodden and slow. He was very tired and cold, as cold as he ever got on Losapas, but he made no move back toward the hut.

"That girl you killed . . ." Woodrow paused a moment, expecting to be cut off. "It has nothing to do with that, does it?"

"Don't psychoanalyze me," Markin said, and Woodrow surprised him by laughing. It was a short, sincere laugh, almost as if he were laughing at himself. "I'm sorry," he said. "When I was in Japan I found out there were quite a few American men over there who never went home after Vietnam. I've spent a lot of time trying to figure it out."

"Why bother?" Markin said disgustedly.

"Because my son is one of them."

Markin stared straight ahead into the darkness above the womb of the ocean, looking through the sheets of rain as if he expected to see the face of Jatsos there, laughing at him. Dozens of times in Vietnam he'd seen lives saved or lost by millimeters. On his last day in country, only hours before he himself was wounded, he'd seen one of his closest friends shot in the neck by a sniper, the bullet hitting him at just the right angle to sever the artery. His friend had bled to death in seconds with a corpsman above him, leaning on a soaked compress, muttering through clenched teeth, "One quarter of an inch. One fucking quarter of a fucking inch." He'd seen a single step mean the difference between someone losing a leg and walking away unhurt; he'd heard stories of mortars falling right on top of someone's head, an impossibly accurate shot, the work of a sadistic God. But his own life had been spared by the same cosmic lottery, a piece of shrapnel driving into his hand instead of his heart, one round from an AK-47 grazing his skull just beneath the line of his helmet, cracking the bone but leaving him alive, more or less whole.

And now it was happening again. Woodrow could have decided not to get off the plane in Owen Town, could have inquired of someone else on the street, someone who didn't know there was an American on Losapas. He could have missed the *Micro Dawn*, could have arrived on a day when the weather wouldn't be keeping the ship in port. He could have been the type of person who didn't ask questions like these, or someone whose son had returned from Vietnam, alive or dead. Mahalis could have chased him away, as he chased away all the other American tourists who landed here.

Everything happens for a reason, a sailor on Guam had told him once with great conviction. He could hear the man's voice as clearly as if he were standing right next to him. He could try to tell himself he believed it, too, but he knew from long experience that it wouldn't work. God's gloved hand, he thought, had made itself into a fist.

Woodrow was watching him, waiting. They were both asking the same question of the world, and it was a waste of time. The world would not answer. Its creator did not feel obliged to explain.

"Maybe it's something you can't put into words," Markin said.

"I need to put it into words."

"What does your son say about it?"

"Nothing. He wouldn't even come home for his mother's funeral."

Markin swallowed with difficulty. There was something he had to ask now. There would be no other right time or right place. He had to carry this conversation to its end. "You don't take it personally, do you?"

Woodrow gave him an incredulous look. "Of course I do. How could I *not* take it personally? I'm his father." He switched on the flashlight, shone it toward the water, and took a deep, quiet breath. "Even Jatsos' father took it personally."

The surf looked magical; in the thin beam of light it leapt and twisted like a white serpent. The intense anger Markin had felt toward Woodrow for violating the sanctity of his small world was suddenly gone, blown out over the dark sea like a leaf. There was nothing else Woodrow could do to him now.

A tremendous gust of wind tore along the beach. Markin watched a coconut roll lopsidedly into the water.

"That was quite a story Mahalis told," Woodrow said when the air had settled. "Is that what the missionaries teach them?"

Woodrow was backing off now, Markin thought. He let him go. What had already been said was enough; the conversation would echo in his mind for months. "Mahalis changes the story a little every time he tells it," he said. "I don't think he has the heart to crucify Jatsos, so he changes history to suit his tastes."

"A good system," Woodrow said.

They stepped into the rain and took the wet path back to the hut.

6

"ANYTHING ELSE I should know?" Woodrow asked as they approached the landing beach the next morning.

"Watch us," Markin told him. "Remember to aim in front of them so they'll swim into it."

Markin had to work to keep the doubt from his voice. Woodrow was over sixty. When they reached fifty-five, Losapan men stayed out of the water; by sixty most of them were invalids, their bodies worn out by work and sun and the insidious intestinal parasites they carried. By sixty-five, almost to a man, they were dead.

He thought of Woodrow getting up from his mat that morning, stiff-jointed and stooped, a fresh scar fishhooking across his abdomen like the signature of death, that shadow in his face.

They'd breakfasted on leftover rice, salt fish, and coffee. For a while Markin had held out some hope that the weather would keep them ashore — the last of Ellen's winds still licked at the treetops — but the early cloud cover dissipated, the sky went suddenly blue, and they were faced with a typical Losapan morning: hot; still; patches of shade shrinking to spots at the base of the coconut palms. Mahalis appeared in the clearing, grinning, and the case was closed.

Somewhere in the course of the night, a night marked by fits and snatches of disconnected dreams, something had changed inside Markin. He awoke to the startling realization that he was not sorry Woodrow had found him. It took him the first hour of the day to come to terms with this; he kept waiting for Woodrow to say or do something to prove him wrong. But Gene made no attempt to go back to their conversation of the night before. He sat on the front step cradling his coffee mug, talked about his impressions of Japan and Owen Town, asked Markin about the Boston area and what it was like to grow up there. But his questions were general ones, the casual inquiries of a new acquaintance. Even when he told an anecdote from his days in boot camp — included Stevie in it — Markin sensed no hidden agenda. By the time Mahalis appeared, a vision of enthusiasm, from behind the water tank, Woodrow was beginning to remind Markin of his father's older brother, Leo, a kind, rough man who spoke English with a strong Russian accent and dropped dead one hot July afternoon at the Holy Name Society picnic.

"You might see a reef shark or two," he told Woodrow as they came out of the trees behind the church, "but they'll leave you alone unless you're bleeding or holding a live fish. Stay away from anything with tentacles."

The landing beach was already hot. On the *Micro Dawn*'s lower deck tarpaulins were being untied, and a handful of early risers stood at the white rail, watching the fishermen on shore.

"We have an hour," Mahalis said in Losapan. He adjusted Woodrow's mask and snorkel, they checked one another's arms and legs for fresh scratches, and then, too quickly for Markin's taste, they were submerged.

Markin and Woodrow followed Mahalis' huge blue fins toward a cargo ship that had been wrecked on a shoal a decade before. The moment he reached it, Mahalis dove and surfaced with a fat *pula* wriggling on his spear. He killed the fish by crushing its skull with his back teeth, and strung it around his waist before Woodrow even realized something had been caught.

Markin floated next to Woodrow, observing his struggle with the *kumi* and the expression of wonder in his blue eyes. Within a few minutes Woodrow had learned how to shoot the spear, and after watching him make a neat fifteen-foot dive to recover it, Markin swam around to the far side of the rusted hull and let himself relax. In the deeper, wilder water off the back beach the reef had been worn smooth by the rasp of surf, most of the underwater foliage torn up by its roots, fish forced down into the few sheltered spots or out into deeper water. But here on the lagoon side the coral was a comb of activity, its craters and niches alive with reeds, crabs, eel eyes. Fish glided along in schools or singly, the larger ones giving him wide berth, the smallest — bright blue and no bigger than a fingertip — nuzzling his mask. In this translucent green world he felt completely alert, completely at home. Each inhabitant had its defense system: venom, camouflage, speed, hidden barbs. There was no hatred, no waste. Even in the bitterness of death, a shark devouring a yellowtail, he saw no malice, nothing political, nothing wrong. He wished he could hold up this perfect undersea world and everything he knew about it and everything it did for him and say to Woodrow, *This* is why I stay here. Show me one thing in America that could replace this.

Without exerting much effort, Markin managed to spear and kill four squirrelfish, enough to fill a frying pan for lunch. He made a lackadaisical circuit of the wreck and, rounding a bulge in the coral, came upon a happy, pale-skinned, sixty-year-old

Marine in floppy pants taking practice shots at a sea cucumber stationed on the bottom. In the distance Markin could see Mahalis, a string of fish hanging from his belt. Two black-tipped reef sharks floated into view there. Woodrow saw them and turned to look at Markin, but in that moment the sharks swam gracefully back into the blue depths. Mahalis watched them until they disappeared, then he moved a few yards closer to shore so that the three men now formed an equilateral triangle: Mahalis still farthest out, in thirty feet of water; Markin close by the wreck; Woodrow standing on a ledge of brain coral, his thinning hair moving this way and that in the surface ripples. The sight of the sharks had frozen him in place momentarily and he found himself surrounded by a school of blue-black *nilanil*. He looked around, bewildered, the fish so close some of them brushed his shorts as they passed, then suddenly remembered his spear. Fitting the forked end against the *kumi* and pulling the spear back so that the tip was close to the crotch of his left thumb, he drew a bead on a *nilanil* and fired. The spear passed behind the tailfin of its target, sped on, and losing altitude, pierced the midsection of a fish near the base of another terraced coral wall. Woodrow watched the impaled fish flapping wildly as it sank, raising sand clouds from the bottom. He dove, retrieved it as if he'd been spearfishing since the Japanese occupation, and swam back to his perch with the spear at arm's length.

Markin was so absorbed in this spectacle that he failed to notice anything was wrong until Woodrow turned slightly, exposing his catch. Writhing near the point of the spear was a lionfish, a pound and a half of potent venom, its foot-long, red and white quills waving near Woodrow's arm. Markin paused an instant in a hypnosis of disbelief, and then he was in motion.

Woodrow, too, appeared to be hypnotized. He fixed his eyes on the lionfish, noting with great curiosity how it refused to die, how it writhed and squirmed on the metal pole, moving a quarter or an eighth of an inch at a time, waving its quills like wands, sliding toward its captor instead of away from him. With both hands he held the spear out and slightly down, then shook it, but that only seemed to infuriate the fish. It continued moving toward the bare hands, the tips of the beautiful quills only a few inches away now.

From a distance of thirty feet, swimming as hard as he could and trying to signal Woodrow at the same time, Markin watched Woodrow's hand reach forward tentatively and touch the tip of the nearest quill. Instantly the arm jerked back, and Markin waited for Gene to do what anyone else would have done: drop the spear. But Woodrow held on. At the base of each of those quills was a sac of venom. If Woodrow's finger had pressed down hard enough on the quill, he'd be in agony in a few minutes, his fingers swollen like sausages, the skin stretched until it looked like it would split open. Markin had seen someone get a good dose of that venom only once, when Ancha was stung in the inlet three years before. He did not want to see it again.

Mahalis reached Woodrow first. He grabbed the spear, lifted it carefully out of the water, and tossed it up on the coral. Markin took Woodrow by the arm and the three of them scrambled onto the reef.

For a minute they huddled there, peering into the water to see if the wriggling fish had attracted sharks. Markin watched the pulse pounding on the side of Woodrow's forehead. "You all right?"

Woodrow nodded shakily. He touched the tip of his left index finger and glared at the lionfish gasping on the coral near his feet.

Mahalis leaned over and examined Gene's wound, pressing the skin around the puncture with both thumbs, forcing a drop of blood. He looked up and pronounced perfectly one of the few dozen English words he knew: "Poison."

"Christ Almighty!"

"He means venom," Markin said. "It depends how hard you pushed, how much of it got inside you. I have some ointment back at the hut. But we'll have to wait and see how bad it is."

For three or four minutes Mahalis worked on Woodrow's finger. He squeezed from the palm up, forcing out a few red drops. When no more blood appeared, Mahalis put the finger in his mouth and scraped his teeth down its length. He sucked and spat several times. Finally, after checking Woodrow's eyes and pulse, and pressing several points on his arm looking for pain, he pronounced the wound a mild one.

Through all this, Woodrow remained enthralled by the lion-fish. Out of the water, it had lost its color. Now it gasped on the spear, a purplish, fleshy lump sprouting limp tentacles. "Christ," he said. "And I was worried about sharks."

"Watch," Markin told him.

Mahalis lifted the spear by its barbed end and swung it like a baseball bat so that the lionfish flew off and landed with a plop on the lagoon's surface. It floated there for a few seconds, swimming weakly, sending circles of ripples like radio waves out into the surrounding water. The ocean swirled a few feet away, there was a soft splash, and Woodrow's fish disappeared.

Mahalis joined his friends at the landing beach. The two Americans returned to Markin's hut, where Woodrow changed quickly out of the wet shorts and dabbed ointment on his finger. There was some discomfort between them, an impending dis-tance.

"I'll send you a note when I get back." Woodrow pulled a folded piece of paper from his pants pocket. "Is this the right address?" Markin glanced at it and nodded. "Leo Markin," Woodrow read. "That's who Steve told me to ask for. You don't use the first name."

"Right." For some reason the disclosure embarrassed Markin. When he'd enlisted, he'd decided that "Leo" didn't sound manly enough, and he'd asked his friends in boot camp to call him by his last name. In Vietnam he'd been known only as "Mark" or "Markin" or "the Marksman" and the first name had fallen into disuse, a label for a person who no longer existed. He looked away from Woodrow and moved toward the door. "We'd better get going. The launch driver won't wait."

Unless there was an unusually large number of passengers going aboard, the Japanese launch driver would make only four trips: two for cargo — mostly handicrafts and copra to be sold in Owen Town — two for passengers. By the time Woodrow and Markin got to the landing beach, the cargo had already been loaded and the first run of passengers was being ferried out to the ship. They joined the crowd and watched in silence. One by one Losapans climbed the rope ladder, the women stopping to clutch bright skirts around their knees, the men handing up bags of clothing, an occasional tattered suitcase, parcels of taro wrapped in breadfruit leaves. Smiles and waves went from deck to shore but there was a sense of abandonment in the air.

As the empty launch turned and began its final approach, Ninake stepped through the crowd and stood in front of Woodrow. "Remember Losapas," she said, adorning him with a necklace of pea-sized, brown and white shells.

A flicker crossed the wide face. Woodrow seemed not to know whether to embrace her or take her hand. He settled at last on a short bow, and she and Mahalis and those nearest him bowed back in unison. Markin offered his hand and said, "I'm glad you came out."

"So am I," Woodrow said. "Any messages?" Without thinking, Markin shook his head. Woodrow turned to Mahalis and held out his slightly swollen left hand; in it was a Swiss Army knife. Mahalis looked puzzled.

"It's a gift," Markin explained.

"*Pwata?*" Mahalis looked at Woodrow, then at Markin.

"He wants to know why."

"Tell him I enjoyed spearfishing more than anything I've done in forty years."

Mahalis smiled at the translation and cradled the knife in his palm. "*Olei le,*" he said.

"It means you're going," Markin said. "You're supposed to answer, *Olei nomw,* you're staying."

"Olay num," Woodrow said. He looked at Markin a final time, then climbed in beside the driver. The motor growled and sputtered, and the launch kicked away from shore.

Too late, Markin realized he had a message. "Tell Stevie I love him," he yelled. Woodrow waved as if he hadn't heard.

A hundred pairs of eyes followed the launch as it rose and fell on the gently rolling surface, growing smaller with each minute, finally nosing up to the *Micro Dawn* like a tugboat. The passengers ascended, the launch was hauled up on deck and lashed in place. Dreamlike, as slow as the movement of the tides, the white ship hoisted anchor, turned, and moved off toward Namulo and the western atolls.

Late that night Markin and Ninake lay on their backs in the warm hut, touching only along the length of one arm. Markin could not make himself fall asleep. His mind kept forcing on him old memories and he kept resisting them, fighting a battle of will he had not had to fight in a long time.

Ninake rolled over and rested an arm on his chest. "Do you think Gene will visit us again?" she said, her voice so quiet it seemed not to come from her body at all but from the warm, still air around them.

"Probably not."

She sighed, and Markin knew she was deciding whether to stay and sleep for a while or go home to her daughter. There were things she had trouble talking about, too — with him, at least. The man who had fathered Marcellina, for example, was a mystery, some kind of island secret. Markin did not know whether he was living or dead, whether he and Ninake had been married or not, how long he had stayed around. In six and a half years she had never mentioned him and he had never asked. Sometimes, though, he detected in her face the shadow of bad history, an expression of the most profound resignation, as if her hopes had been whittled down to accommodate only the offerings of each day. He knew the feeling, the discipline of not allowing yourself any dreams, and now he was finding out what happened when that discipline was lost.

She took hold of his shoulder and pulled them closer together. "Maybe we will visit Gene," she whispered, as though it were a great but impossible adventure, a fantasy. Woodrow seemed to have affected them in identical ways. The unexpected arrival, the quick departure, the fact that he had blended into their lives so mysteriously and with such apparent ease — eating, sleeping, spearfishing like an islander — had somehow converted America from the abstract to the actual. People could go there and come back. Markin thought of his disability money, compounding itself in the bank account in Owen Town, several thousand dollars by now. He thought of the snapshot tucked between the pages of the paperback Bible on his night table.

"We could visit my father," he said, shocking both of them.

Long ago, in response to their questions, he'd told Ninake and Mahalis that his father lived in America and that they hadn't seen each other for years — a common situation on Losapas, where children sometimes moved to Guam or one of the other districts and were never seen or heard from again. But this was the first time he'd ever mentioned the possibility of visiting him, taking Ninake along, the hostage who would ensure his return.

Startled out of her half sleep, Ninake lifted her head and studied his expression. "We could go," she said resolutely. "I would not turn into a different person."

He glanced at her, then stared up at the dark ceiling. "I know you wouldn't. Of course you wouldn't. When I said that I was only joking. My godfather and Gene —" he started to say, but she was already asleep and traveling.

His tired mind jumped from image to image, searching for something. He heard rats squealing and scratching on Ulua's roof and one of her dogs baying pitifully, yelping and whimpering as if it had seen or smelled its own death in the night. The noise roused the island's other dogs, and within a few seconds a chorus of barking sounded from the interior of the island. Markin heard Ulua's door squeak open and slam shut and her muttered, gravel-voiced threat: "Bark again and you will be dinner for me tomorrow night, mongrel. One more sound and I will get out the big pot and start the water boiling."

He remembered: "They eat dog on those islands," Warren, the old sailor, had said to him across the darkness between their hospital beds. "The women run around practically bare-assed." It had been a hot, sticky night on Guam. The hospital's air-conditioning system was not working well and neither of them could sleep. The old sailor had a history. He had captained a PT boat, fought his way across the Pacific as far as New Guinea, been wounded there, then spent twenty-five years wandering through steaming Asian ports, poor and sickly but otherwise unfettered. He was in the naval hospital on Guam for the eighth time and had developed a system for dealing with the sleepless nights and the pain and the various invasions his body was forced to endure in the name of healing: tubes, needles, enemas, x-rays, pills. When his torment became unbearable, whatever the hour, the sailor would reach around in his memory and bring forth another exotic tale. Markin had no choice but to listen. He would sometimes be riven from a feverish sleep by the rough voice (not unlike Ulua's), made to endure someone else's memories.

But on the night he was remembering now it was not pain or heat or Warren's stories that were keeping him awake. That morning the doctor had told Markin he would be released within a week, and the prospect of going back to Averill Beach terrified him. How could he face Angela and his father and his friends, and pretend to believe in the life they were living? How could he possibly get married and settle down and play at being part of that life, bounce babies on his knee and mow the lawn on Saturday afternoons? From the moment the doctor left his bed-side he spent all his time thinking of places he might escape to —

Thailand, the Canadian wilderness, South America, Australia — imagining new lives for himself there. He remembered something someone in his platoon had said about the Trust Territories of Micronesia, and that was what he mentioned to the old sailor. Warren had never been to Micronesia; all of his battles had been farther south. But he had, in his travels, come across a few Micronesians who had left their homes in Truk or Ponape or Yap for the promise of cash jobs in Malaysia or Singapore.

Markin asked to hear more about the islands, and every detail Warren provided — the sailing canoes, storytellers, beautiful women — became part of a fantasy life, a new start. Warren did nothing to disillusion him. "I'll tell you one thing, though," he said on this night. "You go down to one of those atolls, boy, you live like those people for a while, and you'll *never* come back to the world. Believe me. You'll be there for the duration."

Markin had believed him. For seven years, six months, and four days he had believed him.

# PART TWO

# 7

BETWEEN FIVE O'CLOCK,
when the workday ended, and sunset, when Mahalis and his
family gathered beneath the thatched shelter for dinner,
Markin liked to sit in the expanding patch of shade behind his
hut and carve. His tools — crosscut saw, chisels, mallet, whet-
stone, jackknife — arrived by mail order from Guam; his mate-
rials consisted of driftwood that had washed up on Ayao's western shore. Whenever he came across a piece he liked, he'd carry
it home and set it beside the hut. In time this collection got so far
ahead of him that it became a kind of open-air museum, and the
people on his end of the island would stop to admire it and to
speculate on the fate of certain pieces. The Losapans came from
a long tradition of woodworkers — the old sailing canoes had
been ornately carved and painted — so Markin's hobby seemed

perfectly natural to them. The difference was that their artistry was used to adorn something practical, such as boats, doorways, and tackle boxes, while his was purely frivolous, beauty for its own sake. To the Losapans this endowed the sculptures with an exotic appeal, and the demand for them was so great that Markin had to make a list of orders to avoid offending his friends and neighbors. He'd given Ninake his best work, a small, polished pair of leaping dolphins cut from mangrove wood; Mahalis owned an abstract piece that resembled three warriors standing shoulder to shoulder; Ancha, who cut Markin's hair once a month, requested a replica of a dugout canoe, complete with miniature outrigger and paddle. No money ever changed hands, but after a delivery Markin would come home to a bunch of bananas hanging in his hut or a freshly caught yellowtail in a pan on his doorstep or children waiting with gifts of shell jewelry.

He thought of his carving only as a hobby, but he knew the list of advance orders and the collection of driftwood served also as proof that he was here to stay. And even after all these years, that held some kind of special meaning for the Losapans; it changed the way they saw him. In the past all *Re Wons* — American, Japanese, Spanish, German — had come to Losapas for short, often violent visits and then left, always taking some of the island with them, leaving a scar. But from the beginning Markin had come on different terms, asking nothing except to be allowed to live as they lived. All he had to offer in return was his continuing, exotic presence — a negligible payment, he thought, on a huge debt. But it seemed to be enough. A *Re Merika* was choosing to live on Losapas; it gave the islanders a special status in the eyes of the outside world.

Sometimes the tap of his mallet attracted an audience, but on this Saturday evening, as the island was settling into its Sabbath, he worked alone. In his hands a dry, two-foot coconut log was changing shape. It was to be a surprise for Elias, and Markin was glad for the lack of company. He'd been working half an hour, boring straight down into one end of the billet, when he heard someone cry out in the clearing. He stopped tapping and listened. Coming over the top of the hut, muted by the concrete and the distance, but unmistakable, was Ulua's foghorn voice: "Ship! Shi-ip! I see a ship sailing toward Losapas! Shi-ip!" It had been three weeks since Woodrow's departure, and every man, woman, and child on Losapas knew it would be at least another ten days before they saw the *Micro Dawn* again. Markin grinned and returned to his chiseling. Ulua had finally been undone by the heat, finally flipped, sailed over the edge of her own horizon. She was seeing boats in the clouds.

But when he'd put down his tools for the day, dumped a bucket of spring water over his head, and was coming around the front corner of the hut, Markin too saw a vessel moving into the lagoon. He knew immediately who the captain was. Only one man in the district was crazy enough to bring a motorboat into waters so treacherous, in light so slim.

"Louis!" Ulua bellowed. "Louis is here!"

Louis' unscheduled visits never raised the island to any fever of celebration. For one thing, he carried no kerosene, medicine, or food, only the rare piece of mail he might have discovered in the dusty back room of the Owen Town post office, or if he'd been exceptionally lucky, a small grouper or tuna. For another, he had managed, in the course of a fifteen-year acquaintance with Losapas, to estrange himself from half the population. He borrowed money for his fish business and forgot to pay it back; he used the island's only motorboat and scraped it against reefs or returned it littered with banana peels and empty Pepsi cans; he talked to women — all women, whether married or single, young or old — as if their only purpose in life were to quench his legendary sexual thirst. Louis' face was an adventure map. Two front teeth had been knocked out in a brawl on Guam; a pink, jagged scar ran from the bottom of his left eye, across the nose, down to the right corner of his mouth, a memento, he boasted, of a bar fight with two Ponapeans over a fifteen-year-old Indonesian prostitute. His jaw had been broken in New Guinea.

In the course of his wanderings Louis had spent enough time

around Americans to pick up much of their language and some of their ways, and in small doses Markin enjoyed his company. He caught sight of Mahalis squatting in front of his house, watching Louis cruise briskly through a minefield of coral knobs he could not possibly see. Markin scuffed his foot on the sand. Mahalis looked over. They both shook their heads and smiled.

By the time they arrived at the landing beach, Louis had already anchored his twenty-eight-foot *Pirate* and was paddling ashore in the leaky outrigger canoe he kept lashed to the bow. Mahalis and Markin helped him drag it up onto the sand.

"Thank you, my friends." Louis bowed to Mahalis and shook Markin's hand. No sooner had he sat between them on the coral sea wall than he was up again and feeling around in the bottom of the canoe. He returned holding a cardboard box and an envelope in one hand and a ten-pound red snapper in the other. He presented Mahalis with the fish. "Miako can make *sasimi*," he said, displaying his broken smile. Markin accepted the box and the letter. "These were at the post office for you, Mister."

"Thanks for checking, Louis. I'll buy you a beer next time I'm in."

The box, he knew, contained something he'd ordered months before from the dive shop in Owen Town; it would go well with what he was carving for Elias. The letter was a surprise. He tilted it this way and that in the fading light until he was able to make out the return address. Like a true Losapan, he kept his feelings from his face. "What's the news from Owen Town, Louis?"

The captain of the *Pirate* shrugged and pulled a crumpled pack of Camels from his shirt pocket. Several other Losapans had come down to the beach. Louis eyed them warily. "You may not be able to buy me a beer next time you're in," he told Markin. "Some fools are trying to get a prohibition law passed."

"Trouble?"

Louis sucked on the cigarette and blew smoke over his shoulder. "Sure, trouble. The kids can't hold their liquor. They come down from the hills with machetes on their belts. There was a rape. The sheriff quit."

Mahalis shook his head sadly.

"How is the fish business?"

"Eh, Mister, the fish business is like a woman — wonderful when she's good, terrible when she's bad, unpredictable the rest of the time." This was Louis' standard line, and it drew the usual smiles from the men on the beach, softened his reception a bit. "How's my Ninake?" he said, meeting Markin's eyes for the first time.

"Fine. Go within fifty yards of her and I'll sink your boat."

Louis' laugh was an oily snicker. He raised his palms and looked away. "My fights are in my past," he said. "My fights are in my past."

As darkness fell and the banter floated back and forth, Markin knew Louis would begin hinting around for a meal and a place to sleep. He had put him up many times, warning Ninake away in advance, staying awake much of the night listening to Louis talk of his hilarious seductions and his brawls. It was not a bad way to be kept awake, and Markin weighed his options for a minute before he gathered his mail and stood. "Thanks again for these, Louis."

"Going to bed already, Mister? Have a woman waiting?"

"Good night."

"Okay," Louis said, switching to English. "Good night. Seeing you tomorrow."

Markin took the shore route back to the clearing, shadowed by a small sense of guilt. Louis had made a special trip to the post office for him and he had all but ignored him. Usually he was more generous. Tonight he had a letter from Stevie Palermo in his hand; he needed to be alone.

A trace of light remained in the hut, enough to distinguish silhouettes on his night table and the American flag on Stevie's stamp. Markin sat on the pandanus mat, breathing the harsh, sweet smell of frying fish and listening to the laughter of women working in the clearing. There were no continents on the map across from him now, only shadows, tones of gray. Soon even these blended to black and the shrill ringing of crickets announced night. He found himself drifting back to Averill Beach, remembering a late-August Saturday with the sun ready to go down and a breeze coming up off the ocean, carrying the first taste of fall. His father was out in the back yard with Stevie, playing bocce; he could hear the *thunk* of the wooden balls and an occasional happy shout.

He had been in a restless mood all that summer, painting houses, working two nights a week at the dog track, struggling to imagine a future. The track closed in October, at about the same time the painting season ended, so he saw no future there. He and his friends talked about enlisting in the Marine Corps, about starting a car repair business, about enrolling in college that fall (he and Nicky DeAngelo had been accepted at Northeastern University), but all their talk seemed to come to nothing, vaporous notions at a time when he needed something solid. That day he had worked around the yard until five, called Angela, showered, shaved, and promised himself he wouldn't think beyond the weekend. Nicky was out with Janice Cosso; they were all supposed to meet at Stevie's Place at ten.

His father let him use the car, a six-year-old Pontiac convertible. Top down, muffler grumbling, he drove it along Stadium Avenue, up the hill to Angela's house, killed the engine, and sat by the curb, taking in the sweet evening. Angela's neighbors were sitting out on their front porch; he could hear their quiet conversation and the *click* and *tink* of ice in glasses. The dusk was touched with the scent of a fresh-mown lawn.

After a while a screen door creaked and slapped. Mr. Panechieso appeared on the sidewalk with a glass of iced coffee in one hand, his belly distended by the evening meal and pressing tightly against an immaculate sleeveless undershirt. His voice was like stone dropping on stone. "Nice night."

"Perfect."

"She's almost ready, Leo."

Carmine Panechieso was a mason. Six days a week from April to November he laid walks, pointed chimneys, designed and built stone walls. He could drive down almost any street in Averill Beach and see small monuments to himself, proof that he had lived, worked, found his place. On Sundays he took his family to the nine o'clock mass at St. Lucy's, ate roast beef and ziti for dinner, spent the afternoon working among his tomato plants or sitting in the shade with the *Sunday Herald* or watching a football game on TV. If any one person represented the solidity he was looking for it was Cammy Panechieso, but lately even that had changed. Cammy had lost his younger brother at the beginning of the summer and the death seemed to have undermined his whole personality. At the wake Cammy had stood next to the casket like a deaf-mute, his hands folded in front of him and his eyes staring off into the sad distance.

Now he leaned against the car and looked down the street at nothing. Markin looked, too, and from their small masculine discomfort grew something indestructible, a real connection. Or so it had seemed to him then. The feeling stayed with him long after he and Angela had sat through the beach traffic and parked. It was there somehow among her smells and the black shine of her hair, the fragile print of her jacket against his arm. As they sat on the hurricane wall, drinking milk shakes and watching the seagulls circle, something whispered to him, made him believe that he was blood-bound to this city and its ways, that there was a place for him here, he was family. That night he intended to ask Angela to marry him. He'd been thinking of it since long before graduation, planning it in earnest all summer. The moment with Mr. Panechieso had confirmed him in it: it was right, the right thing.

He and Angie loved the beach, and they lingered on the hurricane wall, listening to the waves rumble in and roll themselves flat in the darkness, a pale line of foam catching the streetlight for a moment, then fading. Behind them the neon excitement of the strip was drawing tourists from all over New England. They could hear the Gypsy barker in front of the Dodgems, smell popcorn and onions, pizza, fried dough, pepper steak. In an hour they were expected at Stevie's. He would have to pose the question before then — or afterward in the convertible in front of her parents' house. He formed the words in his mind a hundred times but went the whole night without speaking them.

A year went by without his asking. Something he could not make sense of slipped like a phantom between him and Angela, then him and Mr. Panechieso, him and his own father. Monsignor Calliselli told him it might be the devil. The Marines offered him an honest way out of Averill Beach. Sixteen months later he was in Vietnam.

In Nam he thought often of the beach, made a nightly prayer of remembering it, lifting a detail out of the past, holding it up to an interior light, passing his memories around the platoon the way others passed snapshots of girlfriends. On the worst nights, when he was covered in mud or red dust, when fatigue and fear had turned him into a robot, strands of cloth and skin patrolling an evil darkness — on those nights he spoke to himself in whispers of the beach in August, Saturday nights at Stevie's Place. He reconstructed conversations, whole parties. At such times the rule of reality did not apply. Broken relationships could be mended by a thought, mistakes undone between breaths, hometowns and family altered to suit your mood. Living in the Glorious Past, one of his friends had called it, a bad habit, something you resorted to when the present went sour.

Louis' laughter echoed across the clearing, followed closely by Mahalis' mellifluous voice. Markin waited until they were well past the hut before lighting his kerosene lamp. Since Woodrow's visit he'd found himself returning to that habit, glorifying the past, losing his grip on the present. After one particularly restless night, when he'd dreamed he was having dinner with the Panechiesos and Angela was passing him a bowl of breadfruit, he'd taken the snapshot of his father and stuffed it away in his seabag. For a single peaceful week that had worked. He'd been reinstated to full residence on Losapas, to living in the Glorious

Present. Now his godfather had sent him a letter with the American flag and fireworks on it, and even the handwriting smelled of a New England summer. He cursed quietly.

On those rare occasions when he received a letter from the other world, Markin liked to linger over it, savor it, open it in the privacy of his hut. It was the one area of his present life he kept from Mahalis and the Losapans, though on occasion he'd bring out a wrinkled postcard of Boston or a picture of his father's house and pass it around, his contribution to the evening's entertainment. He checked the envelope to see that there were no photos, then slit it open with the blade of his jackknife and pulled out a scrap of soft white paper, a piece of cocktail napkin, it looked like. He held it up to the light and could barely make out the message printed there.

> Leo:
>    I hope you get my package that I sent right after the Fourth of July when I was thinking about you all day.
>    Leo, Im not much of a writer. Im sorry.
>    I just was thinking of you so strong today I had to write. I know your father wrote you but I wanted to write too. He's a tough guy, your father. Dont worry. He'll bounce back.
>    We still miss you at the Place.
> Love, your Godfather, Stevie

Markin reread the note three times, then blew out the kerosene lamp and sat in the darkness with his eyes closed.

Bounce back from what?

Two hours later, when Ulua's window went dark and Markin felt sure her dogs had settled in for the night, he pulled on a shirt and slipped out into the clearing. In Mahalis' front room a lamp still burned. From inside the house came the sound of Louis' voice — a steady murmur punctuated by lewd chuckling — and for a moment the scene drew him. Louis always made him think of the person he'd set out to be when he left Guam: a nomad, a man with no real connection to anyone. He thought of Warren, the old sailor, and wondered where he might find himself on a night like this, in what hot, noisy city, regretting what? He folded Stevie's letter and pushed it into his shirt pocket. For the two seconds it took him to draw and expel a breath, an old, stale fear stirred inside him, then he was moving through the leafy darkness behind his hut, headed east.

The moon had not yet cleared the tops of the coconut palms and Markin was not carrying a flashlight, so the going was slow. Each cautious step he took sent the creatures of the night — coconut rats, lizards, robber crabs — scurrying and scrambling for cover. By the time he reached the eastern end of the island, the moon had risen enough so that he could see the metal roof of Ninake's house. A square of yellow broke the near wall. She was sitting in a pool of light in a corner, stitching a hem on a child's skirt. He tapped on the windowsill and she motioned him in.

Ninake and Marcellina shared their small house with Belinda, Ninake's older sister. The living quarters were divided into two doorless cubicles: a sleeping room and the dirt-floored outer room, where Ninake sat. She could not spend the night with him or have him visit without Belinda knowing it, and Belinda could not know anything without passing it on to Ulua, who would broadcast it island-wide. Every time he stepped into the house in Belinda's presence, Markin felt as if he were walking onto a movie set where every word he said, each scene, was being recorded. Scene one: here is the strange *Re Merika* with the scar in his hair coming to visit, carrying a string of fish so small they are hardly worth cleaning. Scene two: here is the strange *Re Merika* knocking on the door with a fistful of banana flowers, making up with his sweetheart. Scene three: here is the strange *Re Merika* sneaking into the house at midnight with his lips twisted like a gecko's tongue and an envelope sticking out of his pocket.

But Ninake was alone in the room this time and Markin squatted next to her without making a sound.

"Why are you pretending you can't talk?" she whispered, letting her hands rest in her lap.

"I got a letter from America," he said, taking the scrap of paper from the envelope and showing it to her, watching it tremble in his hands. "I am going back. For a visit."

She gave him an enigmatic look, took the scrap of paper into her hand, and tried to make some sense out of the words. "Will you go for a long time?"

"You can come. We can go on this ship and come back on the next one."

She looked down at the skirt, then at the envelope, then back into his face, and he saw that she was playing for time, hoping, just as he had hoped, in the days after Woodrow left, that the possibility of leaving Losapas would just disappear.

# 8

"CHURCH," Louis said, a thread of disdain in his voice. "It is hard to understand people who go to church."

They were standing in a block of shade next to the deacon's house, leaning back against the plywood wall, watching Losapans in their Sunday clothes gather in groups of three or four around the perimeter of the sweltering clearing.

Markin was able to give the conversation only part of his attention. "I go," he said after a pause.

"Only when Deacon Paradise is away. That makes a little sense to me. What I don't understand is people who sit in there listening to him talk for an hour, then come outside believing they will go up to heaven because of it." Louis ogled a group of smartly dressed girls standing near the church door. "Maybe they believe listening to him is payment for their sins." He thought a moment. "Maybe it is."

As they watched, Ancha's old uncle, Efilo, shuffled across the clearing carrying Markin's mallet. He approached an empty scuba tank that hung from a crooked palm tree and struck it twice, waiting between blows for the sound to fade. A few more people left their conversations and went through the doors of the whitewashed church.

"And I don't understand people who are married."

"What are you talking about, Louis? You were married."

"Twice." Louis spat as if he had tasted something bitter. "I don't understand why I did it."

"You did it because you met a woman you wanted to spend most of your time with."

"No, Mister."

"You did it because you wanted regular sex instead of having to hunt around all the time."

"I like hunting around."

"You did it because everyone else does it and you didn't want to feel left out."

Louis shook his head. "I think about this very much, Mister. All the time I am out on the sea alone I think about it. Why do people get married? Why do they go to church?"

"You're a *philosopher*." Markin had to switch to English, and though Louis nodded, he was sure the word made no sense to him.

"I was born on Awaniku."

"The southern atolls."

Louis grunted. "On Awaniku the women dig taro and the men clean fish. On Losapas and all the northern islands the men dig taro and the women clean fish."

"So what?"

"I think," Louis said in the most earnest tone Markin had ever heard him use, "that there is some island where no one gets married or goes to church, where everyone is like me and you,

Marr-keen. Maybe Merika." Louis smiled and wagged his head back and forth, imitating a gesture Losapans made when they didn't understand something but found it amusing. "When I was a boy I sailed into Owen Town with my father, and while he was with his friends I sneaked away and ran down to the harbor to look at the boats. There were some Merikans there. I couldn't speak Merikan then but they took me on their boat and showed me everything — Merikan food, clothes, the magazine with the naked girls. *Playboy*."

"How old were you?"

"Probably eleven. I found one picture there . . . the woman was looking at me like she needed sex."

"Only one?"

"This woman needed sex with *me*. The men knew it. They cut the picture from their magazine and gave it to me. I still have it in my boat . . . What is *slaku*?"

"Masturbate."

Louis squinted. "It is a hard word. You will have to write it for me. I *slaku* when I look at that picture. First time."

"You know what the deacon would say about that."

Louis pondered a moment. "Fuck the deacon," he said.

"All women in America aren't like that, you know. They don't all go around naked, looking at you like the women in *Playboy*."

"I know," Louis said, but he sounded unconvinced.

Efilo shuffled across the clearing for the third time and dealt the scuba tank a final, resonant blow.

"What are you going to do afterwards?" Louis asked.

"I have to talk with Mahalis."

"About what?"

Markin almost told him. This morning, for some reason, he had the feeling that Louis was the only person on the island who would really understand what this was about. Louis sailed his boat into the lagoon in twilight. He went spearfishing off the back beach during typhoons. They were both forever trying to prove to themselves how fearless they were — the true sign of a man who believed, deep down, that he could not be forgiven.

"I have to give him some money for the coffee he bought last month."

After a moment Louis grinned. He was used to being lied to and he raised no protest. "Taka has invited me for a game of cards," he said.

"What time?"

"Now." Louis looked up at the sun and Markin watched a droplet of sweat slip along the smooth pink scar and onto his jaw. The droplet hung in his sparse whiskers a moment, glistened, and dropped.

"What about church?"

"I don't go."

"Never?"

"Never," Louis said, laughing. "Not even when Deacon Paradise is on Afanu saying a funeral mass. Not even if Deacon Paradise was in heaven saying a funeral mass — for my mother and father. You should come play cards, Marr-keen."

"Afterwards."

"Afterwards is too late." They walked out into the sunlight. "I have won all of Taka's money by then."

"In that case, come by the thatched shelter and I'll win it back for him."

"You are bragging like a *Re Merika* now, Mister." Louis said, then he paused, frowned, and looked down at his toes. Markin knew what was coming. "My friend," Louis continued, in English now. "I need to ask if you can borrow me a little money."

"How little?"

Louis coughed once and looked at the church. "Twenty beeg ones."

"In my hut, in the drawer of the night table, in an envelope."

Louis turned to face Markin and shook his head in disbelief. "Mister!" he said, amazed. "You will let me go there and take it myself?"

"Why not?"

Louis searched his face for another few seconds, then burst

into a roll of great Gypsy laughter, which Markin was certain could be heard inside the church.

There were no pews. The women knelt to the left of the center aisle, and their half of the high-ceilinged chapel was alive with color: orange, red, yellow, and white print skirts, rings of flowers in shining black hair. On the right side knelt a smaller number of men, most wearing a white, short-sleeved shirt and the only pair of long trousers they owned. Markin chose a spot in the back row, placed his sandals side by side in front of him, knelt on them, and leaned his weight back on his heels. His mind would not be still.

Deacon Morinae (also referred to as Deacon Paradise because of his frequent references to the Promised Land, the Place of Eternal Rest, the Garden of Eden, and other imaginary states, which captured little of the Losapans' interest) had taken the motorboat to Afanu for a funeral mass, so the altar was graced only by a large frayed Bible, a chalice filled with coconut milk, and four columns of ship biscuits that a priest in Owen Town had blessed.

Miako began the first hymn and everyone but Markin joined in. He closed his eyes and listened, not wanting to spoil the harmony with his timbreless, two-note gasp. On those Sundays when Deacon Morinae was not present to nourish his flock with one of his tedious homilies, the service consisted only of the reading of the appropriate Gospel, and Holy Communion. There was an excuse to fill the hour with song, and the Losapans made the most of it. They went on and on, repeating all the verses the missionaries had taught them and adding several of their own. Marcellina ended the hymn, finally, on a high, joyous note, and the congregation sank into a reverent silence.

The sacrament of confession was available to the Losapans only rarely, when the priest from the District Center made his rounds, so Deacon Morinae had determined that the quiet moments after the first hymn be used for contemplation of one's sins. Markin closed his eyes and bowed his head, but instead of his sins, what came into his mind was a vision of St. Lucy's, the church he had prayed in as a child in Averill Beach, a dark, cool, simultaneously threatening and beautiful place, the place where he'd gotten most of his ideas about what it meant to be alive. He could picture the oak pews, the carpeted middle aisle, the ornate brown marble altar decorated with vases of flowers and the American flag. A mural of Jesus ascending from a circle of his disciples covered the domed ceiling. At either end of the altar rail, banks of votive candles flickered in tall maroon glasses. He and his father had often slipped into the church on weekday evenings to light a candle for his mother's soul — he could still hear the sound of coins dropping into the metal offering box and echoing against the enormous ceiling — and on Sundays when he watched the quavering flames he was always surprised at how many other bereaved sons, daughters, husbands, and wives there were among the worshipers, how many other people had problems only God could solve. Halfway through the mass his father and three other men left their seats, met in the vestibule, and marched up the middle aisle holding the long-handled, felt-lined offering baskets. When his father came to the pew where he'd sat, he always tapped his son gently on the chest as he slid the basket past, and it was that small gesture of love, not his sins, that Markin found himself meditating on after the first hymn.

Olapwuch stood in front of the congregation, hands on the Holy Bible, gray-streaked hair tied back and crowned with a circle of yellow flowers, breasts resting on the edge of the altar. In her hoarse voice she began to relate the story of the changing of water into wine at Cana — Jatsos' first miracle. There was no false enthusiasm in her tone, none of the deacon's sentimental smiles, pleas, and uplifting intonations. What she was reading was simply the truth: in order to please his mother, the spirit who created the universe had changed water into wine at a wedding feast; there was nothing in the story to be either proud of or skeptical about. She closed the book and returned to her place.

Her reading was followed by another contemplative silence, another long hymn, a prayer said over the biscuits and coconut milk, and then two lines — one male, one female — formed in the center aisle. Markin sat alone against the rear wall and watched the first man break a biscuit in two and hand half of it to the first woman, who put it into her mouth, then took another biscuit and handed it to the second man, and so on until the lines shrank to nothing and the body of Jatsos, like so many stars, had been divided up among the island's Catholics. All through the final hymn — the longest and most beautiful of the three, the same one the family had sung for Woodrow — Markin tried nervously to raise up a prayer to the God of his childhood, a plea for strength. It was a useless effort. He still could not get beyond the conviction that the God of his childhood had stopped listening to him the day he left his father and Angela and went off, so willingly, to war.

Mahalis, Markin, and Elias walked home from mass together at an island pace: lifting the left foot, letting it swing slowly through the air, straightening the knee, and allowing the foot to drop onto sand, lifting the right foot, swinging it ... Their heavy-footedness seemed appropriate on the Sabbath, when the women did not cook and the men did not fish and the heat lay on undistracted minds like a heavy penance. This morning the slow pace gave Markin time to phrase his words. He waited until they had passed the cluster of iron-roofed houses, then forced himself to speak. "I am going back to America," he said quietly. "For a visit."

Elias was holding on to his left hand, and Markin could see that the boy was cocking his head as if he hadn't quite caught the words. Mahalis only nodded.

Elias released the hand and skipped a half step ahead of the others so that he was walking sideways and looking up into Markin's face.

"It is important that you take Ninake," Mahalis said.

Markin was astounded. Mahalis' byword was *Esse lefil-ifil.* It's not important, it doesn't matter. When Markin failed to kill a single crab in hours of trying, when he lost lures night-fishing off the beach with a hand line, when he offered to increase his rent payment, Mahalis' response was always the same: *Esse lefil-ifil.* Now, at last, something seemed to matter.

"I am taking her," he said. "We'll be gone one or two ships."

Mahalis nodded again, and the curtain descended. Markin had envisioned sitting down with him and spilling out the whole history. He'd spent hours deciding how he would say it, how he would describe Vietnam and Averill Beach, what words he could use to explain why he'd finally decided to go back, what guarantee he could offer that he'd return. Now all that was pointless. Generations of living in a tiny, closed society had bred in the Losapans an automatic disguise reflex: their real thoughts and feelings traveled like crabs in deep tunnels, avoiding the light. If anything at all showed in Mahalis' eyes it might have been a fleeting trace of doubt, a faint premonition that this "visit" would be permanent.

They were passing Hermon's house now, and Elias was tugging at Markin's shirt, trying without success to utter his name. "I have a favor to ask before we go," Markin said, keeping his eyes away from the boy.

"Anything."

"I want you to give Elias permission to spearfish with me when we come back."

"Marr-keen," the boy gasped.

Mahalis stopped and turned, and the curtain disappeared. It was the only time Markin had ever seen him have trouble speaking. After a moment he said, "I give my permission."

Markin steered Elias into his hut and handed him the cardboard box. Elias placed it on the floor, sat, and holding it steady with his feet, opened the flaps, tore out the balls of paper, and shook the box free of a black mask and orange-tipped snorkel. The boy's abdomen was puffing in and out like a bellows and his hand had gone suddenly clumsy, but by pressing his stump against the glass he was able to hold the mask to his face and bring the black rubber strap over the top of his head. Markin reached around behind him and adjusted the snorkel. The easy part, he said to himself. Elias stood, peered around the room as if he were underwater, spotted one of Markin's spears standing in the corner, and reached for it and the *kumi* without thinking. His left arm was already moving to position its thumb, but there was no thumb, no hand, nothing but a fingerless arm that ended a few inches below the elbow and could never, even in the kindest imagination, be used to hold a *kumi* and guide a spear. The boy looked up at him through the glass. Markin took a breath, reached beneath his table, and lifted into view the palm log prosthesis he'd stayed up most of the night to finish. The hollowed-out log ended in what looked like a spread thumb and forefinger. He had cut two slits in the top end and, with a length of surgical tubing, had fashioned a sling to fit over the boy's shoulder. "It's almost done," he said.

Elias raised the mask onto his forehead and studied the contraption warily, as though it were a math problem or a book. He looked briefly into Markin's face, then back at the makeshift arm. He leaned the spear against the table, took hold of the palm log with a trembling hand, and pushed it tightly up over his stump. Markin showed him how to arrange the sling, and Elias hooked the *kumi* and spear in place and looked up again, his face twitching as if it were about to break apart. "It will work, Marrkeen," he said. "We will spearfish. You and me."

ON THE MORNING he was to leave Losapas — a Ship Day of terrible proportions — Markin awoke before sunrise and walked out to the back beach. Clouds scudded across the sky, catching feeble streaks of bluish light; the air was wet and cool. He sat on a slab of coral stone and watched the sea awaken.

His life once again seemed painted with a peculiar shade of subtle violence, as though he were fated always to make decisions that led him away from any kind of settled calm, as though he were constitutionally unable to let well enough alone.

The sun appeared, yellow breaking blue, and that was the world, always tearing itself open, risking some new order. There had to be a lesson in it.

When Markin returned to his hut, Ancha was waiting for him,

sitting on the floor of the inner room, sweating vigorously as he always did, holding a gift of three new handmade lures. In great detail he told Markin everything he should know about the lures: what times of day each should be used, which kinds of fish they would catch and why, what size line he should tie them to, and how to let the line run loosely between his thumb and forefinger so he could feel the fish nibbling and sniffing and be ready for the strike.

When Ancha left, Markin went outside to wash and discovered Lawrence waiting at the spring behind the hut, holding a piece of mangrove root — from a place on Ayao where the spirits bathed, he said — suggesting Markin might want to do some carving during the first big rainstorm in America, keep himself from getting bored there.

A few minutes after Lawrence left, Olapwuch came padding up to the front window with a cigarette in one hand and a leaf-and-twine belt over her shoulder. It was important, she told him, to wear the belt on the ship, get some sea spray on it: the brine and sun would dry the leaf stems and make them strong.

They all cautioned him to be kind to the ocean spirits, to drop a sweet piece of pandanus over the stern every evening just before the sun went down. All of them assured him they would watch out for Marcellina in Ninake's absence, that he and Ninake shouldn't worry. And they all touched him lightly on the shoulder and left with the ancient salutation, a simple statement of fact: "*Olei-le.*" You are going.

While Markin was trying to find room in the full seabag for the lures and the mangrove root, Mahalis and Elias came into the hut as they usually did, without knocking. They stood quietly near the door and watched Markin dump his clothes onto the mat and repack them.

Elias seemed to have lost the power of speech. His father spoke for him: "You will be back in two ships?"

"One or two. It depends on how soon we run out of money."

"We have something for you." Mahalis took five twenty-dollar bills from his back pocket, fanned them like playing cards, and extended his arm. "It is from Miako. She told us to give it to you."

Markin hesitated a moment. What Mahalis held out so casually in his hand represented a year's work, everything he and Miako could save in twelve months of cutting copra and weaving mats. Markin pretended to look closely at the money. "What's this?"

Mahalis examined the bills now, too. "This?" he said. "This is Merikan food."

"Americans eat this?"

Mahalis nodded. "That's why they're so thin and their eyes are green."

Elias giggled, but Markin could see the pain in his face, and in Mahalis' face, too. He could feel it in himself. "It's a strange race," he said, unsure of his voice. "A strange island."

"*Ewer*," Mahalis said. "Of course. And it is very far away. So take this in case the *chet* brings you back only as far as Ponape. I have a good friend there, Ege. He likes Merikan food. Give him this and he will bring you and Ninake back in his *mota*."

Ponape was six hundred miles to the southeast, and both of them knew that no one, not even Louis, would attempt such a trip in an open motorboat. Both of them also knew that Markin had more money in the bank in Owen Town than Mahalis and Miako would be able to save in a lifetime. Markin took the bills and folded them into his mildewed wallet.

Mahalis insisted on carrying Markin's seabag to the landing beach, and Elias went to Ninake's house and insisted on carrying her things, too, though they were rolled into a cloth bundle that weighed only a few pounds. As the launch driver ferried his first load of passengers from beach to ship, Mahalis stood on one side of Markin, Elias on the other, none of them quite sure what to do next. Shaking hands was not a Losapan gesture, bowing was too formal, embracing out of the question. The closest the language allowed them to come to farewell was *olei-le, olei-nomw*. It did not suffice.

The launch driver ran his boat up onto the beach with a

grating sound Markin could feel in his belly. Mechanically, he touched Mahalis and Elias on the shoulder, waded into the water, put one hand on the gunwale, then made himself turn and look for Ninake. She was kneeling next to Marcellina at the top of the beach, stroking the girl's hair and brushing tears from her face. Beside him he could sense the launch driver, also watching, impatience radiating from his tanned, pinched face like a bad smell. In a minute all the other passengers were on board, but Ninake was still talking to her daughter, still explaining and promising. Finally, she stood and started down the sand, and Marcellina clutched her leg and dragged along beside her, sobbing louder and louder as they approached the edge of the water, streams of tears running down her cheeks. Markin made himself watch.

Ninake stopped and knelt in front of her daughter again and ran her hands slowly down the length of each arm until she was holding the tips of Marcellina's fingers. "*Kete osukosuk,*" Markin heard her say in a voice that had been ripped apart. "Don't worry."

"I am leaving," the driver announced. He reached out to engage the motor and Markin caught his wrist and twisted it until the man cried out. The other passengers stared. Markin let go immediately, hoping Ninake hadn't seen. In a moment she was standing beside the launch, waist-deep in water. He helped her aboard and they moved away from the beach in a gentle, rolling ocean, accompanied the whole way by the driver's muttering and the wails of the girl stranded on shore.

When the passengers were aboard and the launch and anchor had been raised, the *Micro Dawn* turned and pulled slowly away from the landing beach, its huge diesel engines grinding up to quarter power, where they would remain until it cleared the lagoon. Markin and Ninake stood at the stern rail, watching the water spitting and kicking near the propellers, following the white wake back into the shallows, where it spread and flattened and broke like a frayed ribbon. Their friends on shore seemed to be squeezing together. Mahalis, Miako, Olapwuch, and Elias had all blended into one brown huddle now, leaving Marcellina standing at the edge of the water, alone.

Markin wondered if Ninake would find anything in America that could possibly be worth this price.

In twenty minutes the *Micro Dawn* passed through the cut in the big reef. Its engines went to full power, choking out their black, foul breath. The jostling of the open sea commenced, and like a piece of green fruit tumbling slowly off the edge of the world, Losapas sank out of sight. Ninake stood beside him for a few more seconds, as if hoping the island would reappear, then, without saying anything, she went to sit with a group of Losapans who had already staked out a section of the sheltered sleeping area and were unrolling mats and unwrapping parcels of food. Markin remained at the rail, locked in a trance of self-doubt, staring down at the purple flying fish that burst out of the water and coasted along eerily for a few seconds before being drawn back to the place where they could breathe.

# 10

THEIR FIRST three days at
sea passed uneventfully, the weather typically hot and still, time
slow. A subtle discomfort had established itself between them
during the trauma of leaving Losapas, but gradually and steadily it disappeared — a word, a touch, a moment standing together at the dark rail, watching men fishing with hand lines.
The other atolls on the *Micro Dawn*'s route — Mulo, Namulo,
and Afanu — looked much like Losapas, and Markin and
Ninake chose not to disembark. Late in the afternoon of the
fourth day the ship encountered rain and rough water. That
night no one slept, and the next morning a hundred tired outer
islanders watched as a dark spot on the horizon swelled and
separated into the seven green peaks of Owen's Lagoon. Those
who had never been to the District Center before were given

space along the bow rail. They stood close together, rendered speechless by the height of the islands, running their eyes from base to peak in disbelief. When Ninake finally left the rail and came over to stand beside him, Markin saw the smile he had not seen since a week before they'd left Losapas.

"It's not what I thought it would be," she said. "Not at all. I want to climb to the top."

"We have two days before the plane leaves. We'll do everything there is to do."

As the *Micro Dawn* entered Owen's Lagoon through the northeast cut, its passengers saw, at first, exactly the same miragelike land European explorers had come upon four centuries before, a nation of pyramidal, jungle-covered mountaintops standing up out of a transpicuous blue-green sea. The spell cast by this vision, which seemed to have arisen out of nothingness, captivated them until the ship made a sharp turn west into the mouth of Owen Town's harbor. There, all at once, they were assaulted by the stink of sewage and rotting fish; the sight of rickety metal outhouses lined up along the low-water mark; dilapidated shacks squatting on poles in cluttered yards. Animal and fish entrails and paper litter — the effluent of dockside restaurants — twisted below them in eddies of scum. Ninake looked into Markin's eyes as if he knew the reason for it or had the cure, and he could think of no way to tell her that this was what much of the world looked like. This was the footprint of mankind's passage across the earth.

They descended the *Micro Dawn*'s gangplank into the disorder and heat of Owen Town, lifted their luggage into one of the pickup-truck taxis waiting on the wharf, and endured a short, breakneck ride — Ninake's first — to the Honolulu Hotel.

The Honolulu had been built not long after the end of World War II, and it stood garishly at the edge of the jungle like a stained pink hatbox at the back of someone's closet. Markin stayed there on his annual visits to the District Center because he liked the shabby, homey feel of its rooms and enjoyed being pushed back against some of the memories the place held for him. In the spring of 1970 he'd arrived by freighter from Agana, still unsteady after his long hospital stay, twenty-five pounds below his enlistment weight, and having only a vague idea what he was looking for in this hot, stinking city. The second night in town he sampled *apwut,* a local delicacy made from breadfruit paste that had been buried in the sand and allowed to ferment for six months. He ran a fever within a few hours and spent two days going back and forth between the bed and the moldy bathroom.

On the third morning, weak and disoriented, he found his way downstairs. The hotel coffee shop was furnished with relics of 1950s America, textures straight from his childhood: Formica-topped, metal-edged tables, chairs with red vinyl cushions. He sat near the window and looked out on a febrile street, watching it oscillate, wondering what had made him want to settle in a place where the food was hallucinogenic. After what seemed like an unconscionable delay, the two-hundred-pound waitress shuffled across the room and sat beside him, her fleshy arms moving like gelatin on the table top. "What do you want, *Re Merika?*" she asked languidly in English.

"Two breakfasts."

She laughed. "We have Merikan-style. Eggs, chuse, toast, ham, bothaytoes."

She brought the overflowing plates and sat with him for a time, staring, saying nothing, taking obvious pleasure in his appetite. When he finished, he carried his coffee mug to the counter and watched her running tap water over the cutlery and dishes, painstakingly scrubbing them with an oversize sponge, wiping them dry with a clean cloth napkin. She worked deliberately, with a kind of efficient laziness, from time to time raising her eyes to assess her undernourished customer. "Where are you going?" she asked him when she was done with the work.

"I'm staying here. Owen Town."

"You have work here? Anshineer?"

"No work. I'm thinking."

"Thinking?"

"Thinking and eating."

"You eat here then." She put her hand on his wrist. "The food is clean here. We cook the water."

The simple gesture had a peculiar effect on him. He felt as though muscles in the center of his body that had been in spasm for two years all released at once. Since leaving Angela and Averill Beach, he'd been part of a harder world, a world of canvas and metal and rules, boot camp, Vietnam, then the painful hospital routine. It was a narrow existence, rigid, monotonous, tightly controlled. The waitress, Xenifia, bore no sign of that discipline. Black hair fell in a loose braid down her back; when she walked, her hips seemed to float along beside her, bound only gently by the laws of physics. She spoke a throaty, soft-edged English and taught him his first words of the local dialect: *monga,* eat; and *moueur,* sleep. That afternoon he climbed back into bed and, for the first time in years, dreamed of his mother. She was at their kitchen stove, cooking him an egg for breakfast, giving him some instructions he could not quite hear, something about school or what they were going to do after school. When she turned from the stove and came toward him he saw that she had the face of a Vietnamese girl. On the plate in her hands was an eyeball and its attached muscle, cooked in blood.

For a week after that all he did was *monga* and *moueur* and make short excursions into town. The nightmare never repeated itself. Gradually some structure emerged from his idleness. Mornings he'd eat a large, American-style breakfast and exchange language lessons with Xenifia. Between customers she would tell him about the history of the islands and he would help her solve the puzzle of American tourists (why, for example, they persistently asked her for "pepa" with their eggs when even children knew that "*pepa*" meant penis; why the women walked around in trousers, showing the outline of their thighs; why the men pointed their cameras at everything). He'd spend the hottest hours of the day away from the city, hiking the dusty roads that reached back into the jungle or, when his strength began to return, climbing up to the hillside caves the Japanese had used for gun emplacements during the war. At night he'd eat in the coffee shop again, then linger there talking in two languages with Xenifia's friends, a clique of tough, unemployed young Micronesians who, like himself, were caught between the way things had been and the way they would be. It had seemed like the perfect place to live, except for the fact that every day at five P.M. an Air Micronesia 727 flew in from Guam on its way to Hawaii and the world to the east. There were, people said, plenty of empty seats — all you had to do was pay and climb aboard. He had enough money in the Owen Town bank to buy a ticket, to go back to his father and Angela, to his former life. Every day he'd had to make the same decision over and over again. It had been like ripping the scab off a wound at twenty-four-hour intervals. After a while, he could no longer stand the pain.

Seven years later, as he and Ninake climbed the hotel's dank stairwell, those days came back to him, a mixture of recuperation and confusion. He thought of Xenifia (the desk clerk said she'd had a child and moved to one of the other lagoon islands), of her Micronesian friends (who'd been replaced by a new set of young men — different faces with the same bitter, puzzled eyes), of dysentery and skin lesions, all the intermittent pain of his slow physical recovery, all the beauty and wonder of the lagoon islands. The room he and Ninake were shown to smelled of mold and damp carpet but felt like home.

They sank down together on the sagging bed, exhausted.

"Almost all the women here cover their chests" was the first thing Ninake said when they were alone.

"In America, too," he told her. "We'll go out this afternoon and buy some clothes."

*

After a nap and a shower they went to the bank, then shopped in the glass and concrete department store that had always reminded Markin of the discount warehouses in Averill Beach: dresses, shirts, and bolts of material piled carelessly in bins; mildewed dressing rooms with bubble gum and graffiti on the walls; salesgirls, hands on hips, staring dully out the front window at the road. He had watched, year by year, as Owen Town adopted the modern concept of work. Adolescents who once would have spent their time learning the arts of fishing and weaving were now earning two dollars a day for standing in air-conditioned buildings punching cash registers. Even years ago it had bothered him. Now it made him want to catch the next ship back to the outer islands. It made him think of smashing the plate-glass windows and letting in the hot air, real air, of tearing up the asphalt road, planting trees, filtering the harbor clean again. Ninake was always beside him, watching his face, studying the salesgirls' expressions, sniffing and fingering their cheap cloth. He felt he had to prove something to her. He had to show her the other side of this, the comfort and luxury; otherwise there would be no reason for her to go any farther.

After they returned to the hotel, showered again, and changed into their new clothes, Markin suggested they have dinner at the Americana, Owen Town's fanciest restaurant.

He had been inside the Americana only once, almost seven years before, for a lonely Christmas dinner. The place had not aged at all. It sprawled at the end of a gravel driveway, guarded on three sides by an impeccable lawn lined with coconut palms. Next to each tree, for the benefit of the hotel's mostly American clientele, the management had placed small white signs in English:

CAUTION:
Coco Nuts Release When Ripe.
Please Donot Stand Beneath Trees.

Inside, they were shown to a table that looked out on a strip of clean beach and several of the lagoon islands — Etal, Udot, Fenilan. A waiter lit a candle between them and brought a plate of papaya and melon. They saw shadows stretch across the beach and watched Etal turn black-green, purple, gray, then disappear.

"Is Merika like this?"

"It's much bigger. Some parts are flat, like Losapas. Some are tall, like the District Center. The part we're going to is in between, the houses are big and close together and there aren't many trees. You saw the picture of my father's house."

"Big," Ninake said. She looked around her at the cloth-covered tables, the American and Japanese tourists with their sport jackets and jewels, and the district's only elevator, which made a sound like a spear striking coral each time it returned to the lobby. "Will you be able to spearfish there?"

"Probably not."

"Will we have a boat?"

"No."

"Will the women need help with the cooking?"

"There aren't any women where we'll be staying," he said, and Ninake laughed as though it were a joke. How could there be no women? How could you have a house without women? What kind of life would that be?

The meal was served, and he showed her how to cut steak using a knife and fork. With two fingers she picked up the first piece she cut and put it into her mouth. He watched as she chewed uncertainly for a long time, then spat the ground-up cube of beef back onto her plate.

"You're supposed to swallow it."

"Okay."

She scooped up a dollop of whipped potato, put that into her mouth, and licked her fingers clean with a loud smacking of lips, a gesture considered high praise by Losapan cooks. Two tables away a middle-aged American couple stared. Markin counted silently to five, then turned and faced them. "Staring is bad manners," he said, just loud enough for them to hear.

"So it is," the man said. "Forgive us."

Ninake continued eating like an outer islander, using her fingers for everything but the cutting of steak, which she accomplished only with great concentration. Her clumsiness reminded Markin of himself when he'd first come to Losapas, discovered the new movements and unspoken rules, tried to open a coconut with his bare hands and make conversation with the women as they walked along the paths. He'd felt like a child in an adult's body, a frustration he wished he could spare her. The American couple finished their meal and left. A few minutes later the waiter appeared with a bottle of red wine. "Compliments of Mr. and Mrs. Auerbach," he said, nodding at the empty table.

Ninake sipped the wine, puckered her face, then drank the whole glass down quickly as if to avoid tasting it. Five minutes later she stopped eating and looked up at him from underwater.

"You're drunk."

"I like it." She touched her forehead and lips to see if they were swollen. "Where is the *benjo*?"

Markin took her arm and led her across the lobby. "I can't go in there."

She gave him a bemused look, then pushed through the door. Markin paced back and forth in the lobby, feeling self-conscious, giving the waiter and the desk clerk reassuring nods, avoiding any movement that might be taken as a dash for the exit. Other female diners passed in and out, and finally, when he'd begun to wonder if it might, after all, be possible to be sucked into a toilet and drown, he pushed open the door and saw Ninake standing wet-eyed in front of the mirror, unable to tear herself away from her own reflection.

"I have changed into a different person already," she said when she saw his face appear beside hers. She burst into tears and watched herself weep. "I have become a *su-fanun*."

On Losapas *su-fanun* was the supreme insult. It described a person who neglected his or her responsibilities, someone who made life more difficult for others. A husband who abandoned his wife and children was a *su-fanun;* a chief who failed to govern properly was called a *su-fanun* behind his back; Louis was a *su-fanun,* perhaps the ultimate *su-fanun.*

"You're only a temporary *su-fanun,*" Markin told her, making a weak attempt at humor. He put his hands on her shoulders and began a gentle massage. "For two months. You only feel this way because you drank the wine."

She unbuttoned the front of her new dress and let the air wash over her nipples. As he slid one hand beneath the material and gently massaged her breasts and throat, the door opened and the desk clerk pushed his head timidly into the room. He was an old man, no taller than Mahalis, and above the shirt collar his skin was sun-lined and coarse. He paused a moment before addressing Markin. "Where is she from?"

"Losapas."

The man nodded. "I am guarding the door."

They sat for an hour over coffee and dessert, waiting for the alcohol to wear off. Around them foreign diners continued their decorous ritual: menus were opened and studied, boiled water poured into glasses, meat cut, bread buttered, coffee sipped, all accompanied by polite conversation and a studied gentility Markin had forgotten. Choosing the Americana had been a mistake. More than any other place in Owen Town, it pointed up the differences between them, exaggerated Ninake's already distorted view of America, encouraged both of them to imagine the worst. They rode back to the hotel standing in the pickup's bed, leaning on the cab and each other for balance, letting the cool night air carry away a chaff of disappointment.

In their room they stood side by side at the window, looking out over the town. At that hour Owen Town's skyline was little more than a collection of haphazard silhouettes, a lighted window breaking the darkness here and there, but the scene suggested mystery — alleys and dark streets; solitary travelers in town for one night on their way across the ocean; new, unimagined worlds. In some strange way it freed them.

"Why did you stay here?" Ninake said without taking her eyes from the window.

"In this hotel or in Owen Town?"

"In Owen Town. What made you stay here instead of going to Merika?"

"I was unhappy," he said, thinking that the word did not begin to describe it.

"About what?"

"I had been in a war."

She said nothing for a moment, and he guessed she was remembering stories her mother had told her about the Japanese occupation, the only war Micronesians knew. Her mother had been raped, forced to live with and serve a Japanese officer, abandoned in her fourth month of pregnancy when American Marines liberated the islands.

"You never told me that," she said. "Did you have a girlfriend there, in the war?"

"No."

"Children?"

"No."

She was silent for a long time, and he waited for her to ask if he'd had a girlfriend in America. "I had a husband," she said, a long exhalation belying the matter-of-factness in her voice. "Samichi."

Markin's throat tightened. "From Losapas?"

"Yes."

"Is he still alive?"

"I don't know."

A taxi pulled up in front of the hotel. They heard a muffled exchange of words, a door slam, then saw two red lights rush off toward the center of town. Seven years, he was thinking. Seven years. On Losapas they could have gone seventy years without telling each other these things, and it would not have mattered.

"He left to go to Guam when Marcellina was a baby. He said there was work there and that he would come back in a few months with money. Other men had gone and come back. Lawrence, Ancha, Tieli."

"And he didn't come back?"

"Not yet."

"He was a fool."

"He was a boy," she said. "The way Louis is a boy. He and Louis were friends, as close as you and Mahalis."

"Did they go to Guam together?"

"No. Louis had already been to Guam. He took Samichi as far as Owen Town in his boat and Samichi flew in a *chet* to Guam. Louis says the last time he saw him, Samichi was getting on the *chet*."

"Louis is another fool," Markin said, but he was secretly, selfishly glad.

Ninake shook her head, still transfixed by the dark scene below. "He is just young. Elias and Marcellina are older than he is."

"Does Marcellina remember her father?"

"She was almost three. She remembers. Right now she is at home, thinking, 'My mother is also going to fly away and abandon me. What did I do wrong?' "

# 11

THE NEXT DAY, as the cloak of early-morning mist burned off, Markin and Ninake rode a taxi up to the concrete fortress the Japanese had built on the summit of the island's tallest hill. In the early 1940s the fortress had served as a communications center for the Imperial Navy. After the war it had been purchased by the Catholic church, and now neatly dressed girls and boys crossed its lawns carrying schoolbooks, looking tiny and incongruous beside the thick, shrapnel-pocked walls. On the edge of the school grounds a grassy slope faced out over the northern part of the lagoon. Markin and Ninake sat there in the shade of a breadfruit tree for most of the morning, eating slices of coconut and drinking from a bottle of well water, gazing down at part of the enormous surface of sunlit ocean that separated them from Losapas. For the first time since boarding the *Micro Dawn*, Markin felt the power of an old unself-consciousness and naturalness binding them together again. He wanted to package the feeling and carry it with them to Averill Beach.

"Do you remember the time I sewed your hand?" Ninake said, watching him pop a shard of coconut meat from the brown shell with the tip of his knife.

"I think about it every time I look at the scar, every day."

"You were brave with the pain."

"Was I?"

"I could see it was important for you to be brave."

"So you went easy on me?"

She laughed and her breasts bounced beneath the new white blouse.

"You were extra gentle when you stuck the needle in, is that it?"

"I am always gentle. But with you I was especially gentle."

"The soft *Re Merika*," he said, and she smiled distractedly.

"Marr-keen?"

"What."

"Were you brave in the war?"

"Not always."

"Were you hurt?"

He paused a moment, reminding himself of a resolution he'd made when they left Losapas, then pointed to the long scar above his ear.

"This?" She fingered the scar for the hundredth time, her forearm resting on his shoulder, their faces only a few inches apart. "You told me that happened when you were a boy, that you fell against a tree."

"I didn't want to tell you I was in a war."

"Why not?"

"I was ashamed."

"Because you weren't brave?"

"No."

"Why?"

"Because I killed people." Watching her face, Markin realized that the idea was an abstraction to her, just as it would be to everyone in Averill Beach, mere words. They were sitting so close together he could trace the blood vessels in her eyes, count the pulse in her temple, see the small decorations of age above her dark eyebrows and around her mouth. No expression formed in the muscles there, no hint of judgment found its way to the surface. He wondered if there was a way to make her understand.

"Do you want to have children?" Ninake said, as if it were a natural extension of the conversation.

"Why do you ask me that now?"

"People want to know."

"Which people?"

"Some people," she said, and when he kept looking at her she added, "Ulua."

"What does Ulua say?"

"That we are cursed."

He could have swum back to the island and strangled her. "What does Miako say?"

"That we have to summon Pwa."

"And what do you think?"

Ninake hesitated only a second. "That you just don't want to be a father now."

"And that's enough to keep you from getting pregnant?"

She looked at him closely. "Of course."

Somehow, Markin thought, what was buried always found its way to the surface. He considered denying it, telling her about his parents, who in ten years of trying had produced one child. But he knew the idea of inherited infertility would make little impression on her, would sound like an excuse. Which, in a way, it was.

"Did you have a wife in America?"

"A girlfriend."

"What was her name?"

"Angela."

Ninake spoke the strange name beneath her breath several times but could not work the combination of consonants. She asked him to repeat the name, and he did, and she tried saying it the way he said it and could not.

On Losapas, Markin thought, it was easy to trick yourself into believing that no place else on earth really existed. Except for the one day a month when the ship appeared on the horizon, and the six or eight other days a year when a Japanese fishing boat or someone like Louis happened by, Losapas was a world unto itself, unseen and unseeing. Cloth and batteries, tools, medicines, and canned food appeared from somewhere else, but their source was a secondary reality, another spirit world.

Woodrow, he thought, had broken that spell. With Woodrow, for the first time in years, he'd had the urge to talk about the other world. He felt it coming up again in him now. All the secrets wanted out.

"Are there other things?" Ninake said, reading his mind. He had the feeling she was going down a list of questions she'd been compiling since their conversation at the window the night before.

"There are things I haven't told you."

"What things?"

"Things I did in the war."

"Tell me," she said, and inside him, after a short moment of rumbling and hesitation, the top of the crater split open.

As soon as he began, he realized it was impossible to start talking about Vietnam without first providing a minimum of background. This was not Woodrow he was talking to; he could not simply tell Ninake he'd raised his rifle and put several rounds through the heart of an innocent ten-year-old girl. That would be no more truthful than saying nothing. First he would have to make her feel what it was like to arrive in Vietnam, what it felt like for someone from his island to step out of an airplane into that unbelievable heat, what it was like to realize — not in his mind but in his throat and chest and stomach — that he had been sent there to kill other people, who had been sent to kill him. Once he'd accomplished that (and it required some time; he had to stop every minute or so to explain a word or an idea, describe something alien, like a helicopter, by comparing it to something she knew, like the small Navy planes that flew over Losapas once or twice a year, exciting the whole island), he had to describe to her what it was like to meet men who had really killed other people, who'd seen their friends killed and maimed, men who'd lived next to death for so many months that you could see it stamped on their faces, you could hear it in the way they talked. He had to take her with him into the jungle night, a night of bizarre noises and strange smells and a darkness that held, simultaneously, great calm and great horror. He had to keep her there for weeks at a time, weeks of incredible boredom and incredible excitement, incredible fear, weeks of eating food from cans, sleeping in holes in the ground, sweating and bleeding and not being able to wash; nights of picking leeches from his legs and watching hideous lesions grow on the skin between his toes. As he went on with the long story — in a language not made for such stories — he discovered that his muscles were clenching again, not in an obvious way, but subtly, deep inside him, and he began to struggle to make the story real enough for her and not too real for himself. He didn't mention, for example, Shevolovich's eyeball hanging from the tree branch, dripping, and the rest of Shevolovich scattered in wet red pieces in the bushes. He didn't mention the things that happened to the Vietnamese girls found with ammunition, what a poncho felt like with blood and dirt on it, what the skin of a burned child looked and smelled like, the way the earth could shudder, the ways a man could scream.

And, knowing it was impossible, he didn't even try to convey the humor of Vietnam, the beauty, the tricks your mind could play there.

In the magazines he'd bought when he lived in Owen Town, he'd read articles about returning Vietnam veterans; he knew the stories of Marine lieutenants loose on the streets of Los Angeles or St. Louis or New York, a pistol in their pocket and a scalding memory in their brain. Never, in all the years he'd fenced with his own demons, had he thought of himself as being similar to those men, but now he saw he was not so different. Other realities lurked just beyond the present time and place, only a thin film separating them from the present. Anything could summon them, and once summoned, they were no less real or horrifying or shameful than they'd been in the past. Logic said time should wear them thin, and for the most part that was true. But certain scenes were burned so deep into the brain they could not be worn away; nothing diluted them. The whining scream of a fighter jet twenty feet above the treetops, the glint of its metal snout, the chemical stink of napalm; those things were as accessible to him now as they had been eight years before. He only had to turn his mind in that direction and there it all was.

And then, in the middle of his story, Markin suddenly decided to tell her everything. If she knew any of it, she would have to know all of it. He had to find a way to describe an F-4, and she had to see it, feel it reduce a village to smoke and splinters in a matter of seconds, hear the roar as it disappeared. She had to understand what it felt like to know that people wanted to kill her, the actuality of that.

After a year in the jungle — three quarters of an hour of uninterrupted talk — he had to take her through one last day, down one long, winding, red dirt path, through the blackened remains of a tiny hamlet, through the vision of a friend's neck bursting blood, the corpsman kneeling above him like a desperate lover, the earth around them soaking red, the great helicopter carrying the body away as if returning it to a truer world. She had to walk the last two klicks with him, sweating and stinking in the late-afternoon heat, absolutely exhausted, accompany him down the last part of that path toward the last village, a line of men behind him wound so tight they might have exploded instead of breathed, walking at the pace of ninety-year-olds, making absolutely no sound. She had to see what he saw, the elephant grass at the bend in the path, the still, merciless sky, banyan trees standing dark green in the end of day, impassive as Oriental sentries. She had to hear the noise and she had to know it was a footstep and turn and see the young girl, black-haired, cinnamon-skinned, dressed in a loose white shirt and black trousers, stopping on a bare slope with a basket on her head, then flying backward and down as if hit by a typhoon wind, her bare right foot twitching, a fountain of blood where her shoulder had been, the straw basket rolling crazily down the slope toward him and stopping in a dirty puddle three feet away, circling there once and standing upright. Ninake had to sense the speed at which such things could happen. Finally, and most importantly, she had to know what had been inside him at that moment, that instant when he believed he could have stopped himself from squeezing the trigger and did not. She had to understand what that did to him, how the underbrush erupted after that, how he ran forward, not wanting to live. She had to understand what it had meant to try and keep one place pure in himself through almost a year of that war and then to see it destroyed, to know that, in the end, in the last tally, the war had ruined him. He wanted her to see what even Woodrow hadn't been able to see: that moment had tainted not only his future, but his past as well.

When he was done he drew a breath and made himself turn and face her. He looked hard into her eyes, trying to determine whether or not she had understood. What he saw there, as clearly as he had ever seen anything in his life, was that he had made a terrible mistake.

He turned away, feeling as empty as the scuba tank Efilo struck to call the Losapans to church. He could not bring himself to face her again but reached out for her hand. She squeezed his fingers and seemed to him to be trying to understand all of it, to be struggling to stretch her imagination into places it had never been, make a connection between the man she had known for seven years and the man now sitting beside her.

They sat on the knoll in absolute silence for what seemed like hours, until the sun was directly above them, shooting tiny arrows of reflected white light from thousands of leaves. It seemed to Markin that each second brought with it a small wave carrying particles of sand onto a reef, building up an island between them. By the time they stood and walked across the schoolyard again and caught a taxi back to the oven that was midday Owen Town, that island was too tall for them to see over, the jungle too thick to admit light, the distance between them too great to be bridged by the human voice.

He was completely American now, once again, cut off from the people of the soil.

# 12

OWEN'S ISLAND, the main island of the District Center, was shaped like a crescent moon, with Owen Town occupying the northern tip. At the opposite pole, marking the final destination of the tortuous dirt road that began at the capital, was the village of Sapuk, a ragged congregation of wood and thatch and corrugated metal huts that perched on a hillside above the southeastern cup of shore. Sapuk's hundred or so houses were owned by people who still lived much as the outer islanders lived. They either did not want or could not get the cash jobs offered at the other end of the island, eight miles and one hour away. They survived by fishing, harvesting the trees, sometimes selling a little marijuana or a few handicrafts, sometimes signing on for a week of slave labor in the holds of Chinese cargo ships or on government road crews.

All of the eleven outer islands were represented in Sapuk. There was a Namulo house, a Ruo house, several Afanu houses, an Awaniku house, the people in these houses connected by blood to one or more of the families on each outer island. When a family from Ruo visited the District Center, it was assumed they would sleep in Sapuk (few of the outer islanders could afford a hotel in Owen Town), at the Ruo house. There was always room on the floor, and the extra hands were welcome for cutting copra or net fishing. Mahalis had been staying at one of the Losapas houses when Markin first met him, and Markin knew that he and Ninake were obliged to put in an appearance there before they boarded the jet for America. He would have preferred to take a taxi to Sapuk, visit with her relatives for a little while, then come back and sleep in the city. But the hotel, with its air-conditioned rooms and indoor plumbing, seemed to make Ninake uneasy, and after the trauma of their hour in Vietnam that morning, he was wary of asking too much of her. Once they arrived in Averill Beach, there would be more than enough adjustments for both of them.

After lunch and errands and two hours of fighting off a dark, persistent silence, they carried their parcels out of the hotel lobby and caught a crowded taxi for Sapuk. The pickup bounced and skidded and splashed through mud puddles left by a recent downpour, leaving the city behind and moving twenty years back in time with each mile. The flight to Honolulu left in twenty-seven hours, and Markin could feel himself growing shakier as the time ticked down. His belly seemed to have been colonized by a nest of wasps, and he remembered how as a boy his problems had always attacked him there, just below his navel. The affliction visited him on Halloween, at amusement parks, on the morning of the first day of school. For two days after he learned his mother had been struck and killed by a trolley car, he hadn't been able to eat; he'd sat in his room with the venetian blinds closed, sobbing quietly, feeling like someone had run a carving knife into his midsection and was sawing it back and forth there.

Next to him, Ninake was sinking further and further into her own apprehension, a Micronesian melancholy characterized by enormous stretches of silence and a certain faint knitting of the brows. She spoke in sentences of one or two words. He did what he could to comfort her, from time to time letting their shoulders touch, making attempts at humor, going out of his way to avoid any mention of the frightful island called America. Once they were on the plane, he told himself, things would be better.

Ninake's cousins lived in one of Sapuk's larger houses, a twenty-foot-square plywood box on the edge of a stream that fell from the hills into a clean blue bay. There were a few women and children in the front yard when they arrived, and in accordance with island custom, no one was introduced. There was no hand-shaking or bowing or formalities of any kind. Ninake simply came up along the path by the stream, walked into the yard with her *Re Won* friend, put down her cloth sack near the front step of the house, handed over a bag of rice they'd brought as a gift, and started talking with one of the women as though they'd last seen each other an hour before.

Markin tried to follow suit. He left his seabag near the step, took a drink from the rain barrel, and wandered behind the house, where three men sat near a steaming caldron. Without looking at him, one of the men smoothed a spot in the grass, motioned for him to sit, and placed two breadfruit there for him to peel. Squadrons of brown flies filled the air, buzzing around the caldron, pursuing their small sweet feasts. But in spite of them, and in spite of the rusting roof and littered clearing, Markin felt that the house and yard were holy, invested with peace. The work these men were doing had been done in almost exactly the same way for twenty generations. Their ancestors had sat here cross-legged on the same sandy soil, pounding breadfruit with coral pestles to make *apwut*, sweating, waving at flies. In all those centuries no one had thought to build awnings or screens, invent insect repellent or special tools. Micronesians changed things inside themselves and let the planet be. It reminded Markin of what had drawn him to the islands in the first place; it gave him hope that much could be solved within himself, no matter what the surroundings. He took it as a sign, telling him to press on.

"The moon will be round tonight," the man beside him said after they'd worked half an hour. He handed Markin a slice of warm breadfruit and a piece of fresh copra and motioned for him to eat. "It is a good time to take a trip."

By Micronesian standards the man was a giant, six feet tall and built like a weightlifter. The muscles in his arms jumped as he worked the copra knife. Sweat trickled from his face. He smiled constantly.

"You are going to Merika tomorrow."

"How did you know?"

The man laughed good-naturedly. "Everybody knows. Everybody talks about you and Ninake."

Markin kept himself from wondering aloud what everybody said. They worked diligently, peeling off the rubbery breadfruit skins and tossing them into the bushes, chopping and mashing the soft pulp, then wrapping it tightly in breadfruit leaves and tying the flat bundles with twine.

"I want to go to Merika someday," the muscular man said, wiping the handle of his knife on his pant leg. "People are rich there."

"Not all of them."

"They all have cars."

"Most of them."

"They're rich." The man stretched his smile, as though he were very happy for all the rich Americans. "I want to walk down the street in New York with a roll of money big as this" — he held up one of the breadfruit — "in my pocket. I want to be a cowboy and love all different kinds of girls."

The fantasy sounded like something Markin had heard before, a dream nurtured in the quonset hut downtown where American westerns were shown on Friday nights and argued about afterward over Philippine beer in the Wharf Bar and Lounge. "Do you know Louis?"

"*Ewer*," the man said, nodding drops of sweat, like seasoning, into the mound of food in his hands. "Everybody knows Louis. He is on Awaniku now, catching lobsters for the Japanese company. Twelve cents a pound. Good money."

"Do you know how much a lobster dinner costs in America?"

"How much?"

"Twelve dollars a pound."

The man stopped working and made his eyes round. "*Fak-kun?*"

"Really."

After staring another moment in silence the man said, "Bad for us, then. Bad for *Re* Micronesia, good for *Re* Japan." He chuckled happily, as if it were a joke on someone else.

At sunset Ninake's aunt called them to dinner. One of the men had caught a huge grouper that afternoon. The women steamed it over their own fire, and it fed the whole family: four men, five women, Markin, Ninake, three small children, and one skinny dog, who minced around the edges of the group, begging handouts. After the meal the family remained outdoors near the dying fire — the flies were gone and the smoke chased off most of the mosquitoes — making quiet conversation while darkness fell. The meal sat in Markin's stomach like a stone. Occasionally Ninake would meet his eyes across the shadowy circle, but there was no way of guessing what her glances meant. He wished he'd waited two more days to tell her about Vietnam.

Near seven o'clock the muscular man, Samwen, invited Markin to hitchhike into town with him for a drink. Markin declined, and told Ninake he was going to take a walk down to the dock.

Barefoot, he moved carefully along the slick, starlit path, trying to steer his thoughts away from the next day. Where the stream emptied into the small lagoon he turned left, followed a dirt road for fifty yards, then turned right onto the long stone pier the Japanese had built for their torpedo boats. He'd heard the stories about this pier. He'd met people in the District Center whose relatives had died working on it, pushing boulders out of the jungle in the midday heat on empty stomachs while the Japanese soldiers sat in the shade with their rifles across their knees, sucking oranges and making jokes. When he lived in Owen Town he'd often come out here to swim with the children of Sapuk because it was the cleanest water on the island and because, unless the tide was high, the shape of the reef kept out most of the sharks. It was eerie being on the pier at night, though, surrounded by blackness and the sound of lapping waves he couldn't see. The sky seemed very close, and the moon, shrinking and losing its color as it left the horizon, was a bright bulb burning only a few hundred feet away.

Markin sat on the end of the dock and let his toes dangle near the water. Eighty yards in front of him the moonlight caught a line of surf at the reef, drawing a halo of phosphorescence there that reverberated along the horizon. He fingered the scar on his left palm and recalled a hot Saturday morning when he'd been on Losapas less than two months. He and Mahalis were on Ayao cutting copra, and he was holding half a husked coconut in the sweaty palm of one hand, working the tip of the copra knife beneath the white meat. The nut slipped sideways and the knife sliced through the flesh at the base of his thumb as though it were a ripe pear. Blood sluiced from the wound, soaking his forearm and shorts in seconds. Mahalis wrapped the hand in a compress of breadfruit leaves, tied a T-shirt tourniquet around the wrist, and ferried him across the inlet to a shack near the church. Inside was a long table and a few thinly stocked shelves. "Lie down," Mahalis told him. "I am going for the doctor."

He knew there wasn't a doctor within seventy sea miles of Losapas, but he lay there waiting, sweating, trying to keep from passing out. It must have been over a hundred degrees in the small metal shack. He watched the corrugated roof go in and out of focus, and as the minutes passed, his imagination presented him with old visions of infected wounds, amputated legs, splintered bone, and bloody muscle.

Finally, the metal door creaked. A shaft of sunlight fell across his legs and a young woman stepped up to the table and slowly removed the leaves and the bloody tourniquet. He could feel the wound reopen and begin to ooze. Through a haze of heat and semiconsciousness he heard the woman going through boxes and bottles on the shelves, placing objects on the table beside his head, breathing nervously. He'd seen her several times among the friends Miako sewed with. She'd always been accompanied — shadowed — by a pretty four- or five-year-old girl, and assuming the woman was married, he'd always avoided looking too long at her bare breasts and finely shaped face and the mane of black, unbraided hair that hung down to her waist. But he couldn't help noticing, even then, that she seemed to look out on the world from a distance, a solid place, a place far removed from his own angry uncertainty.

She took hold of his wrist and carefully sponged away the dried blood, her face knit in concentration. "I will have to sew it," she said when the raw edges of flesh would not hold together. She made a stitching motion with one hand and watched his eyes.

His palm was beginning to throb and the stifling heat seemed to be pressing down on him, pushing sweat in waves along his forehead and temples and into his ears.

The woman held up a nearly empty bottle of Xylocaine so he could read the label. "We have only a little medicine against the pain."

"It's all right."

And it was all right. Whether because of the anesthetic or a natural immunity to the pain of a fresh wound, he wasn't sure, but it was bearable. The stitches hurt, but not enough to prevent him from hiding his grimaces when the woman glanced up; and when the cut was sewed tight and she was turning his hand gently this way and that, wrapping the palm and wrist in gauze, he let himself feel something else. He hadn't been touched by a woman in over a year.

During the following week the pretty, long-haired doctor stopped by his hut every morning and checked to see how the hand was healing. After her short visits, he'd rest his forearms on the windowsill and stare out at the lagoon, thinking of Angela and the way he'd abandoned her, pondering a pointed remark Mahalis had made to him on the night of the accident: "The woman who fixed your hand today is a very good woman," he'd said in the middle of a conversation about outboard engines, "a healer. She is Ninake."

On the day after the stitches were removed, he stopped Ninake in the clearing, thanked her again, and fumbled through his Losapan vocabulary searching for a certain word. "Do you have a husband?" he said at last, as the little girl at her side glared up at him.

Ninake shook her head once, as if she weren't sure.

"Will you walk with me tonight?"

"When?"

"After the children are asleep."

"Where?"

"On the back beach."

"No one walks there at night. The spirits are there."

"If we see any spirits we'll turn back."

She laughed, took her daughter's hand, and left him standing in the hot sun.

That night, when most of the kerosene lamps had been extinguished, he went out and followed the path to the back beach. Ninake was not there. He walked up and down the beach, superstitiously avoiding the hermit crabs that scraped around his feet in great, migratory waves. After half an hour a shudder passed through the crab population. Something, a dog perhaps, scampered across the stones and into the underbrush, and he turned and saw Ninake moving like a shadow up the beach.

They walked along the rocks flanked by surf and dark trees,

and he thought of the stories Mahalis had told him, ghostly tales of spirits who prowled that beach at night, sweeping people up into the world beyond the stars, a place haunted by eternal loneliness. Other dark nights came back to him. He remembered pressing his face against the dirt of a lightless jungle, listening to the ominous pop of mortar tubes, beset by fear, exhaustion, and a merciless, hopeless solitude. Ninake, too, seemed to have known that kind of aloneness, seemed steeped in it. It drew him to her.

They had not been walking long when the moon broke the horizon. They sat on a flat rock and watched it rise. "Last year the ship brought us a *zhenerator* from the District Center," she told him, using the English word. "We watched a movie of two Merikans walking on the moon, jumping and playing like boys." She paused and considered the rising melon of light. "Mahalis said it really happened."

"It did."

"Merika," she said, as if the word were an idea, something magical. "My mother used to tell us a story about the day the Merikans came. She said they had fast metal boats with guns in them and the guns fired and the Japanese were screaming and dying like fish on the beach, trees falling on them. The Losapans ran and hid on Ayao or went out in their canoes. Then airplanes with guns in them came. In three days the Japanese were either all dead or they had all sailed away to Ruo. Seven years of suffering, she used to say, and it ended in three days because of the Merikans."

"A lot of Americans suffered, too," he told her. "A lot of them were killed on these islands."

"But people here remember only those three days. They still call Merikans *Re Won,* the men from above."

"We're no different from other men."

"In some ways very different. In some ways exactly the same."

Both of them were comfortable with silence. They watched the moon make its slow ascent, sending a ribbon of light across the water toward them. After a time, heart hammering, he reached out and laid a hand on her thigh. She did not move. The hand crept a fraction of an inch closer to her hip. She stood and led him into the trees.

And that was the way it worked, Markin thought, watching the shimmering reef. He happened to go swimming off this pier one day and he'd met Mahalis; he happened to cut his hand and he'd met Ninake. He happened to be born in a place and time when young men were going to war and it had led him down a certain stretch of path on a certain afternoon in a certain frame of mind and the girl had happened to come walking out of the trees at just that moment. You bounced from one coincidence to the next, foolish enough to believe you had control over your life, taking every breath for granted.

He heard a footstep on the pier and knew who it was without turning around. She came up and sat beside him.

"This is where I met Mahalis," he said after a minute, hoping to retrieve the comfort of the morning. "I was swimming here one afternoon and I saw him come in from the reef with his spear and *kumi* and a belt full of fish. I asked him to show me how to spearfish, and he invited me out to Losapas."

Ninake put a hand on his thigh but said nothing. Her cheekbone and lips were lit by the moon, the eyes cast in shadow, focused on some far-off scene.

"What's wrong?"

"Nothing."

"Ever since I told you about the war you've hardly said a word to me."

"It was such a terrible story."

"Do you wish I hadn't told you?"

"No. I wish I did not ask."

"That's over." He put a hand on her hand. "That was a different person." The words sounded hollow, even to him.

They watched the moonlight sparkle on the waves for a few minutes, then she said, "I want to go in the water."

"What do you mean?"

"I want to go in the water now. I can never go in the water at night on Losapas because of the sharks."

"There are sharks here, too."

Ninake started unbuttoning her skirt, then stood and stepped out of it. "Samwen said they don't come in near the dock at night." She pulled him to his feet and unfastened the snap on his shorts, tugged the zipper down, and let them drop to the pier. Motioning for him to follow, she climbed down the ladder and stood there chest-deep, the tops of her breasts floating in the warm sea. No one goes in the water at night, Markin thought, as he felt for the slippery stone rungs with his toes. There were stonefish to step on and lionfish that liked to float in on the shore currents, even if the sharks did avoid the shallow water near the dock — a theory he doubted. When his feet touched the sandy bottom, Ninake put her arms on his shoulders and found his eyes with hers. She began running her hands lightly up and down his back, fingering each vertebra. A car passed by on the road, sweeping its only headlight across the bay, but they paid no attention. She climbed astraddle him, legs crossed behind his back, for once hiding her eyes, kissing his neck and shoulder, letting herself slide gently down his hips. Holding her, he tried to stop time. He did not want to move, he did not want to think about the morning, or their flight, or what waited for them in Averill Beach; he did not want to think about anything but this moment, medicine enough for a lifetime of illness. Ninake began to stir slowly, like the sea, swaying gently from side to side, surrounding him with a warm tide, pressing her breasts against him, squeezing his hips with the insides of her thighs. He held to the wet flesh of her back and listened to the quiet slap of their waves hitting the pier, feeling the warmth coming up inside him steadily, unhurried, filling his worried stomach and his legs and arms, moving up into his throat and mouth. He took her hair between his lips. He began moving with her, letting their bodies separate, then come together again, churning up the water now, making a small typhoon in the edge of the bay. She let herself cry out when she came, startling him. The sound bounced along the shore like a voice coming from each tree in succession, one long, vibrating syllable after centuries of silence, an amazing thing.

When she stopped moving he held her tight against him and looked over her shoulder at the dark silhouette of coconut palms a quarter mile off. After a moment he realized she was shaking. He thought at first, for an instant, that she was laughing at something, at the sound she had made, or the fact that they were making love here in the dark water, like adolescents. It wasn't until he tried to lean away from her that he realized it was not joy shaking her, but grief. Her chest was expanding and contracting in short spasms of misery. She would not let him look at her.

"*Use tongeni,*" she sobbed into his ear.

He ran his hands up and down her back, too quickly, fighting a small panic. "Yes, you can," he said quietly, still trying to look into her eyes, still meeting resistance. "Sure you can. It's nothing. It's just —"

"No," she said, sobbing steadily now, trembling in rushes, but still squeezing their bare chests tight together so he couldn't see her face. "I can't."

She leaned away from him finally and stared hard into his eyes.

The water and cool air had taken on a dreamlike quality for him; he felt that he and Ninake were part of the same body. He remembered that in all their time together he had never once talked her into, or out of, anything.

"I tried," she said, still crying, her lips still quivering. "Mahalis said, 'Try, try, it is important for Marr-keen.' He said, 'Don't worry.' She paused for a moment but could not quite catch her breath. "I tried. I left Marcellina . . ."

Markin closed his eyes and rested his forehead against her face. He did not want to try to understand anything anymore. He would live instinctively, second by second. Against all reason and probability he was still linked to this woman, flesh to flesh. He tried to concentrate on that feeling, to fix it in his memory. That was what he would have to take back with him to America.

# 13

MARKIN SAT in a plastic chair in the Honolulu International Airport, wearing the expression of a man who has encountered a vision. Around him thrummed a world of frantic purposefulness, a gleaming city of noise. He could not get used to the order and speed of it.

Strange things caught his attention. He observed that the corners of the building were perfectly straight, the floor perfectly flat and clean, all the surfaces hard, polished, flawless, and lifeless. Sitting there in running shoes, jeans, and a new dress shirt, he felt like the tattered edge of the world's cuff. Yesterday afternoon he'd been wealthy; now the humid Oahu morning found him with four hundred dollars and an extra plane ticket in his pocket, feeling like a vagabond who had stumbled out of the railroad yard into a twenty-first-century rush hour downtown. The air smelled of a constant, invisible competition.

A woman hurried past, not a Micronesian woman in a loose skirt with long, streaming hair and fleshy arms, but a narrow-waisted, tight-skirted, short-haired, made-up glimpse of beauty, carrying a neat blue suitcase and drawing behind her, as if in a boat wake, two sturdy, perfectly dressed children, a boy and girl. Fascinated, Markin watched them until they disappeared into a crowd at the check-in counter. A robot's voice was speaking over the public address system. Coteries of uniformed stewardesses wheeled their belongings toward the exit. Jets taxied along the runways; now and then a muffled roar would shake the building and Markin would see a tube of metal lifting into the sky, trails of gray exhaust, a painted tailfin. In the cafeteria he'd rediscovered water fountains, butter, steaming food in metal bins, sandwiches in plastic wrappers, machines that beeped and whistled, shuffling lines of tired men in suits, and hordes of tourists in colorful shirts. A young man with scrubbed cheeks and a tie had accompanied him across the lobby, speaking of Jesus and money. The newspaper in Markin's lap was full of puzzling names and references. Who was Son of Sam? What was a neutron bomb? Even the baseball box scores were peopled by aliens. If he'd had a picture of Ninake in his wallet, he would have taken it out and used it as a reference point, a compass. He was lost in this world.

After a time a middle-aged man in a wrinkled brown suit took the seat to Markin's left and immediately set to drumming his fingers on the top of one thigh. "Hate flying," the man said, watching the nose wheel of a 727 settle softly onto the runway. "Hate it." He glanced at Markin's face for a second, then looked away. "California?"

"Massachusetts."

The man made a series of rapid nods. "Going home to see your girlfriend," he said. "I can tell."

"I just left my girlfriend," Markin said, though he didn't think of Ninake that way. Angela had been his girlfriend. Ninake was something else, a spirit guide perhaps, a healer, his female half, his wife. Still, he had left her; nothing in the morning could hide that.

"Where?"

"Owen Town," he looked to see if the man understood. "Micronesia. The Territories."

The man nodded again before being distracted by another landing. His eyes followed the fuselage to the end of the runway as if watching for an explosion or a sudden collapse of the landing gear. "Micronesia," he said, shuddering. "Christ save us from ever having to fly through Micronesia again. Missed the direct flight to Guam one time. Had to island-hop. Oh, Jesus. The Truk Lagoon? Ponape? Majuro? Dirt runways the length of my pecker. Radar stuck to the top of a palm tree, for Chrissake. On Truk the pilot goes diving in there between the mountaintops like the Jap antiaircraft is still operating. No thank you." He waved an arm. "The take-offs. You're racing and bumping down this strip of dust, and the second the goddamn nose gear lifts up you see the runway go blue and there's this wall of green mountainside in front of you. Valium time," he said, slowing the tempo on his thigh. "Martini time."

"Where are you flying to?"

"Guam," the man said. "Business. Sell batteries."

"That's not a bad flight."

"Eight hours in the air. One stop, Johnston Island. They won't let you get off the plane. Where you headed again?"

"Los Angeles, then Boston."

"They have showers in L.A. I was on one of the buses there though, the ones that take you from the plane to the terminal. And the driver was tuned in to the control tower. Constant talk. One plane after another landing, taxiing, turning, waiting to take off, taking off. The controller was talking like a speed freak: do this, do that, take this pattern, get ready for this, that. Unbelievable. There's just too much going on now, too much traffic in the skies. Just too much."

Markin nodded his head agreeably. After a few minutes the

man got to his feet and, tossing a "good luck" over his shoulder, hastened off toward his gate, leaving Markin alone again in the midst of the whirl. He considered cashing in his ticket and catching the return flight west, leaving America to its high-speed citizens, returning to more familiar demons. But it was only a fantasy and he knew it.

The flight was announced and Markin stood and made himself move in the direction of the boarding gate. In a strange way what he felt now reminded him of what he'd felt going into combat. After a certain critical moment the dreaded thing created a magnetism of its own. It drew you forward. It immersed you in everything you weren't ready for.

# PART THREE

# 14

TIRED, his muscles stiff from more than twenty hours of sitting, Markin lifted the shade and looked down on the forests of western Massachusetts — folds of green broken by veinlike rivers and roads and patches of field. As the jet moved closer to the city, these fertile stretches began giving way gradually to the blacks and grays of paved lots and superhighways, and he pressed his forehead against the window and watched for Boston's bunched, metallic skyline. At last the city appeared, larger than he remembered it, shouldering up through a belt of yellow smog, then slipping away beneath the wing like a glass and steel phantom. In a moment the plane was over ocean once again, banking in a tight circle — north, then west, then south toward Logan. When the jet leveled its wings the curve of Averill Bay and its strip of amusements and fast-food stands were there beneath him, looking like a set of old teeth in a huge jawbone. Markin ran his eyes back and forth along the Boulevard. Most of the white wooden buildings were suffering from advanced decay; in his absence there had been some extractions: here and there an empty lot pocked the ramshackle row. Just before the plane left the Boulevard behind, he caught sight of Stevie's Place and noticed that the corner where the Escapade was supposed to be was now marked by a pile of charred wreckage. For two seconds, looking back through the window behind him, he watched a crane picking apart the rubble. Then the scene was replaced by the homes of Beachmont and East Boston, another, smaller flash of bay, and the white numerals of the runway rushing beneath the wing.

The jet shuddered when it touched down. Its engines thundered, clouding the air with heat, making the control tower and hangars wobble like desert visions. At the end of the runway the plane made a neat U-turn and rolled gracefully back to the terminal, where it sighed a final breath and was still.

Markin waited for the cabin to empty, then stood, exhausted and excited, and stepped down the aisle and through the door. In front of him briefcase-wielding businessmen marched along the portable hallway and he followed them, pursued by a shadow of misgiving.

As always, exhaustion and fear made him sharp: the rivets on the walls were shining; he could hear someone's shoes squeaking and smell the thin scent of jet exhaust floating in sterile air. At a turn in the corridor he realized he was walking with short, quick steps, almost marching, watching anxiously for the door. In Vietnam he'd had a thousand fantasies of this moment, seen himself stepping off the airplane in uniform, decorated, being swept up in a crowd. Angela and her parents, his father, the guys from the corner, Stevie, one or two of his father's old cousins from Watertown. In the fantasy they were all laughing and smoking and clapping him on the back. Angela would not let go of his hand. Even his father wanted to hug him.

Subconsciously, Markin still half expected it, and at first the boarding area disappointed him. There were people waiting, but no one waiting for him. No one knew him or cared that, finally, eight years and ten months after leaving this airport to go to war, he was here once again, coming home. If he'd called, his father would have been here, acting like it was no big deal, pretending his son had been away eight weeks, not eight years. He'd get a hard handshake and a once-over look and that would be it; they'd fall back into their old acts, too cool and proud to really connect.

But Markin hadn't called, hadn't warned his father or Stevie. He needed to be alone for this first half hour, and he was holding to the thin hope that when his father opened the back door and saw him standing there, the shock would break through something in both of them, allow them to say things to each other they'd never been able to say.

Markin retrieved his only piece of baggage from the conveyor and stepped out onto the sidewalk. The first driver in a line of yellow cabs dropped the seabag into his trunk and signaled for Markin to sit in front. They raced out of the airport at what seemed an incredible speed, death-defying, worse even than the taxi drivers in Owen Town, who had to contend only with pigs by the roadside and potholes the size of shallow graves. Here, so close together Markin felt their door handles would touch, fleets of yellow and red cabs, limousines, and loud buses sailed along the access road as though racing toward the last few parking spaces on the continent. Before he had time for a thought, they were already on 1A, passing fields of gray fuel tanks lining the harbor to the left and the thirty-five-foot crucifix by the Catholic nursing home on the right, rocketing toward a row of billboards large as drive-in-movie screens, instructing him to park, eat, buy jewelry, fly to Florida. He was tempted to ask the driver to stop, let him sit by the side of the road for a minute, and catch his breath.

At the next traffic light the driver looked over at him, flexed the triceps of his driving arm, and tried to start a conversation.

"Home on a little R and R?"

The phrase caught Markin's attention. He turned to look. The man was in his late thirties or early forties. His black hair was swept back from a receding hairline and his nose was large and angular, eyes dark brown, skin the color of light oil. An Italian face, he thought. A paisano.

The driver flashed him a quick smile. "I seen the seabag," he said. "Semper fi." He reached out his hand and demonstrated a firm grip. "My brother's in the Corps. Flies choppers down in Pensacola."

Markin nodded. The man would be from East Boston or Revere, possibly even Averill Beach, though he didn't look familiar. It was fertile territory for the recruiters. Almost in spite of himself Markin found that he was settling into an unspoken camaraderie. The way the driver pronounced his *r*'s, bringing the lower lip up and growling it out of his mouth in "Marines," making it into an "ah" in "semper"; the way he hung his wrist over the steering wheel; even the flex of his black eyebrows, which made him look puzzled and angry and ready to laugh all at once — it was all part of the language of their upbringing. There was some kind of beautiful and immediate telepathy between them. They were of the same blood.

The cab jerked away from the light and led a mad race past the brick housing projects and toward the trailer park where the people from the horse track lived. They passed a rusting quonset hut with a neon sign out front, a seedy little place called the Riders' Club. The week before Markin left for Vietnam, an Averill Beach patrolman had been murdered there, shot in the face from six feet away. It seemed a strange memory to surface in his first hour home.

Markin watched the roadside speed past, loosely connected swatches of memory assaulting him. He remembered Stevie telling him once — after a wave of gangland killings had washed across Averill Beach and the city was being maligned in the Boston papers — that there were Italians and there were guineas. "Guinea" was a fighting word. Markin himself had gotten into a scrape or two over it, and he was surprised to hear Stevie use it. "Your guineas," Stevie said, "give the rest of us a bad name. Your guineas go into the mob, and so everybody connects the mob with the Italians. Your guineas are loud, crude. So people think the Italians are loud and crude. But the real Italian people have respect for themselves. They have class. They have what you'd call dignity. I used to always think of that when I was climbing into the ring, Leo. No matter what happened, I told myself, I'd hold on to my dignity. I wouldn't disgrace my people."

Approaching Averill Beach, Markin believed he could sense both the extremes of his people here, the best and the worst. He could picture the particular forms of good and evil taken by the Italian-American personality. Here, in the wooden triple-deckers between the railroad tracks and the highway, lived dark-haired saints and dark-haired satans and thousands in between, decent men and women whose lives were bound by clear borders: family loyalty, Catholicism, patriotism. Family, God, and country.

Half of him felt perfectly at home with it.

"Grow up in AB?" the driver asked.

Markin said that he had.

"Now *there's* a town."

Markin was still staring out the window, taking it all in, but something in the driver's voice made him perk up his ears. A tone of warning sounded in his memory.

"You don't find any of 'em there," the cabbie said mischievously. "Not in AB."

"Any of who?" Markin asked, not looking at the man but guessing the answer, already remembering all of this as though he'd been away only a week.

"Your darker races," the cabbie said, and he turned to check Markin's expression. "Course, there's your element down Shirley Ave. now, if you count them. Your Cambodiams and Vietmese. You can call them colored."

"My wife's colored," Markin said, turning to look into his eyes, thinking that the skyline and the billboards and the car styles had changed but this had not. He saw the man start to laugh and then catch himself and concentrate, like a student driver, on the sharp curve into Otis Circle. They turned west on Atlantic Street, past the funeral parlor where his mother had been embalmed, past blocks of aluminum-sided houses behind lawns not much bigger than parking spaces — old, well-kept, two-family homes with chimneys and sharp roofs, a few shrubs out front. He couldn't take his eyes off them.

In the center of the city the driver had to reduce his speed, offering his passenger, in slow motion, a panoramic view of the community of Averill Beach. The low hills and fields and woodland had long ago been sliced up into blocks separated by busy streets, each block sectioned off into narrow lots holding houses that varied from one another just enough to preserve the sense that real life was lived here. There were good lawns and bad, stockade fences, hedgerows, small plastic pools; there were gardens and flower beds in their last weeks of life, gaudy birdbaths and statues of the Virgin, driveways and garages for the five-year-old Chevys and Pontiacs and Fords. To Markin, the whole jumbled scene bespoke a certain tattered elegance. In its own way it was perfect.

But on Broadway he came upon signs of a new disease. The neat storefronts he remembered were spotted with peeling paint, some of the windows covered with metal grates. Broadway's only new buildings, two gleaming glass-and-brick banks, made everything else seem slightly shabby, rough around the edges, unkempt. The brick fire station with its three wide doors had not changed, but the street in front of it was completely clogged with traffic, trimmed with paper litter. Two MBTA buses crept along no faster than a person could walk. The driver leaned on his horn twice before the taxi was finally able to escape onto Stadium Avenue. "Christ." He glanced at the meter and then switched it off, sixty cents early.

Stadium Avenue seemed better. The small trees that had been planted in the early sixties were in the midst of a healthy adolescence and the houses were better kept. But there was no one on the streets. Noontime, and not one pedestrian in a city of fifty thousand on a warm September day.

He had the taxi stop a hundred yards short of Wilson Street. They got out, the driver opened the trunk and handed him the seabag. Markin paid him and included a tip. The driver shook his head and held out three one-dollar bills — his tip plus some change. "No tip," he said.

"Why not?"

The driver pushed the money into Markin's free hand and started around the corner of his cab. "No tip this time," he said, stopping to look at his passenger. "I learned somethin'." Before Markin could argue with him, the cabbie had ducked into the front seat and was off, having kept himself from disgracing his people.

Seabag on his shoulder, Markin went the final three blocks of his ten-thousand-mile journey on foot, expecting to see or be seen by someone he knew. An old man in a porch chair nodded at him, but the face was unfamiliar. A Doberman trotted along with him on the other side of a chain-link fence. Another MBTA bus huffed by — a driver, forty empty plastic seats, and two white-haired women. The small market at the corner where his mother had sent him for bread and milk and penny candy was now an accountant's office, a grid of metal bars over its front windows.

Markin turned the corner onto Wilson Street and stopped. Two houses up on the left was the old willow tree and the swinging metal plate with his last name on it, creaking, as always, in the slightest breeze.

His father's house looked freshly painted, dark green with cream trim, and to Markin's eyes it stood out from the twenty or so other homes on the street, which seemed to blend together in a confusion of gray roofs and drooping black wires, cracked and slanting pavement, old porches, parked cars, trash barrels. Sidewalk weeds clutched to thin seams of dirt in the pavement like survivors of an asphalt flood.

He started forward again, paying attention to his breathing and the hard thumping in his chest, wanting to do it correctly now after all this time. He wiped his right palm on his trouser leg, lifted the fence latch, went along the narrow flagstone walk into his father's back yard, up the four brick steps. The storm door was new. He rapped on it and waited a century for the sound of footsteps on the kitchen linoleum.

Then his father was framed in the doorway, indistinct behind the screen, looking thin beneath his shock of white hair, just standing there, staring, as if in a dream. Markin saw him swallow, and he swallowed, too. The picture went out of sharp focus. He heard a small *click* as the screen door was unlocked and pushed open.

"Hi, Pa," he said.

His father held out his hand, the same ring with the green stone — looking too big now — the same hard grip, the same slate-blue Russian eyes. But small things were different. Half puddles stood in the bottoms of the eyes. The mouth was set in a line, but Markin could see the muscles working to keep it that way, wrinkles flexing. After a minute, certain of what he was seeing, his father spoke: "The war is over."

Markin dropped his seabag and hugged him, breaking the distance between them, feeling an old man's bones beneath the sweater, fragile as a fall leaf. His father was thumping him on the back as if counting off the years, and he thought that, whatever else happened or didn't happen on this trip, this, just this, was worth the pain of leaving Losapas.

# 15

THEY FELL automatically into old postures. Markin took his former place at the table, barely able to keep his eyes open, while his father shuffled around the kitchen. He was at the sink, then at the stove, opening and closing the refrigerator and the familiar white cupboards, doing the only thing he knew how to do to show he was happy to have his son home again. Markin watched every move. In a few minutes there was a meal in front of him: a salad with oil and vinegar, Italian bread, a bottle of beer, some leftover eggplant parmigiana, oily and steaming on a clear glass plate. Although he'd been served breakfast on the plane less than two hours before, Markin forced himself to eat. This was the ritual his mother had taught them and which they repeated in memory of her. It was a rite performed constantly all over Averill

Beach, the Italian mass, affection in the guise of food, love without language for people who never seemed comfortable using mere words for anything important. In the end, Markin thought as he ate, his father had become more Italian than the Italians, than his mother would have been, than the neighbors were. Even the Russian accent, a source of shame to his father for sixty years, appeared to have been conquered.

His father watched him eat, his watery eyes following the fork from plate to mouth, then inspecting the face, neck, shoulders, and arms, returning to the scar above the ear and to the left hand, which did not move as easily as it once had. "You're all right," he stated after a time.

Markin nodded with his mouth full. When he was finished and had started in on his second beer, he returned the inspection. His father's body seemed to have grown not so much older as slightly smaller, making the nose and ears and blue eyes stand out, rendering the soft white hair even more impressive. Markin could still see him in front of the hall mirror, an oval hairbrush in each hand, brushing with hard, rhythmic strokes until he felt he looked distinguished enough to face his welding job at the GE plant. He could see his father standing near the front door and placing the gray felt hat gently on his head, adjusting it with his thumb and middle finger, then patting his son on the shoulder and stepping out into the world. In the face across from him Markin could see what he'd been too young or immature or full of himself to see in all the years he'd lived here — he could see another life.

"How are you, Pa?"

The stone eyes shifted and found the wall, and for a moment Markin did not know what was happening. His father seemed about to start crying. The eyes came back, clouded but steady. "They mugged me, Leo."

"What do you mean? When? Who?"

"Who knows who." The eyes went away again and the old face seemed to shrink, brows pulling in toward each other, eyes and mouth narrowing.

Markin put his beer bottle on the table without looking and it toppled and struck the plate. His father straightened it up, sponged at the spilled beer, and carried the plate to the sink. "I went down Broadway for the paper," he said over his shoulder, and it seemed to Markin he had been waiting months for the chance to tell this story. "Two o'clock in the afternoon. I was coming back. I turned onto Wilson Street. I was looking up at the new paintjob on the house, and they cracked me over the head from behind, blackjacked me. They took my wallet with the picture of your mother."

"How many of them?"

"Who knows? One, six, I never saw them. Two o'clock in the afternoon. In front of my own house." His father stopped washing for a moment and twisted his neck to look at his son. "And they never found who it was. No suspects. Case closed. The Averill Beach police."

"What about all your friends on the force, Pa? Joey Bianco, Eddie Mer —"

His father turned back to the sink. "Retired."

"Tommy Mario?"

"Tommy was killed down the beach, Leo. Last year. I didn't want to write you that."

Markin looked past his father, out the kitchen window at the slate roof of the house where Tommy Mario had lived for fifty years. Something twisted into a hard fist in his stomach and he could feel the muscles in his hands and arms and neck awaken to the first sparkle of adrenaline. On Losapas he'd spent years wondering how someone like himself could have *volunteered* to go to war. Now, in a matter of seconds, he understood it perfectly. He was back.

"I was in the hospital two weeks."

"And you didn't write?"

"Of course I didn't write. Did *you* write when you were in the hospital? What was I supposed to say? 'I'm in the hospital with a headache, Leo. Come home and hold my hand'?"

"You don't know how to ask for help, Pa."

"When the day comes I have to ask for help I'll go down the beach and take a long swim. Straight out."

"Thanks."

"You're welcome."

"What did the doctor say?"

"I had a headache for two weeks. Sometimes I forget things now." His father stopped, as if he wanted to say something more and couldn't find the words. He draped the dishcloth over the oven handle, leaned on the sink, and stared out the window. Markin watched his shoulders shrug once. "I fell backwards," he said angrily. "I fell on my ass. On the bottom of my backbone." His father looked at his hands. "The nerves there," he said, and he tried to turn and face the table but could not move. "The nerves were crushed. I . . . I lost control there. I'm like a kid now. I wear a diaper now almost all the time."

Involuntarily Markin's eyes drifted down below his father's belt, then he made himself look at the table top. He picked up his fork and squeezed it in his fist, and there was a roaring silence in the kitchen until his father turned on the faucet and started wiping the sink clean again.

"Every Sunday I go to church and I ask God to let me forgive them. I say, 'Let me forgive them. Let me forget about them.' But it's no good, Leo. Every time I . . ." His father looked out the window at Tommy Mario's house and seemed to have to squeeze out the last words with all the muscles in his upper body. "I want to find them and kill them. I want to find them and kill them with my bare hands."

The words reached Markin through layers and layers of weariness, not just the weariness of a week of travel but something else, the weariness of some battle he'd thought he'd never have to fight again. He understood now that his father did not really mean what he was saying, but that didn't matter. What mattered was that he hadn't understood it before and that his father still didn't understand it. In Averill Beach, saying something like that in front of your son was the same as coming right out and asking him to do the killing. It was a test.

Markin's head was spinning. He felt he had somehow known about this in advance, that it was perfectly consistent with coming back, part and parcel of the decision to leave Losapas. Leaving Losapas meant coming to this: this burning up in his belly, this hopelessness, this old man standing here neck-deep in misery, a stubborn, dying, good man surrounded by a wonderful, violent, and slowly decaying city. Except for Parris Island, this was the only America he'd ever known, and he loved it and was tormented by it at the same time, so that in his confusion he fell back on the habitual responses. Already — and he'd been home how long? an hour? — he felt his voice and posture changing. Both he and his father were slipping back into their customary roles, as if neither of them had learned a thing in eight years. After the first few minutes, all the surprise had drained away. His father hadn't even asked why he'd suddenly decided to return — the question Markin had been bracing himself for all the way across the continent. It was as if he'd gone away for a weekend.

Markin thought of Woodrow asking: What keeps you from going back?

He looked up and the eyes were on him, blue and dry and asking of him the same old thing: not that he be good, but that he be loyal. It was the rule of Averill Beach, the essence of Vietnam, the very thing he wanted to flush from his life.

# 16

MARKIN slept fifteen hours, waking at noon in light the texture of early morning on Losapas. He turned to feel for Ninake beside him and rolled off the bed onto the floor.

Downstairs he poured himself a glass of water and admired the chrome faucet. He turned the new TV on and off twice, toyed with the remote control, glanced at the lingerie and automobile ads in the *Herald*, sniffed the strange, odorless air. Through the kitchen window he caught sight of his father out in the garden, feeling for ripe tomatoes among a tangle of dying yellow stalks. For a while Markin just watched him work, the deliberate movements of old age striking him as proper, more careful, more precise than the movements of a younger man. He thought of Woodrow flying out to Japan, and tried to figure the odds of his father ever coming to visit him on Losapas. One in five trillion, he thought they might be. To his father, to everyone here, Averill Beach was the center of the universe. There were no maps on the walls of this city and no need for them. Boston was five miles away, and like another country; you needed a visa to go there. If you were from Averill Beach, you were from a separate place in time, a place with its own rules and codes, America's own outer island.

His father got to his feet and lifted the basket of vegetables, and Markin went into the back yard to meet him. "I'm going out for a little while, Pa. I want to see Stevie."

"Stevie's not there today. He went to Canada."

"Canada?"

"Canada, Montana, somewhere down there."

"I want to see the beach anyway."

"Do what you want. I'm cooking for supper."

"I'll be home before supper."

His father grunted. Markin touched him on the shoulder and the old man frowned.

He left the yard and walked toward Broadway, along the same route the taxi had traveled the day before, imagining Ninake beside him, trying to see Stadium Avenue as she would see it: strange trees with very small leaves; painted, numbered houses large enough for fifty people to sleep in; sheets of pavement covering the soil; no smell of rotting plants and dung; no children running around naked chasing chickens; no people at all except those visible inside the cars that hurried past.

He wondered if, secretly, in some hidden part of himself, he'd hoped Ninake wouldn't come with him, if, from the moment they'd stood together at the rail of the *Micro Dawn* and watched Losapas drop off the world, he'd been afraid of what she might see in him here. The idea upset him. At the corner of Broadway he went into a jewelry store and, after pondering for a few minutes, selected a thin gold bracelet and asked the saleswoman to put it in a fancy box. He carried the box two blocks south to the post office, where he stood at the glass table beneath a poster that said the Marines were looking for a few good men, and wrote:

> Ninake:
> I miss Losapas. It is cool here and I think about you every minute.

There was no way to say "I love you" in Losapan, no word for "love" at all. On the island, lovers whispered "*U pe remw,*" which meant literally, "I would die for you." He printed that at the bottom of the card, glanced up at the pink-faced Marine — ready to die for something else — and brought his gift to the window.

It wasn't much, he realized as the parcel was being weighed — a forty-dollar loop of metal and a card with a few lines of handwriting on it. She might not receive it for weeks, might not receive it at all unless she happened to check Losapas' box at the post office in Owen Town. Still, it drew a clear line between him and Samichi, the other man who had left her, the *su-fanun.*

As Markin was leaving the post office, it occurred to him that one of the people Ninake might bump into in Sapuk or at the post office in Owen Town was Louis, who would be in and out of the District Center, sleeping in Sapuk and Monoluk and Weichap, hunting for fresh women, sopping up stray information like a sponge. It was September thirteenth. The *Micro Dawn* left for the northern atolls on the twenty-seventh of each month. Fourteen days. If Louis found out Ninake was going to be in Owen Town alone for fourteen days, he would follow her around, offering boat rides to the lagoon islands, perhaps even back to Losapas, suggesting she'd been abandoned again.

Markin climbed the post office steps a second time, bought a blank postcard, addressed it to the Wharf Bar and Lounge, Owen Town, Eastern Caroline Islands, and printed a short message in English on the back:

Louis:
    Castration by copra knife is a very painful experience.
                        Your American Friend, Markin


On the sidewalk in front of the post office the planet was spinning too quickly. There were horns blaring and engines racing, plumes of bus exhaust, people hurrying along without looking at each other, too many signs in the windows, too many choices, too much on his mind. A rusted Oldsmobile pulled into the No Stopping zone and a fourteen- or fifteen-year-old boy got out on the passenger side, a Red Sox cap pulled down over his forehead and two manila envelopes clutched in one hand. Except for the fact that he was not in school, there was nothing at all unusual about the boy. He had the shadow of a mustache, legs too long for his body, the look of someone carrying inside himself a world he could never articulate. He ran up the post office steps two at a time and slid the envelopes into a blue metal box, a self-conscious, ordinary adolescent. But Markin was fascinated. He watched the boy as if watching a younger version of himself. The baseball cap made him think of Fenway Park, a place he'd completely forgotten. The boy's torn jacket brought back memories of fights on the playground at McKinley School. The golden cross around the boy's neck, which swung and bounced as he jogged back to the car, had the peculiar effect of making Markin realize that one of the things Vietnam had done to, or for, him was to strip him of all his old points of reference. His Catholicism had been devastated in Vietnam. His trust in the military — a kind of religion — had been shattered. The canons of Manhood, Family, Patriotism, had somehow come to seem insufficient — not wrong necessarily, just incapable of providing the kind of ultimate answer he was looking for, a rule by which he could live. After Vietnam he was on his own, floating among the wreckage of old half-truths and approximations, Losapan superstitions, theories of various sorts. He no longer had any spiritual moorings. And that was something no one in Averill Beach would be able to understand.

The teenager ducked back into the car and slammed the door, and Markin moved quickly toward Beach Street, going past DiMaggio's tavern, past the two new banks, past the library and the traffic circle, trying to get to the ocean as fast as he could. At the pastry shop where he and his father had sometimes gone for coffee and doughnuts after mass, he turned right and found himself in Southeast Asia again. Shirley Avenue: he was taller by a foot than anyone on the street. Everywhere small and very quiet people were going about their business in the Oriental shops and groceries that had sprung up on both sides of the street. He listened hard but did not catch a single phrase of Vietnamese, nor could he remember any of the words on the signs in the shop windows. It was as if his mind would not admit to knowing them. Waiting at the corner for the light to change, he made the mistake of trying to start a conversation with the man beside him, a young Vietnamese, someone he might once have spoken to or fought for on the other side of the world. The man took a step away and looked down at his feet, and Markin was enveloped in a cloud of savage memories that would not leave him until he reached the Boulevard and the hurricane wall. Even then he had to stand and look out at the water for a long time before his thoughts would settle.

When he was a boy the beach had been the treasure of his inner life. This was where he retreated when he wanted to escape the din of the city, touch something that spoke of another realm, something beyond the world of competition and rush. This was where he and Angie had come to make and talk about love, where his friends gathered, where, when things were bad, he could take a swim in the cold Atlantic and make the world fresh again. Beyond the arc of sand, the surface of the bay shifted in soft undulations and he was tempted to tear off his clothes and race into the water, dive deep, run his chest along the gray bottom — anything not to lose hold of the feeling of Losapas.

A tanker crept across the horizon toward Boston Harbor, and he could almost hear Ulua's croaking voice penetrating the walls of his hut on Ship Day mornings. He could feel the chill come over him, the dread, the sense that his own history was sniffing along the trail behind him.

Now he heard Woodrow ask him again: What keeps you from going back? The question coiled and twisted in Markin's mind like a writhing snake, and he saw that there were some problems you didn't solve by thinking. You didn't kill the snake in your mind by talking about it, analyzing its powers, worrying the possibilities. There were times when you had to *do* something. Right or wrong, frightened or not, you just had to take one step in the darkness. And so he made himself turn and start walking north, toward the very center of his former world, the heart of his love and the heart of his fear.

Stevie's Place had not changed at all. The small dining area was crowded, filled with the murmur of conversation. Quietly, Markin took a table near the window and let his eyes move across the marble-topped bar, the plain gray mugs and dishes that looked like those in the Honolulu Hotel coffee shop, the black-and-white boxing photos on the walls. Like someone going through old family photographs, he took in the jukebox, the wide-screen TV, the rows of beer cans and whiskey bottles and Stevie's Golden Gloves trophies lined up on shelves behind the bar. Stevie Palermo was his father's closest friend. Stevie's family and his mother's family had come from the same mountaintop village northeast of Naples, and Stevie, who had never married, had been a fixture in Markin's childhood, a constant, welcome presence in the empty house. On his birthday, Stevie would drive him to Boston and buy him a pair of ice skates or a baseball glove or cleats for the next football season —always the most expensive skates or glove or cleats the salesman showed them. In the days when his allowance was twenty cents a week, Stevie gave him five dollars for every A on his report card. When he left for Vietnam, Stevie was at the house two hours early, pacing the back yard as if *he* were the one being sent to war.

At the airport he nearly broke his godson's ribs hugging him goodbye.

Markin looked out the window and the memories would not stop. When he'd started the eleventh grade, Stevie had decided he was old enough to drink and had allowed him to sit at the bar on weekends and have one or two beers. As if it were happening at that moment and not twelve years before, Markin saw himself coming through the front door with his new girl, Angela Pane-chieso, showing her off, and Stevie wiping the bar, pretending to withhold judgment just as an uncle or father might, then serving both of them beer in coffee mugs, the same mugs he could see now at the next table. He seemed to be sitting inside his own history: he could see himself, feel himself as a teenager, standing outside, ogling the motorcycles and GTOs parked against the curb; even younger, walking in here with his father on Saturday mornings and sitting at the counter as the two men talked, being served a cold glass of milk with bubbles on top and flat English muffins grilled in butter, watching his father and godfather and wondering, even then, what he would have to do to prove he was just like them.

The waitress, too, reminded him of things past, of someone, a scene he couldn't place, another snapshot in the family album. She set down his water glass, pulled a notepad from her skirt pocket and a pencil from behind one ear, and asked him gruffly what he wanted.

He ordered the Boxer's Breakfast. The waitress pursed her lips in studied boredom, exactly like the beach girls he'd chased fifteen summers before. He half expected her to shift a wad of gum from one cheek to the other, swear, spit, light up a cigarette. She turned on her heel, strutted across the room as if she knew he was watching her, smacked the kitchen door with one palm, and disappeared.

Markin turned to look out the window again, taking in the expanse of the ocean, letting it calm him the way it had always calmed him. He found himself carrying on a peculiar inner dialogue. Stevie loves you, he told himself. He was the one who brought you back here — through Woodrow, through the letter. He doesn't care what you believe in now or don't believe in. He's your godfather, he loves you. But another voice reminded him that Stevie Palermo was a man of symbols, carefully arranged and supported so that they reinforced his perception of the world. Stevie was one of the most loving and generous people he knew, but the borders of his love were clearly marked and strictly guarded.

After several minutes of this internal debate Markin sensed someone coming across the room toward his table. He was afraid to look. Perhaps it was Stevie after all, summoned home from Canada by some old telepathy. Then, unbelievably, a live memory was taking the seat across from him, a pair of protruding ears and an obliging smile right out of the fifth-grade class picture. "Billy Ollanno," Markin said, shaking the offered hand.

"You know it, pal. It's the kid Bill. What the eff are you doin' here?"

Markin did not know what to say. He fished around for his lost Averill Beach personality and finally found some words: "I practically used to live here. Stevie's my godfather. What are you doing here?"

"Friends of the family," Billy said, smiling the fifth-grade smile. For a moment Markin could see him trotting up the first-base line in a Little League game, as happy with a base on balls as anyone else would have been with a home run. Billy was clutching a mug of coffee in both hands, but the size of his pupils and the red, worn-out look around his large eyes spoke of some stronger drug.

"What's going on?"

"Still here in the old town," Billy said proudly. "Went away for a while on a minor rap, but I'm straightenin' out now, workin', you know."

"Prison?" Markin said, too loudly. A man and woman at the next table looked up at them, and Billy sipped his coffee before answering.

"Deer Island." He shrugged and turned down the corners of his lips. "Six months. It ain't as bad as people make it out to be. So what about yourself? We heard you was wounded over there, and then we never seen you again."

"I haven't been back."

"Somebody said you was dead."

"I wasn't."

He and Billy had never been close friends — no one seemed ever to have been very close to Billy. He had always joined in happily, was always tolerated, never taken very seriously. Still, he was a part of the past, a living connection to Averill Beach, and Markin felt both glad to see him and unable to remember a single hour they'd spent at ease with each other.

"So where you livin' now, Leo?"

"An island. Out in the Pacific. Way out."

Billy reached across the table and slapped him on the shoulder. "So *that's* where you got that dynamite tan. An island in the South Pacific, huh? Man, I knew you'd do somethin' interestin', if anyone would. I knew it. The South Pacific, huh?" He shook his head in wonder. "You back for good now, or what?"

"I don't know."

"You married?"

Markin shook his head. "You?"

"You kiddin'? Me? Never happen, man. Live free or die."

They exchanged smiles and shifted their eyes.

"Jeez, I feel like I gut a million things to tell ya," Billy said after a few seconds. He scratched his chin with the rim of his coffee mug. "Lemme think where to start . . . Andy Mielovski died over in Vietnam. You knew that, right?"

"I didn't even know he went."

"Yeah. Left a wife — no one we knew. Lemme see. Suzanne's married to a guy from Saugus. They have two or three kids. Joey Manasone's doin' okay. Four kids. They thought he might've caught cancer for a while there. He did catch it, I think, but they got it out of him in time. He stuck it out in the old hometown,

has a house up on the Heights. Who else ... Ah, Jimmy Di-
Bianco left — nobody really knows where to — he was away for
a few months with me. Nice kid, too. Jeanette got a job workin'
as a model in Boston. She lives over there now. I just seen her in
an underwear ad in the *Herald*. She's doin' good. Mario sells
wrenches for some company on the South Shore. His old girl
Linda is married to a cop in Everett. Who else ..."

Markin knew who else but he couldn't bring himself to pro-
duce the name. The waitress brought an enormous breakfast —
eggs, sausage, pancakes, home fries — and placed it in front of
him coquettishly, smirking, meeting his eyes briefly before leaving to take another order.

"Remember her?"

"Almost."

"Lisa Orsi. Angie's friend. Your Angie."

Markin concentrated on his food. Billy was staring out the
window, squinting into the light. It appeared he was getting
ready to start in on another subject, and Markin couldn't let the
opportunity pass. "What's she up to?" he said as casually as
possible.

"Angie? You haven't seen her? What's the mattah wit' you,
pal? You avoidin' the old bunch?"

"No," Markin said, though that was precisely what he'd been
thinking of doing. "I just got in, that's all."

"Well," Billy said, embarrassed. "She's married. You knew
that, right?"

"To Richie."

"Right. Richie Mowlen. They have one or two kids. Thinkin'
of splittin' up, from what I heard. An' between me and you,
everybody in the city is rootin' for her to just dump the guy. He's
bad effin' news."

Markin felt something, some hope unconnected to reality,
jump in his chest. "Is she still around?"

"Still in AB, yup. Lives up on the Heights, too, near Manasone. Bay Ave. someplace. Richie was drivin' truck for a while,

and he always had it parked up there, right in the middle of the street, the jerk. I used to go by there once in a while to see my cousin, have to practically drive up on the sidewalk to get by."

"She doesn't ever come down here anymore, does she?"

"Nah. Hardly nobody comes down here no more, nobody we know. It's all strangers here now, bikies, dopesters, a few homos. Stevie ain't even here now except on weekends. You know how it is. People start havin' their families. No one ever sees no one around hardly. I seen Angie about as much as I seen you, except you live in the South Pacific, that's your excuse." Billy laughed loudly, checked Markin's face, then chuckled and sighed. "I knew you was too smart to stay around here, Leo."

Dimly, Markin remembered this part of the Averill Beach code. Moving away meant you were disloyal but wise, someone to be envious of in certain unguarded moments.

"I heard about your old man," Billy said, and this, too, seemed to cause him embarrassment.

Markin tried to swallow the piece of sausage in his mouth. Billy Ollanno knew more about what was happening in his father's life than he did; that was the kind of son he'd turned out to be. The small particles of peace he'd been able to rescue from among his old memories were scattered like spores in a breeze.

"Cops ain't doin' squat about it neither."

"That's what I don't understand," Markin said helplessly.

"Yeah, well, there's a lot here not to understand, pal. That was a lousy thing, really effin' lousy." Angrily, Billy swigged down the last of his coffee, and Markin remembered how hard Billy had once worked to pepper his conversations with the word he now seemed unable to pronounce. He wondered if Billy had gotten religion at Deer Island.

Billy quickly disabused him of the idea. "I hear a lot a talk where I work now," he said proudly. "I'm tendin' bar down the Leopard Club."

"In the Combat Zone?"

The couple at the next table glanced over again.

"You gut it. You should come down some night. I'll introduce you to some of the girls. They're a lot smarter than you think."

"I'll do that," Markin said, though he knew he never would.

Billy seemed to know it, too. An ember of pain shone in his eyes. "I'm not the old Billy no more, you know, Leo. I know some people. I hear things. A lot of stuff goes down most people don't pay no attention to, you know." He looked around the room as if things were happening there no one else could see, then met Markin's eyes. "I'd do anythin' to help you wit' a thing like this. You know I would."

"I know you would." Markin couldn't look at him.

"Well, okay," Billy said. "You better come see me then, or you're a real jerk. I'm there any night but Sunday or Monday. You remember where it is, right?"

"On Washington Street."

"Next to the big movie on the corner."

"Next to the big movie on the corner, sure. I'll come by. Definitely."

"I'll be there," Billy said, producing a smile. "Just ask for Billy O. You'll see me." He tilted the empty cup to his lips again, realized there was nothing in it, grinned sheepishly, and not knowing what else to do, stuck out his hand. "It's good to have you back again, buddy. It's like old times." He squeezed Markin's hand and slipped out of his seat and through the door.

Markin watched Billy move along the sidewalk, glancing from side to side as if into mirrored walls, and he was transported back to the William P. Columbine Elementary School, a three-story, red-brick edifice with arched granite doorways and a blanket-size American flag flying from the balcony. The fifth- and sixth-grade boys were milling about at recess on their half of the dirt playground, some tossing a wiffle ball back and forth, some playing kickball with the big maroon ball that pinged when it bounced, a few of them crouching in a shady corner, examining Aldo Fasco's collection of dirty pictures. Suddenly, in the mysterious way that riots start and rumors spread, word flashed around the schoolyard that Billy Ollanno had been seen kissing Debra DeLeo in the coatroom on the third floor that morning. The story was an obvious lie: no fifth-grader as shy and eager to be accepted as Billy would be caught even thinking about touching a member of the opposite sex. Yet the word spread and, fanned by Aldo Fasco's obscene laugh, caught the attention of all the fifth- and sixth-grade boys. At the far end of the playground, Leo Markin could hear and see Billy stamping his foot indignantly and shouting in a shrill voice, "You lie! You lie, Aldo!" But the protests only made things worse for him. Seeing that he'd struck a nerve, Aldo organized a small parade and led eight or ten boys around the playground, chanting, "Bil-ly and Deb-bie, Bil-ly and Deb-bie, Bil-ly and Deb-bie." They surrounded Billy and, pointing and jeering, maneuvered him toward one edge of the playground.

Markin pushed his way through the crowd and reached the front row just as Billy's back touched the fence. Billy was blubbering incoherently. In his right hand he clutched the new Red Sox cap he'd worn to school for the first time that week and which had earned him a slew of compliments, from Aldo among others. Now Billy's fortunes had reversed. Opposite him, feet planted wide apart, jowly Aldo Fasco continued to lead the chant. Aldo had repeated a grade; though only a year older than his classmates, he was already the size of a high school freshman or sophomore. He had big arms, a porcine chest and belly, the start of a feathery mustache. Markin made his hands into fists and stepped in front of Aldo, his back to Billy, his chest heaving so violently he could not speak. The chanting tapered off. Someone at the rear of the mob yelled "Fight! Fight!" alerting Mrs. LaBrege on the girls' half of the playground. Aldo was smiling; he did not expect to be hit. When Markin rushed forward and thrust both hands against the big chest, Aldo was knocked off balance and stumbled backward toward the mob. One of Markin's friends stuck out a leg. By the time Mrs. LaBrege arrived on the scene, Leo Markin was straddling a prone, bloody

Aldo Fasco, pummeling his chest and arms and head like a boxer in the final round. From that hour on, Billy had treated Markin like a heroic older brother.

It was incredible, Markin thought, how something like that could affect a relationship. A pattern was established, the mold hardened, and everything either person did, every word they said for years afterward, solidified them in their respective positions. Only with great pain or great effort could people step out of the roles they had assigned each other or themselves. He thought of his father and wondered if he would ever be anything more than a son to him.

When the waitress returned with the check they played the game of not recognizing each other. It wasn't difficult — they hadn't exchanged more than a dozen words in high school — but Markin felt cowardly about it and about promising Billy he'd visit him at the bar, about the underhanded way he'd asked about Angela. Averill Beach could do that to you, he thought. It could make you start to think of yourself as a coward, no matter what you had done to prove otherwise. He inquired after Stevie.

"He only works weekends now," Lisa said, affecting a curious look, pretending to wonder who he was, why he was asking. "But he's out of town now anyway, some funeral in Wisconsin or someplace." She hurried off to another table before he could say anything else, and Markin watched her go, wondering how long it would be before she called Angie and gave her the news.

Out on the Boulevard again he felt at loose ends. Jets came in low over the bay, engines roaring, then dropped behind the houses on the top of Beachmont Hill. Retired men sat in parked cars reading newspapers or walked dogs along the hurricane wall, stopping to exchange a few words with each other, taking the edge off their loneliness.

To the south, Markin could see part of the skyline of downtown Boston, a solid block of buildings, another island. He climbed over the wall, took off his shoes and socks, rolled up his pants and waded into the cold water knee-deep. "The sea breathes like you breathe," his mother had told him here, describing the world. She patted his round, little-boy's belly, then tickled him until he plopped down in the water, laughing. "Just like this belly, it goes in and out, but slower. The sea breathes twice a day." She lifted him to his feet, then up so that his face was against her neck and he was staring over the tops of the amusements at a bleeding, golden sky, feeling her arm at the back of his knees, listening to her beautiful voice saying wonderful things he couldn't understand.

# 17

"YOU'RE NOT doing dishes in my house," his father said after supper that night, and Markin was not surprised. This was the way it had always worked. For reasons that were never made clear, his father held exclusive rights to certain household tasks: gardening, cooking, puttying the old storm windows when they were taken down in spring. Markin was allowed to work on the lawn, to paint and help with small carpentry jobs, to vacuum the rugs and set up the Christmas decorations and hang the laundry out to dry. But other areas, the area around sink and stove and garden especially, anything having to do with feeding the family, remained his father's sacred provinces. Markin remembered, too, that it was next to impossible to get the old man to go out for a restaurant meal. Whenever he suggested it, his father balked and stiffened, said he'd planned to make chicken cacciatore that night, fell back on the argument that he'd already bought the peppers and mushrooms, that they wouldn't taste the same if they weren't cooked fresh.

Over the years Markin had learned that, where his father was concerned, it was much wiser to acquiesce than to argue. But tonight he remained standing at the counter, watching him run the water and commence with the ritual squeezing of the sponge.

"Sit down," his father said gruffly when he noticed the new tactic. "Afterwards we'll have a smoke."

"Can I at least dry?"

"No. What's the matter with you?"

Again he took his place at the table and watched his father work, wondering what it would take, what he could do, to break the mold, then wondering if, in fact, it needed to be broken. For probably the fiftieth time that day his thoughts went back to Losapas. He was sitting in the shade of the thatched shelter, sweating, watching Elias and his friend Autei play in the clearing. The ship had arrived two hours before, and aside from himself and the two boys — who had grown bored with the adults' business and come back to the clearing to build cities — everyone was at the landing beach helping unload the launch. He had gone spearfishing off Moon Beach, alone, and was cleaning his catch beside a metal bucket. When the work was nearly done he saw Ninake come out from behind Ulua's house and walk by the two boys, her breasts swinging slightly as she moved, a gentle play of flesh he loved to watch. She gathered up the folds of her skirt, squatted on her heels in front of him, and waited as he clumsily slit open a *pula*'s belly and scooped the innards into his pail.

"That is woman's work," she said.

She turned to look at something near the edge of the lagoon and he sneaked a glance at her. They had been lovers three months, three ships. Beneath the tight, neat fabric of island life they were starting to weave their own cloth, something still loose and free-form, a combination of torn pasts. The memories of his war were finally beginning to disappear. He could close his eyes at night without seeing what was not there. This beautiful woman's steady ocean stillness was working its slow magic on him, and on good days he felt he might be restoring something in her, too, bringing back to life the young girl inside her. He tried not to make any great demands. He was satisfied just to lie on the pandanus mat, holding her, listening to the night sounds outside the window, to talk with her once or twice during the day, make an occasional comment about living together. But something was not right. Ninake never came to his hut two nights in a row, never seemed to give herself completely when they made love. During the day she insisted on keeping their affair hidden — as much as anything could remain hidden on Losapas. In public, she told him, they could not embrace or hold hands or show any sign of special friendship. That was the island way. She would not even talk about living together. When he mentioned it she retreated into an implacable silence. Looking at her, he was sure they were moving toward their first real quarrel — a deepening or a separation.

"Don't you want to see the ship?" she said.

"No." He went back to his work.

"Why not?"

"No reason."

"Everyone else is at the landing beach."

"That doesn't matter to me. I don't have to do what everyone does, do I?"

"No."

"Do you need help there?" he said. "Carrying medicines?"

"There are other men to help." Behind her the two boys shrieked and raced around the sand in circles. "Mahalis was looking for you."

"I went fishing."

"Alone?"

He laid his knife down in the clean sand and watched her,

furious at the unwritten rules. You did not show affection in public; you did not do anything alone; you did not upset the community in any way, tip the perfect, ancient balance. He searched her face and saw that she was angry, too, a very deep, feminine anger that concealed itself by habit, that would never break the surface. "Are you coming to visit me tonight?"

"Probably," she said.

"I don't like pretending."

"Is that why you don't come to the landing beach?"

"No."

"Why, then? Are you afraid of the ship?"

"Of course not."

"Then why?"

"I don't know the reason why," he said loudly, and the boys stopped in their tracks and looked over at him. "I just don't want to see the ship. I've seen it. It's not interesting to me."

"Are you afraid you will get on it and go away?"

"No."

She seemed skeptical. "Are you going to stay here then?"

"Yes."

"For how long? A long time?"

"Forever."

"Really?"

"Yes."

She allowed a small portion of exasperation into her eyes. "Then you will have to be less of an alone person, Marr-keen. You want me to show other people I am with you but it is not easy to be with you. You are with yourself in a small room. No one else can get in."

The words had a curious effect on him. He remembered feeling a huge finger pressing against his chest, very slowly, millimeter by millimeter, crushing the breath out of him. At that moment he understood that he would have to change something fundamental in himself; he would have to bend or the world was going to break him. He saw that he had spent his life after the war trying to find a secure spot, some place or state of mind where nothing could hurt him, some secret island where bad things did not happen, where families were not destroyed and young people did not split up or explode into bloody parts. He had harbored that hope like a private treasure and it had cut him off from people, from the way things really were, made any kind of true connection impossible. "You're right," he told her, squeezing his hands together like a man praying. "What you just said is right."

She seemed only to need to hear that, to have that small concession, a half promise. He could change. That would be enough to allow her to bear the weight of island opinion alone. She put a hand on his hands for a moment, then stood and went back down the path.

His father sat down opposite him, lit two fat cigars in his mouth, and passed one across the table. They puffed out great clouds of pungent smoke until the kitchen was all layers and swirls of gray. "Stevie gave them to me," the old man said, looking at his cigar. "He always asks for you."

"I missed him today."

"Like I told you, he wasn't there today. He's in Canada."

Markin nodded. Canada, Montana, Wisconsin. It was all the same. "I was thinking of Ma today at the beach, how she used to swim straight out so we thought she wasn't coming back."

"*You* thought that," his father said, and he blinked four or five times in quick succession. "You always thought that. You always cried when she did that, whenever she left you. You were sure you'd never see her again." He paused a moment. "In the end you were right."

His father got up, rummaged through a drawer filled with twine, shoelaces, and paper clips, and came back holding a creased photograph. As if it were evidence in a trial, he placed on the table in front of Markin a picture of two young women, his mother and someone he didn't recognize, standing in front of 10 Wilson Street holding their babies.

Markin had never seen this photograph. He studied his mother's face for a long time, looking for something in the dark eyes and wide, pretty mouth, but the image seemed willing to yield only one secret: the passage of time was a fact.

His father appeared to have taken the same lesson from it. "I am going to die," he said across the table. There was no self-pity in the voice, and though the eyes were moist and distant, Markin had the feeling his father was not looking for sympathy. It was something else. What struck him hardest was the matter-of-factness of the statement, its indisputability, as if he were giving some important fatherly advice, telling his son something he didn't already know. "You are, too," his father added, and in this there was a hint of complaint.

"I know, Pa."

"That's right. You knew already. You knew before me."

Markin remembered the wake of the uncle he'd been closest to, his father's older brother, Leo, his namesake, and he recalled the family friends who'd come up to him and said what a shock it was that his uncle was "gone." Mixed with the sadness in their faces was a look of disbelief, as if death were something not only unfair but unexpected, as if God were supposed to give advance notice. The fact that at sixteen he already knew something — such an important thing — that these adults were still ignorant of had puzzled him and made him sadder.

His father was off in a reverie. Markin tried to bring him back. "I missed you, Pa."

His father nodded and a strand of white hair fell onto his forehead. He pushed it back absently. "When your mother died I spent an hour at the cemetery every day for a year. I thought it was something that had only happened to her. I thought it was unfair."

"It *was* unfair." Markin watched his father's cigar smoldering in the ashtray. He took a long drag of his own, exhaled the smoke to one side, and followed the gray cloud as it collected in the light near the window.

"Do you remember," his father said, "how she used to pray all the time?"

"I remember coming home from first grade and opening the gate to the back yard and seeing her sitting in one of the old metal lawn chairs. She was saying the rosary and looking at the pear tree like she could see something there no one else could see."

"She could. She used to tell me . . . One day before you were born we were swimming down the beach. We came out of the water and we laid down on our towel and she asked me if I ever saw all the things going on at once. All the blood flowing back and forth inside all the people on the beach, the sun moving across the sky, everything that was happening in the ocean, all the different living things there, the way the tide came in and out like magic. I said, 'I can imagine it when you talk about it, Theresa, but I can't *see* it, not really.' You know what she used to call it, Leo? God breathing." The old man shook his head as though, thirty years after he'd first heard the phrase, it still puzzled and amazed him. "God breathing," he repeated. "Have you ever felt that?"

"Sometimes. Sometimes on the island."

His father grunted as if he'd suspected as much. "You were different. You were like her. Even your eyes are her eyes."

Markin looked at the photograph and saw that it was so.

"Do you remember after she died you didn't talk for three days? You said later you didn't have time to talk to other people, you had a lot on your mind. You don't remember?"

"No."

"You don't remember for years after that day you used to go down the corner and throw things at the trolley cars — rocks, snowballs? I used to come home from work and find you all alone down there, squeezing your rubber ball in one hand, getting ready to throw it when the trolley came. They almost arrested you once, don't you remember?"

He remembered the red-faced Irish trolleyman chasing him across Stadium Avenue and through the frozen back yards of

Essex Street. The man didn't have a prayer of catching him — he knew every fence and bush in every yard, all the good hiding places. He squeezed into the alley between Mrs. Flynn's garage and her toolshed and listened to the driver run by, puffing breath. By the time the man finally gave up and headed back to his passengers, he'd already clambered onto the low roof of the awning company and was waiting there like a sniper on a cliff. He hit the driver in the back of the neck with a ball of ice, a perfect, one-in-a-thousand shot, guided, he told himself, by his mother's hand. The police came to the house that night and he hid in his father's closet behind the rack of clothes, breathing the mothball air. His father opened the front door and told the patrolman to go to hell, then fixed everything later with Tommy Mario.

"I remember the day you came home and told me Ma was dead."

His father pretended not to hear. "You were always a little bit different," he said, looking down. "Your teachers always told me that — smart, they said, but a little bit different." His father put the cigar in the ashtray, took a handkerchief out of his pants pocket, and blew his nose. "Stevie comes up here sometimes on Sunday nights and we talk about you," he said through the handkerchief. "He misses you like you don't know."

"I missed him, too. I missed you." Markin looked into the old eyes and saw that his father was trying to avoid responding to the remark, just as he had avoided responding to Christmas gifts and the hugs of his late sisters, as if only he knew how little he deserved such love, or as if human affection were some shameful secret that should never be acknowledged. Markin decided not to let him get away with it this time. "I'm sorry I stayed away so long."

"You were in the war," his father said, stuffing the handkerchief back into his pants and looking at a chip in the surface of the table.

"I was wrong not to come back and see you."

"It doesn't matter now." His father made his face hard, a signal that the brief sentimental lapse was over. It was something

Markin had seen ten thousand times, a mask that had always, until this moment, fooled him. One of the spotted hands reached out and took hold of the cigar, twisting it against the rim of the glass ashtray and bringing it to his mouth for a final taste. "Are you going to stay now?" his father said, immediately looking away.

Markin looked away, too, then back. "I have a girlfriend there, Pa."

"What about Angela?"

Markin just stared into the wet eyes, unable to squeeze out a word. His father nodded and twirled the cigar and made himself not care, a thing he'd had a lot of practice at.

"Her name is Ninake. I was thinking I could go back and get her and bring her back here so you could meet her."

His father nodded again, not believing a word of it. He picked up the snapshot and replaced it carefully in the drawer, then stood at the sink as he had the night before, staring out the window.

Markin walked up to the counter and stood beside him. "I love you, Pa," he said, and he could feel the old body tighten.

"Were you a coward over there? Did you disgrace yourself? In the paper it said you have two medals."

"I do."

"What then?"

For a moment Markin thought of telling his father the whole story in detail, opening up to him the way he'd opened up to Ninake, trying to make him see what he couldn't imagine. But he decided one small part of it would have to be enough. If his father couldn't understand that, it would be a waste of time to talk about the rest of it. "I killed a little girl over there," he said. "I couldn't stand to have that inside me." He glanced at his father's face, hoping for some sign, a glimmer of understanding. The face was stone. "I was afraid to come home and have people think I was still the same person."

"You are."

Markin couldn't keep himself from grabbing hold of the bony

elbow. "Look at me, Pa!" His father turned his head and met his son's eyes. "I killed a little girl. I burned people's houses. I slapped people until their mouths bled — old women and old men!" His hands and legs were shaking so much he thought he would be unable to finish. All of that burning hot, murderous year was rising up around him in the kitchen, a city of ghosts. His father pulled his elbow away and Markin grabbed it again, knowing this was the wrong way to go about it but unable to restrain himself. "You can't forgive the person who mugged you. Do you think those people can forgive me — for crippling them, murdering their daughters?"

His father looked away, embarrassed. "That's war," he said. "Stevie went to war. He did things like that."

"Stevie never saw one day of combat."

"You don't understand, Leo."

"I was the one who was there!"

"I would have gone to war," his father said, hitting his chest with his thumb. "I tried three times to go. Three times! They wouldn't take me. I was a master welder, thirty-four years old. I would have given anything to go, to do what you did." The old man fixed him with a look he'd never seen before, an expression exposing anguish so deep, hidden for so long, it had taken on a power beyond human proportion. Markin shuffled half a step back. "Do you know what that's like, Leo? To have all the men go to war and you stay home and work in the factory with the women, making the planes that their husbands might be killed in? Can you understand that? What it's like to go down Broadway and cheer when the men come home and see all the women cheering, wanting to dance with those men, not you? Do you understand?"

Markin felt as though he'd been struck across the face. In answer to his father's questions he could only stand wooden, arms at his sides. He understood, finally. For all their lives he and his father had been bound by a secret pact. The father would pretend — for the sake of his son — to have no fears, no tender places. And the son would pretend — for the sake of his father — to believe him. As the years passed, it became clearer and clearer to each of them that their contract was based on a lie, an impossibility. But they had never learned how to free themselves from it. And, Markin thought, if he ever had a son or a daughter of his own, it would be the same way; it would encrust his life with a subtle, deadly fraudulence.

But strangely, now that his father had finally torn the mask away, Markin wanted him to replace it. He'd seen such nakedness there once before, only once, in this same room, and it was the worst memory of his life, worse, in its own way, than anything that had happened to him in Vietnam. He wanted to reach across the few inches of space and touch the man beside him, but his father was scowling, closing himself off again, and it seemed that, if touched now, his fragile defenses would crumble completely. Instead of a father, he would be left with only a man.

For the rest of the evening they kept as much distance between them as the house allowed. His father sat at the table in the dining room — which they had not used for a meal since the day before his mother died — and wrote out checks to cover his monthly bills. Markin sat upstairs in his bedroom, looking half-heartedly through old school papers. He came across a photo of his third-grade class and found Billy Ollanno there, smiling obligingly at the camera, ready to jump out of his seat and run an errand for someone, anyone.

At ten o'clock his father climbed the stairs and stuck his head into the room. "Don't forget you were going to take the car down tomorrow afternoon and have them look at the muffler," he said, like a father. Markin was happy to see the disguise back in place. When his father wished him good night and went into the bathroom, he stepped over to the dormer window and knelt there, looking down at the street. He would never forget the date: October 9, 1956. He would never forget coming home from school and finding the house empty, something that had never happened before. After wandering through the quiet rooms for a while, he'd gone and knelt on the sofa, chin in hand, looking out the window for signs of his parents. It was late, dusk. He saw Mr. Mastromarino's black car pull into the driveway across the street, watched his neighbors, Elaine and Lora, walk up the sidewalk from the bus stop carrying shopping bags and hurrying because, as usual, they were late. His mother was never late. In the two years he'd been at school he'd never once come home to an empty house, and he knelt there until darkness fell, feeling hungry and unsure.

When his father finally came home, he was alone and his face looked strange, as though the muscles that held it together had stopped working, leaving the bones to float beneath the skin. He sat in one of the kitchen chairs and the boy stood in front of him, hands on his father's knees.

"Where's Ma?"

After a long moment the man said, "God called your mother today."

The boy looked at him blankly, waiting, watching the eyes and contorted mouth. "What do you mean, Pa?"

"God called your mother."

Slowly, meeting tremendous resistance, a thought found its way into the boy's mind. No, he said to himself. No. But the thought was seeping into his brain the way rising water seeps across an almost flat surface — moving into the easiest places first, then filling in. The sight of what looked like tears in his father's eyes was, to that moment in his life, the most surprising and horrifying thing he had ever seen. "What do you mean?" he repeated desperately, though now he was almost certain he knew.

"Mama died today," his father said, and the face fell apart.

From a distance of twenty years he watched the two of them crying: the boy shaking uncontrollably, sprawled face-down on the floor, one hand on his father's shoe; and the man, arms hanging helplessly at his sides, raincoat drooping down along the chair legs, lips trembling, two straight rivers wearing beds into his cheeks.

# 18

A LIGHT RAIN was muttering on the roof and dripping on the metal vent hood near the kitchen window with a maddening *tink tink tink* Markin associated with gray February afternoons when rain melted the ice on the back roof. In the living room his father was sitting in front of the television — it was too wet to work in the yard today — and the game-show laughter and staged applause drifted into the kitchen like a poison cloud. Markin felt the house beginning to infect him with lethargy — the kitchen seemed as confining as a coffin — and he stared out the window, considering his options. He could ride the subway into Boston and walk around in the city (his father said there'd been so much new construction he'd get lost just trying to find the Common). There might be a matinee worth seeing. He could call up some of his high school friends on the chance they wouldn't be at work, walk down to DiMaggio's for a few beers. He could climb up into the attic and look through the boxes of snapshots or throw out some of the old clothes his father had saved for him. He could catch the early act at the Leopard Club and drink with Billy Ollanno.

Bells and sirens sounded in the living room, and the program ended with a circus of music and senseless cheering. The rain kept tapping on the vent hood, and Markin remembered riding with his father on days like this when he was a young boy, the car windows closed against the rain and the windshield wipers tharumping and squeaking back and forth, back and forth, back and forth, the stale air and smell of upholstery making him sick to his stomach. Markin knew he needed to get out of the house, get to the beach again or take the car and drive north for an hour into the woods. He knew it, but he couldn't make his body move. The stifling air and jet lag and television noise had hypno-tized him; nothing seemed worth the effort. Earlier, he'd tried to convince his father to take a ride with him, anywhere, but it seemed the only places his father went now were church, gro-cery shopping, and out into the back yard. He'd even given up the dog track, his one passion. "I get dizzy sometimes, Leo. I don't want everybody at the track to see me fall on my face."

Now there was organ music on the television and Markin heard his father flipping through the channels to find the soap opera he liked. He put on his jacket and went out onto the sidewalk and stood in the drizzle for a minute or two, still drugged. No one else was out. A few blocks away a siren shrieked and faded. Markin started to walk, up Wilson Street this time, past the brick elementary school, which had been turned into condominiums, then down through the housing project where Julius Cosmo had been caught with two pounds of marijuana and a pistol in his trunk and made himself a hero in the eleventh grade. The rain on his face and hair chilled him; he walked faster, headed nowhere. In this part of the city, cars were parked with two wheels up on the sidewalk; overflowing metal trash barrels clung to the curb; old houses stood only twenty or thirty feet apart and seemed to be leaning toward one another, dying together. Most of them, in this section of town, were shabby triple-deckers with lawn chairs and clotheslines and everything else that would not fit in the apartments piled out on their porches. The curtains were drawn, drab in the gray light. But behind them Markin knew the living rooms would be clean and comfortable, plastic saints on the walls, plastic fruit in bowls. The kitchens would be places where you could sit for hours, eating and drinking and talking, creating a warm and beautiful world there that had little in common with the grim view from the street.

He had spent some of the finest hours of his life in kitchens like those. In the Panechieso home, especially, there had been some good times, at least two happy years. He could no longer keep himself from thinking about it.

From early on in the relationship it had been assumed he would be part of the family someday. Angela's mother and father had treated him like a son, Mrs. Panechieso teasing him about his appetite, Mr. Panechieso about his strange last name, asking him which was the Italian half, right or left, saying that was the hand he'd shake. He'd arm-wrestled with Angela's brother, Michael, at the kitchen table, losing consistently, and being teased still more for that. When he graduated from Averill Beach High, the Panechiesos had given him a card with a Saint Jude medallion and a hundred-dollar bill inside, had taken him and Angie to the most expensive restaurant on the North Shore, had bought them the biggest steak, had waited all that summer and fall for their daughter to come home with a diamond on her finger. It was almost worse to think about them than to think about Angie, but he let the thoughts come, let everything pour down on him. He hadn't traveled all the way back here just to run away from it again.

At the top of the rise — Washington Street — he stopped and looked south over the roofs of five hundred houses. Beneath the quilt of gray rain clouds, two low hills broke the horizon near the beach. He could see Bay Avenue running along the Heights like a stripe on an animal's back, the squat gray water tower standing above it, a few trees already turning color. He stared at the scene for a long time, then started walking again, head down, moving now gradually in the direction of the Heights, taking back streets that would bring him slowly, eventually, to the house where Angie lived with Richie Mowlen.

When he reached the bottom of Bay Avenue he started climbing, moving doggedly through the drizzle, not even looking for the house until he got to the top of the hill and then glancing up and seeing it immediately, the name MOWLEN burned on a block of two-by-six, a high school shop project. He looked down at his feet and kept walking, descending now, moving toward the ocean.

Bay Avenue ended two blocks from the water, opposite the elevated MBTA station that marked the end of the Boston subway line. Markin stood on the corner there, hands in his pockets, and watched a string of blue cars rumble up to the platform and stop. The doors slid open, a few passengers emerged and disappeared into the station. Five minutes later what sounded like a schoolbell rang, the doors clapped shut again, and the train rumbled back toward the city. "There's talk of us going overseas," he'd said to Angie in a car parked not half a mile from here, against the beach wall.

"Vietnam?"

He was already a Marine then, home on leave from Camp Lejeune. His hair was short, muscles hard, he'd developed a temper and good posture. "I might not come back," he told her. "Or I might come back in pieces. I don't want you putting your life on hold."

The childishness of it repulsed him now, the false generosity. He thought he might vomit his breakfast into the gutter.

"But I *want* to wait for you," she'd said, unable to look at him. She put a hand up to her eyes, then removed it.

He hadn't reached out to console her, of course. His mind had been ringing with ideas the Marines had instilled in him: discipline, duty, honor. He'd become obsessed with his own ability to conquer pain, to prove himself under fire. Next to that, what Angela offered, what she represented, seemed inconsequential. He was going to risk his life to protect the free world; she wanted to have babies and hang pictures of saints on the wall. That was no life for a man.

He shuddered.

A second string of cars rumbled and rattled out of the tunnel. Markin watched a flock of pigeons burst out from their roost in the trestle beneath the tracks, bank and whirl in a wet, purple flapping, and take up positions on the rooftops nearby. He fixed his eyes on the subway cars, trying to pretend he had never spoken those words or held those beliefs or gone off to war because of them. But it was no use; there was no magic in Averill Beach. When the bell sounded and the doors closed and the train started back toward Boston, his Marine discipline and sense of honor made him turn and start back up the hill. He did not fail to note the irony.

Angela's yard looked like dozens of others on the street: a miniature front lawn enclosed by a picket fence and edged with rose bushes; a ceramic statue of the Virgin Mary sheltered by half a metal bathtub painted sky blue; kids' toys. The gate hinges squeaked, the wooden porch steps flexed beneath his weight. He pressed the third-floor buzzer and waited, wondering what he would say if Richie answered. A minute passed without any sound in the stairwell. He pushed the button again and had turned away from the door when he heard footsteps, then a hand on the bolt. "Who is it?"

"It's me," he said foolishly, nervously.

The bolt snapped back, the door opened, and Angela was standing there three feet in front of him, looking worn and beautiful. "Christ Almighty," she said.

*

The cramped, top-floor apartment could boast of two things. It offered a partially obstructed view of the ocean, and since it was at the rear of the house, its rooms were insulated somewhat from the noise of the street. Beyond that it was bereft of luxury — plain walls, bare linoleum floors. The kitchen was furnished with hand-me-downs, including an old, round-cornered refrigerator Markin remembered from her parents' house. He sat at the table and looked out a window as she shuffled around the kitchen in her slippers, heating coffee, setting out a plate of cookies, locating and lighting a cigarette, doing anything she could to avoid sitting down opposite him.

"How's your mother and father?" he said when she finally joined him.

Her cheeks hollowed momentarily on either side of the cigarette and she blew smoke to one side before looking at him. "Pretty good. They still ask about you."

Some of the tightness in his stomach disappeared. His intestines made a gurgling noise that embarrassed him and he turned away, not wanting Angela to see how much the remark had affected him. He stared at the wall above the cast iron radiator for several seconds before he realized he was looking at a picture of a boy, Richie and Angie's son no doubt, his angry little eyes glaring out at the world. It was so sad it almost made Markin laugh, the tricks life played, passing on to this harmless child a pair of eyes that would bring him trouble all his life, courtesy of his troublesome father. He had never seen Richie when his eyes didn't look angry like that. Some childhood trauma seemed to shadow him everywhere, coloring even his laughter, which Markin suddenly recalled, a bully's laughter, a sound lacking any charity or joy.

He turned back to Angie. She had changed so much! Her mouth and eyes were guarded by lines — narrow, empty moats. Her lips looked thinner, drier. The skin he remembered as smooth and, even in winter, showing a trace of color, was now bone white and drawn too tightly across her cheeks. Her hair looked the same — carbon black and cut so that it hung in a neat half curl on her shoulders — but that didn't help much. At twenty-nine she made a good-looking forty-year-old, and it hurt him to see it and to think that she might have married Richie out of some kind of desperate revenge. "How's Michael?" he said.

She spilled some of her coffee. "Married. Marilyn's pregnant with their second. They have a cute little girl named after me."

"You're a mother now, too," he said. His voice sounded strange to him, higher than usual, false.

"Twice." She almost smiled. "Richie Junior's at kindergarten. C'mon in the bedroom, I'll show you Michelle."

They left their coffees and stepped quietly into a dim bedroom, where sheets and towels were stacked in orderly piles on every horizontal surface and a wooden crucifix hung over the bed. Pressed into one corner was an old crib. Angela leaned over the rail and carefully rearranged the blanket on a sleeping infant. The gesture seized Markin. He was momentarily overcome by the certainty that he had been in this room before and watched this woman bending over their own child. Angie's fingers on the satin hem were fingers from a part of his life that seemed like an interrupted dream. He could see the bra strap outlined against the back of her housedress when she bent over, the shape of her hips, her legs. She seemed to stay in that position for a long time, as if waiting for him to touch her, and he was about to touch her, his hand had already started to move, when she straightened, stroked the nape of the baby's neck, and led Markin back to the neutrality of the kitchen.

"Lisa said she saw you at Stevie's yesterday," Angie said as she refilled their cups. "I wondered if you'd call or anything." She tapped a fresh cigarette out of the pack, lit it, and took a deep drag.

Markin had never known her to smoke, and the new gestures fascinated him. "My father was mugged," he said, unable to take his eyes from her.

What little color there was in Angie's face drained away. She coughed on the smoke and put the cigarette down. For a minute he didn't know what was going on, whether she was that surprised, whether the fact that they were sitting together again had finally caught up with her, whether she was just upset about his father. She seemed not to know what to do or say until she finally managed, "I heard about him, about that," and a few seconds later, "I heard about it." She looked at him, then away, then back. "I'm sorry."

Only ten minutes had passed and already they had run through all the topics he'd prepared on the walk up here. He imagined himself finishing the rest of his coffee and going down the stairs, out into the fresh air, out of her life again. He owed her more than that, but what was he supposed to say? Remember when we used to park my father's old Pontiac against the beach wall and lie there with our bare feet sticking out the window and just kiss and talk for hours? Remember Forty Steps Beach, what a foggy night it was and how scared we were that someone would hear us or see us with our pants off? Remember the time we thought you were pregnant and I was all ready to go talk to your father? Remember Nicky's Christmas party?

For a minute he could not face her. He turned toward the wall and pretended not to see the picture of Richie Junior. What could he say? He's a cute kid? Looks a lot like his dad? Nice eyes?

Angie rescued them both by going into a room off the kitchen and returning with an armful of old snapshots. She placed them on the table and stood at his shoulder, so close he could smell her skin.

It was, for the most part, an unsurprising collection: old friends, scenes from their high school summers, a few shots of Angie pregnant, a few of her holding one-year-old Richie Junior and smiling. There was only one with her husband. They were in a restaurant, dressed in their going-out clothes, looking drunk and happy. An anniversary celebration, Markin guessed. "This is nice," he said. She didn't respond. Near the bottom of the pile he came upon a picture of a young man and a young woman, both in shorts and T-shirts, sitting together at what looked like a picnic.

The man was tanned, brown-haired, well built. One of his arms was curled playfully around the woman's neck, pulling her head against his shoulder. In the margin was printed LEO AND ANGIE, JULY 4, 1967. For several seconds the picture looked up at them like an advertisement for a life neither of them had ever found. There was nothing to say. Angela pushed the photos together and brought them into the back room. Markin heard a drawer open and close and waited for her to reappear. When she didn't return after several minutes, he stood and walked to the doorway. The room was a narrow porch with a wall of windows facing down over the east side of the Heights to the sea. Angela was sitting on a daybed, elbows on her knees, chin in her hands, staring at a saucer on the coffee table. She had been crying, and he sat near the door watching her, feeling a pressure building against his eyes and ears. "How's things?" he said stupidly when he could no longer endure the silence.

"Depends on which things we're talking about."

"What's Richie up to?"

"He was driving a truck for Eastern Freight. They laid him off and he was out of work for about four months, collecting. Then his uncle got him on with the city." She paused, and he could see she was deciding how much more to tell him. At that level, a job with the city would be a dead-end, completely dependent on the re-election of the mayor. You'd have to put election stickers on your car window; you'd have to stand at the polls with a cardboard sign. In return you'd get just enough money to live on, the basic benefits, not an ounce of satisfaction.

"He hates it." She twisted her cigarette along the edge of the saucer until the ash fell like a severed head, rolled an inch, then broke apart. A puff of smoke rose from her lips and drifted toward the windows. Markin knew there was something else she wanted to tell him and he waited, his eyes moving nervously over her face, shoulders, and hands. "We're thinking of breaking up."

"Billy Ollanno told me. I bumped into him at Stevie's. He mentioned that."

There was a terrible moment when neither of them knew what to say or where to put their eyes or what to think. Angie let out a big breath of smoke and looked at her nails. "He was hitting Richie Junior," she said, pronouncing each word quietly without looking at him. "Last winter he gave him such a kick between the legs that his balls turned blue. We had to take him to the hospital."

Markin let the information pass into his memory and settle there. It was almost enough to turn him back into a killer, and he did not try to keep the feelings from his face. When he spoke again he heard his own voice. "Did he ever hit you?"

Angie pretended not to hear, which was his answer. "I was worried about the baby."

"What did you do?"

"I cried. I screamed. I said I'd go to the police. I took Richie Junior and the baby and spent two weeks at Marilyn's. She wants to pay someone to break his legs. She knows some guy —"

"I'll chip in."

A wry smile passed across her face and immediately vanished. "I'm afraid to tell Michael or my father . . . Richie says he won't do it again, ever, that it's over. He swore to me it was just because he was out of work, going crazy . . ." For a moment she looked up at him and seemed to wish she hadn't told him, then she brought the edges of her teeth together — something he'd seen her do a thousand times — put out her cigarette, and went on. "And there were other things." She looked just to one side of Markin's face and seemed to be hoping he would guess, but he couldn't guess. He couldn't think. In her eyes he saw a familiar struggle, loyalty tugging at her conscience. It was a battle as old as the city they looked out on, and in Averill Beach there could be only one possible result. For a few seconds it hurt him to think she would keep something from him to protect someone else, then he felt ashamed for thinking it. She owed him absolutely nothing. Richie, at least, had married her; he'd done that at least, the sonofabitch.

There was a long silence during which Angie seemed to drift away, to lose contact with the world for a moment, then return. "How's things with you?" she said. "We read about the medals and all. I have the clippings."

"That was bullshit, Angie."

"Was it?"

"I killed a little girl, and I went crazy and got myself shot. That's what they gave me the medals for."

She was no more affected by it than his father or Woodrow had been. He had the feeling he could have told her he'd helped crucify Christ and she would have shrugged, blinked, lit up another cigarette.

"I think about you," she said. "You were smart to get away."

"I was selfish."

"Sometimes selfish is smart."

"You were as smart as I was. You're too smart for this."

"You get stuck," she said, unoffended. "If I leave Richie, I'd have to move in with my parents. Nobody in AB would go out with me, because either they'd be afraid of what he'd do or they wouldn't want to get that involved — you know, instant family. I'd have to get a job, leave the kids with my mother. It wouldn't be much better than this."

Markin allowed himself to imagine something, a drastic step to erase the past. He let the idea play in his mind for a second or two, then buried it. "You can change this," he said, but if she had asked him for a specific suggestion, the only one he would have come up with was to leave Richie for good, just get away from him.

She smirked and didn't ask. "What are you going to do now?"

"Stay with my father for a while, I guess, then go back to the island." He started to tell her about Ninake, looked at her face, and stopped.

"Near Hawaii," she said. "Will you ever be back for good?"

"Maybe someday."

"I don't know if I wished you lived around here or not, Leo."

The sound of his name on her lips, what he thought of now as his former name, startled Markin. He was beginning to sense a great weight of shame and regret bearing down on him; he was beginning to lose what little control he'd been able to carry up the squeaking flights of stairs. If Richie had walked into the room at that moment, Markin was sure he would have thrown him through a window. He moved to the edge of the chair as if to stand, but waited, trying to think of an apology, the right apology. He saw that it would change nothing. Certain deeds were etched in stone. You didn't erase them with words. You didn't say five Hail Marys at the altar rail and move on. There was a law in the universe, however shrouded and impenetrable. You paid for things with a geologic slowness, in kind.

Angie was looking straight at him now for the first time since he'd entered the apartment. Her irises were black-flecked blue. "You're thinking you fucked things up for me, right?"

What had earlier been stuck in his stomach was now stuck in his throat, keeping him from swallowing, damming water into his eyes.

"Don't think that," she said, still looking straight at him. "I know why you didn't come back."

"Tell me."

"You'd die in a place like this, Leo. I knew that even before you enlisted. I used to come home and cry about it. My father knew it, too. That's why he liked you so much, because he's the same way. A part of him just wants to take off, travel around the world for a year, go live on an island. I still see it in his face when he asks about you."

This truth pierced Markin as though he'd been shot with a spear; it skewered him to the chair. This was as much forgiveness as he could ever hope to hear and yet it made him feel hollow with failure. The magnitude of his own selfishness sickened him. For a moment he convinced himself that he could have held on to his wildness, his manhood, and still given Angie what she needed from him. But that path was closed to him now, finally, irrevocably.

"You should go see him."

"I should," he said in an unsteady voice, knowing that, Marine discipline or not, he would never be able to do it. Now he could not look at her.

"What happened on Guam, Leo?"

For a second he wasn't sure if she'd really asked the question or if he'd imagined it, but when he looked up she was watching him, waiting — not judging, just waiting — as if once she'd heard his answer, she would be able to stop thinking about it forever.

He felt he was about to explode and scatter pieces of himself all over the small room. "I fell apart," he said. "I lost myself."

She nodded.

He knew it wasn't enough. "I was wrong, Angie."

Angie was shaking her head in small movements. "My father offered to fly me out there, you know. Guam." Her voice caught and there was a long pause before she controlled it and went on. "I was too afraid to go."

He was nodding; in some mysterious way he had known this. She could not get on the plane, he was saying to himself, she could not break the chains of Averill Beach. "I wasn't me," he said. "If you came out there then, you wouldn't have known me."

They fell silent, into themselves. Markin felt the pressure rising through his throat, behind his eyes. The tears were coming up now, sliding down his cheeks. His legs were trembling. He stood abruptly, afraid of what his body might do if he stayed with her any longer. Angie followed him to the top of the stairs. He put his shaking hands on her hips and she held them there.

"Look me up again, all right?" she said, weeping openly now.

He knew he would not be able to say anything else. He tried anyway, and failed. He opened and closed his mouth stupidly, then turned and went down the flights of blurry stairs, stepped out into the daylight, and followed Edge Street down the steep face of the hill.

# 19

FOR AN HOUR Markin wandered aimlessly along the streets behind the Boulevard, a lowland of reclaimed salt marsh, four-room cottages where the carnies lived in summer, drug addicts and drifters the rest of the year. Even when he was a boy it had been a bad place for a walk. Now groups of men loitered on street corners and sagging wooden porches, eyeing passers-by with a quiet malevolence akin to lust. He made a point of walking past each group several times, hoping to elicit just one untoward comment.

But nothing happened. Markin walked and walked through a steady drizzle, hands in his pockets, eyes down, thoughts running back over and over again to the drab apartment on the Heights.

Near one o'clock he found himself at the edge of the five-acre parking lot owned by the Atlantic Dog Racing Association. At the far end of the lot, cars were pulling in through a chain-link gate, taking up spaces near the track entrance. Beyond them stood the grandstand's white bulk, windows like a line of dull eyes, a brick wall surrounding it and the kennels and track as if it were a prison or a monastery or an institute of higher learning. It was an ugly building enveloped in memories; as Markin drew nearer one of them leapt out and took hold of him.

After they had both signed the papers that indentured him to the United States Armed Forces, the Marine recruiter in Everett had told him he would pick him up on the morning of November 29 and drive him to Logan Airport, where he would be put on a plane for South Carolina.

"Where shall I meet you in Averill Beach, sir?" Markin had asked. He had been eager to please, anxious for his new life to begin, worried the Marines would find him unfit or that he would back out at the last minute and humiliate himself in front of the whole city.

"You tell me."

"How about the dog track on Seaview Avenue?" he suggested, guessing it was a location the recruiter would know and thinking it would be appropriate to start his journey to manhood from a place he'd associated, from his earliest years, with his father. After his mother died, his father had made the dog track into a second home, going there three or four nights a week during the racing season. His father knew the owner, was friends with the ushers and some of the trainers. He knew how to bet and when to stop betting.

"Oh-eight-hundred hours," the recruiter said.

At twenty to eight on the morning of November 29, 1967, his father backed the Pontiac out of the driveway and headed toward Seaview Avenue in a nervous silence, keeping both hands on the wheel and pushing an unlit cigar from one side of his mouth to the other. A hundred yards short of the track entrance, his father pulled over to the curb and stiffly shook his hand. "I'll leave you here," he said, by way of a farewell, "so the sergeant will think you walked."

The sergeant didn't seem to care whether he'd walked, flown, or sprinted. He drove Markin to Logan in a plain green government car without so much as grunting, stopping in East Boston to pick up two other recruits, acting like a man who'd never entertained even the smallest doubt about his place in the world, his usefulness, his beliefs. The recruiter had made such an impression on him that years later, as Markin crossed Seaview Avenue and approached the square tunnel that was the dog track's main entrance, he could recall the man's features exactly: aluminum eyes; round, fleshy cleft jaw; rigid bearing.

He had bought that act.

The interior of the clubhouse had been redone, new white and green tiles on the walls of the tunnel, new betting windows, bright ceiling lamps. But the feeling of the place had not changed. It was still a world of cigar smoke and beer, race announcements on the PA system, knots of men and a few women poring over white paper programs, cursing, laughing, glancing up across the infield at the numbers on the tote board.

Markin climbed the stairs to the second level and headed toward the green wooden seats that looked out through enormous plate-glass windows onto the finish line. Section H-3, his father's territory. He took a seat there and immediately regretted it. Once or twice on a Saturday night he'd come here with Angie. They'd sat behind their fathers, taking lessons in what to look for in a dog — weight, class, speed out of the box, determination in the crowded turns — sharing bets for a dollar apiece, sneaking glances at each other and thinking about what they were going to do afterward. It wasn't long — two visits, he thought — before she'd told him she couldn't stand to hear the dogs scratching and whimpering in their dark metal starting boxes, and after that he'd never taken her here again and never been able to come here alone without thinking about her.

He fought now to sort out sentimentality from the real feeling of those times, but it was a lost cause. He was drowning in memories, visions, snatches of speech, haunting moments. It was, he saw, exactly what he'd come to the track in search of: a sea in which to lose himself. But soon it became more than he could bear. He escaped H-3 for one of the open food bars, which offered a view of the first turn and the dilapidated houses on the other side of the wall. The bartender, a tall, stoop-shouldered, balding man wearing oversized black glasses, was someone Markin recognized from 1967, a Russian, another acquaintance of his father's. Vysotski or Vysovski. Vysovski, if Markin remembered right, enjoyed a reputation among track employees as a zealous whoremaster, patron of the Washington Street strip clubs.

The bar had just opened. Markin ordered a bourbon, a beer, and a hamburger. If Vysovski recognized him, he failed to mention it.

On the monitor above the bar, Markin watched the promenade of the eight greyhounds who would take part in the afternoon's first race. Each lead-out boy brought his dog up to the starting judge, who tugged on the animal's blanket and tested its muzzle. Numbers clicked on the tote board, an announcer gave the minutes remaining to post, bells rang, dogs were unleashed and stuffed into their starting boxes, the cloth rabbit began its circuit of the track, metal pole creaking. Another bell sounded and eight aluminum doors burst open, eight dogs thundered past in a flash of haunches and muzzles and dirt, a thousand pairs of eyes followed them around the track. There were shouts of encouragement, curses, rolled programs batted against chairs, thighs, the top of the wet fence that held bettors back from the animals. Markin watched and listened carefully. For once it all made perfect sense to him. This place had almost nothing to do with winning or losing money. The dogs were a sideshow. What was really going on here was spelled out on the tote board, the real center of attention. This was a place you could practice taking chances, practice losing, learn what it felt like to win, even when winning meant nothing more than an extra six dollars and twenty cents in your pocket. You had a car in the lot across the street, or a token for the subway. When the last numbers went up, win or lose, you'd have a place to go back to. You could fail here and walk away.

It was something he'd never noticed before, a new level of understanding. The conversation swirling around the bar seemed to confirm it.

"That six, the pig. Halfway into the turn, she follows her boyfriend to fuckin' Chelsea."

"Fifteen yeahs I been comin' down heah an' I nevah seen anythin' like that. My whole life I nevah seen it."

"Da eight just took a shit."

"That four hasta figya in this. He's been outa the money so long he's due."

"Deuce loves the rail. Door pops open she just sees that rail. Nothin' else mattahs."

They were men and women in golf caps and light jackets, smoking happily though they knew what it did to them, talking about dogs as if they were human, while from the kennels off behind the backstretch came a muted yelping, pure greyhound misery. Markin could see his father, middle-aged, white-headed, circling figures on the program with a stubby yellow pencil, concentrating almost intently enough to forget the fact that he had no wife, one absent child, no future.

He sent the last of the bourbon down his throat and followed it with a gulp of cheap dog-track beer. He stared at the hamburger in its bun on the cardboard plate but could not imagine eating it. One thing was obvious: he'd abandoned the two people who'd been closest to him in Averill Beach, and they'd suffered because of it. That did not seem like a forgivable sin.

Vysovski refilled the shot glass and put another plastic cup of beer on the bar. Markin drank hopefully, greedily, stared at the numbers on his program and the numbers on the tote board, and waited. He needed a break now, a breath of good luck. He was due. An usher approached him and he bet ten dollars across the board on an old dog called Steady Favor. He watched through the window as Steady Favor broke strong, held the lead through the first two turns, along the backstretch, slipped to second on the third turn, to third on the fourth, and struggled home just out of the money, his tongue poking out through the muzzle as he trotted around with the others, confused at the disappearance of the rabbit — though it had disappeared before and would disappear again — waiting for the boy with the leash to come and take him away.

When the race was declared official and the returns were posted, someone took the seat next to him at the end of the bar. Markin glanced up and saw Eddie O'Malley, Stevie's nephew, one of his thick hands extended and a genuinely pleased expression on his face. Markin, too, was pleased. Eddie was Averill Beach at its best, a true friend, a breath of good luck.

"We heard you was back," Eddie said after his first sip of beer. He did not look at Markin as he spoke. That was Eddie's style. After the initial eye contact he always looked where his partner in conversation was looking. If Eddie met people on the street, he would turn sideways and talk to them shoulder to shoulder instead of face to face. Markin had always liked the habit — it made the natural pauses in conversation more comfortable — and today he was especially glad for it. He did not need anyone looking at him too closely right now.

Eddie had been an altar boy at St. Lucy's, a fearless but reluctant street fighter, an All-State defensive tackle for the Averill Beach Warriors in 1965. Markin and his father and Stevie had gone to all the games that year, followed the team to the Eastern Massachusetts Championships, and watched them win, 6–0, the defense led by number 77. Markin remembered the day Eddie stuffed two footballs under his jersey at halftime and pranced and high-kicked with the Chelsea High cheerleaders. He recalled sitting in the grandstand on a freezing Thanksgiving morning,

Stevie chewing high-blood-pressure pills and jumping to his feet and screaming each time Eddie made a tackle: "That's my sister's boy! He's half Irish but I love him, I love that kid!" After the game they'd stood in a crowd near the team bus and applauded as the Warriors emerged from the locker room, Eddie puffing a huge victory cigar and smiling, looking as though he could carry the whole city on his shoulders.

Eddie had not gone to college. There were rumors of secret, excruciating injuries, a hint of academic troubles, but Markin suspected that the prospect of living someplace other than Averill Beach had simply been more than Eddie could face. After sampling various construction jobs, he'd settled into a career as a nightclub bouncer, work Markin imagined him fulfilling with a degree of humor, even tenderness, reaching out a hand to help his clients up off the sidewalk after he'd deposited them there. Eddie, he thought, would have married a girl like Angela the first Saturday after graduation. Markin finished his third bourbon and half the beer.

"We heard you was livin' on a desert island," Eddie said.

Markin couldn't sort out the tones in Eddie's voice: envy, amusement, mere politeness, true curiosity. He hadn't drunk much alcohol over the past seven years — a beer or two on his yearly visits to the District Center — and the boilermakers were already overtaking him, edging his thoughts with a faint, happy light. It seemed that Eddie really wanted to hear about Losapas. Even Vysovski appeared to be cocking an ear in their direction. Markin wondered where to begin. "It's hot," he said, "like a hot day in July, only every day, all year."

Eddie took a thoughtful pull of his beer and seemed to be trying hard to imagine it, a winterless life. Vysovski was standing right in front of them, slicing a lemon. "Snatch go topless?" he blurted out suddenly, the first words he'd spoken since Markin's arrival.

There was a moment of stunned silence. Eddie lifted his eyes and gave Vysovski a look of such disgust that the bartender grew confused and left to serve two middle-aged women at the other end of the bar.

"So what else, Leo?" Eddie said. "It's real hot over there. What else?"

"What else do you want to know?"

Eddie thought a moment. "I want to know," he said, "if it's different from AB."

The third race went off. They watched it on the monitor above the bar instead of turning to see the live action through the window on their left. Eddie said he had a C-note on the six dog, Georgette's Prince Robert, but he followed the race without expression, taking a small mouthful of foam as Georgette's Prince Robert was bumped on the far turn, somersaulted sideways in a spray of wet sand, and loped home far behind the pack.

As the replay was being shown on the monitor, Markin said, "I saw Angie this morning." The words seemed to have been propelled directly from his brain into the air above the bar glasses. Some filtering mechanism he'd always depended on had simply stopped functioning. Alarmed, he concentrated hard on the immediate surroundings, locking everything in place: Vysovski eyeing the hands of the middle-aged women as if imagining what other use they might be put to; this smoky air; this clouded plastic cup and wet black plastic counter top; this side of Eddie's big face — cheek, blue eye, hair the color of a coconut shell.

Eddie swiveled his neck and their eyes met. "You bump into her down Broadway or somethin'?"

"I went up to her house."

Eddie continued looking at him for several more seconds, then turned his face forward again and slowly, as if working his way through a difficult progression of thoughts, began tapping on the bar with the end of his pencil. At last he said, "You're all right, Leo M. You're fuckin' okay in my book."

It was a compliment of the highest order, but Markin would not let himself accept it. Eddie was judging him according to the

Averill Beach code of honor. It no longer applied. Without a word Markin got to his feet and walked away from the bar.

The men's room was loud with pissing and flushing noises and muted race announcements. It smelled of stale spilled beer, disinfectant, and urine, a pungent mix that reminded him, most specifically, of a basement strip club in Agana called the Love Cave. He tried to push the memory away but it hung stubbornly in the air around him, stinking. On the day he was officially released from the U.S. Naval Hospital, Agana, Guam, he'd drunk himself into a stupor at the Love Cave and tried to place a collect call to Averill Beach. He'd gotten a busy signal three times in twenty minutes before some demon took hold of him there in the odorous hallway near the toilet, convinced him to hook the receiver back in place and fish his dime out of the metal slot, made him turn and stumble back into the clamor of the room. A minute later, sitting at one of the wet plastic tables, pretending to watch the stripper on stage, he put his hands up to his face and wept. A Navy lieutenant came over to sit with him. The man had latched on to him earlier in the evening — he seemed to want desperately to be around someone who'd seen combat in Vietnam — and now he tried, drunkenly, to offer comfort. "Everything happens for a reason, man," the lieutenant kept saying. "It all happens for a reason."

But on that day Markin could see no reason for anything, nothing but cruelty and coincidence. He'd seen dozens of his friends killed, a year of his life ruined; the papers said the Marines were being withdrawn from Vietnam; at home the police were beating up college students. He lowered his head to the table and stayed that way for a long time, this same mix of smells in his nostrils, this same sense of shame in his heart. Three days later he cashed in his plane ticket, stuffed his few possessions into the seabag, and caught a freighter south toward the islands the old sailor had told him about. He had never tried to contact Angela again. He had never allowed himself to cry again — until today. He had never been able to make himself believe that things happened for a reason.

Markin splashed cold water on his face and remembered that he'd forgotten to take his father's car to the garage.

It seemed a very short distance back to the bar. Vysovski had set him up with another round, and Markin understood himself to be at the point where he could either stop drinking, have something to eat and a few Cokes, and end the day bitter and sad but more or less sober — or move on toward more complete oblivion.

"I was thinkin'," Eddie said, bending the program so that only the figures for race four were visible. "Maybe we could send a cab up to Wilson Street, get Mr. M. down here for the last few races."

Markin just shook his head. The race went off and ended in what felt like a few seconds, the cheers and groans seeming only stupid now, child's play. The crowd at the bar thickened. Vysovski kept sneaking glances at him.

"What about the cops?" Markin said, the floodgates open again. "They gave up."

Eddie snorted. "This city runs on connections. You know that, Leo. And all your dad's connections are dead now, or too old to matter." He eyed the fifth-race dogs on the monitor and refolded his program. "You know about Johnny Mario's father, right?"

"He was killed."

"Killed? They machine-gunned him down the beach. Quiet Sunday night, Johnny's dad's gettin' into his Caddy with a spucky san'wich. Some guys pull up alongside with shotguns. Took the city two weeks to clean the bloodstains outa the guttah. People say it was the cops takin' out one a their own."

Vysovski was in front of them again, standing with his palms flat on the sink, weight on his arms. He coughed and glanced over Eddie's head into the crowd but Eddie ignored him.

"I nevah thought I'd say it, Leo, but America's goin' down. The beach is like a war zone some nights, like Roxsberry. Dope like you wooden ba-lieve. Kids don't hardly go there to watch the sub races no more. There's even whores down there now. We're sinkin', pal. You done right to get away."

Vysovski poured himself a shot of Johnnie Walker and wet his lips. "Greates' country on world," he muttered.

"A place you hafta come back to," Eddie agreed, though he'd never left.

Markin gulped his beer, thinking about the submarine races. Along the length of Averill Beach's hurricane wall there were a hundred or so parking spaces, and on Friday and Saturday nights teenage lovers parked there, wriggling and squirming on back seats, unbuttoning blouses and unzipping jeans, feeling the heat, doing the handball shuffle. Watching the sub races. The alcohol was helping now; he could smile at the memories. He glanced at Eddie — who was placing another sizable bet with the usher — and wondered what kinds of odds could be had on finding something to laugh at this afternoon. "Remember Nicky's Christmas party?" Markin said.

Eddie's eyes brightened. Vysovski poured all of them another round. In the near distance a woman cackled drunkenly.

"You punched Richie's toot' out," Eddie said. "Funniest thing I ever seen."

Vysovski had turned his back to them and was waiting for the race to start on the monitor, but Markin knew he was listening.

"Richie put his hand on Angie's ass when he walked by, Angie told him to screw off, you decked him. One, two, tree — the whole thing happened in about two seconds."

"Somebody couldn't stop laughing."

"Wanda Petersen," Eddie said. "My date. She did that after we made it sometimes. Started laughin' and coulden stop. She seen her dog get runned over as a kid."

"I was in the bathroom reading an article about Vietnam. I came out thinking, Bronze Star, Purple Heart. Richie had his hands on Angie and the next thing I knew he was under the table looking for his tooth."

"Which he nevah found. Know how I know?"

"No."

"Your eight-two," Vysovski said, watching the rerun on the monitor.

"Because Angie's brother's girl, Marilyn, picked it up and put it in her bra. I seen her slip it in there between her big cleavage and pick up her drink cool as this." Eddie pantomimed a casual drinker. "Michael said he found the toot' in there that night at the sub races. You should hear him tell the story. He says that was the night he and Marilyn fell in love. He says —"

The usher interrupted Eddie and handed him a thick white envelope with a green greyhound on the flap, the kind, Markin recalled, reserved for winnings of more than five hundred dollars. Eddie's face showed no emotion. He handed the usher two twenties and signaled Vysovski to pour a round for the bar. He pushed the envelope to one side of his beer glass and went on with the story. "Richie's friends wanted revenge. I went over to Joey Manasone and I grabbed his arm like this." Eddie squeezed the edge of the bar between his left thumb and forefinger and Vysovski looked up from his work and said, "Coupla hard guys."

Eddie ignored him. "I says to him, 'Hey, Joey, Dr. DeBonato has hours on Friday nights when he has just boys ovah, know what I mean? Why don't you take Richie down there now and get his mout' fixed. Maybe you could arrange for an exam, too, while you're down there.' Joey was all upset, ready to go afta you for humiliatin' his buddy in public, so I pinched his arm again to get his attention and kinda put my hand behind his neck. 'Joey,' I says, 'take off,' and I made such a ugly face Wanda screamed and made me stop."

"Pig shots," Vysovski said, pouring more beers for them. "Coupla macho men."

"I remember Richie going backwards out the door, yelling at me. 'I'll get you, Markin. I'll get you, you fuck.'"

"He still hasn't gotten you."

They were both wearing broad smiles now, chuckling behind watery eyes.

"Mr. Atlas and Tonto," Vysovski said.

Eddie continued to ignore him. "I've nevah been so happy in my life."

Markin searched for something to add to the story. He wanted to cling to the triumph for a little while, but the brief rush began to stumble. He could feel it wobbling, staggering, threatening to fall flat. It was beginning to seem that there was something wrong with the story now. He recalled what he'd really felt at the end of Nicky's Christmas party, after his friends had stopped clapping him on the back and rehashing the events a dozen times. "Richie is Angie's husband now," he said to no one, and the real sorrow in his voice made Eddie turn his head.

"It's a sin, ain't it?"

Vysovski nodded.

Markin's eyes had come to rest on the white envelope next to Eddie's glass. It reminded him of something he didn't want to be reminded of.

"Your own fault, though, Leo M. She was your girl if you wanted her."

"Thanks, Eddie."

"Not probly what you wanna heah, but you woulda been a hell of a lot bettah for her than that guy she ended up wit'."

Vysovski nodded again without looking at either of them. Markin had the feeling the bartender was carrying on his own private conversation, a buried dialogue that periodically burst through the surface and made contact with the outer world. For a moment, in his own hazy inner world, Markin confused Vysovski with Billy Ollanno. He could almost hear Billy telling him, "And every guy in town is rootin' for her to dump him."

"Mowlen," Eddie said disgustedly. "What kinda name is that? Jewish?"

"Irish," Vysovski said. He looked at Eddie and his thin lips stretched slightly into a kind of smile.

"Alex," Eddie said, raising his big head slowly. "I'll take ovah the bar for a while. You go in the back room someplace and mastabate, okay?"

"Mr. Football," Vysovski countered. "Joe Lineback."

"You play sports in the old country, Alex? Whacha do? See who could stand in line the longest?"

"What you do, Eddie? After football."

Eddie deprived Vysovski of an answer and went on. "The only reason she ever even ended up wit' him was because everybody else knew she was your girl and had the class not to ask her out. Everybody but Mowlen. I always hated that guy. Always. Stevie can't stand him neither."

"I don't know," Markin said, but secretly it was what he wanted.

"Well, I know. I work weekends down there now. I know."

Markin was surprised. Stevie had been a professional boxer. He had never needed any help policing his bar. "I was there the other day," he said.

"Lisa told me. Me and her go out now."

"A good kid," Markin said politely.

"Nice person," Eddie agreed drunkenly. Then, after thinking a minute, he added, "Has a beautiful ass."

Vysovski overfilled a beer cup, cursed softly, and shook the foam from his fingers.

"Now don't get all flustered, Alex," Eddie told him. "Three more races an' you can hop the subway into town, catch the animal act at the Leopard Club."

"No animals, Mr. Football. No Irish broads with freckles."

"Have you ever had a real girlfriend, Alex? Someone you don't pay afterwards?"

"You pay before," Vysovski said.

Markin was trying to ignore Vysovski in the same way he'd pretended to ignore Lisa the morning before at Stevie's. He remembered Vysovski and his father standing at this bar drinking beer, carrying on a sparse conversation in their native tongue, a language that had always made him think of worn machinery shussing and clacking in a dim factory somewhere. Some of the words still clung in his memory, *sobaki, skorost, kharasho,* and beneath his drunkenness he worried Vysovski would finally make eye contact and tell him, "I know who you are. I was your father's friend. I used to see you work here. Lead-out boy. I know you."

Markin pretended to study his program, but the numbers and names made no sense: JC's Darling, Julie's Pride, The Black Flash, King William II, Yesterday's Jester. "Remember Billy Ollanno?" he said to Eddie.

"Billy O. now," Eddie corrected without looking up from his program. "He's tryin' a pretend to be Irish."

"Hah," Vysovski snorted. "Who would wanna pee Irish?"

Eddie looked up solemnly, face full of pity. "I didn't say 'pee Irish,' Alex. I said 'be.' That's a letter in the American alphabet you don't know yet. It comes right after A. You'll get to it soon."

"Hah," Vysovski said. Unable to think of a comeback, he jerked his head toward Markin and declared, "Billy O. is mop."

Markin thought it was Vysovski's idea of a joke, or an insult. He smiled politely and went back to pretending to study his program.

Vysovski tapped a finger on Markin's shoulder. Their eyes met. Behind the thick lenses Vysovki's pupils seemed too small, gray shirt buttons on the pale cloth of his face. "Billy O. is mop now," he repeated, as if it were important for Markin to understand.

Markin glanced at Eddie for help, but Eddie was busy with the usher. "Mop?"

"Mop!" Vysovski told him angrily. "Mop! Mop! . . . Mafia!"

It was a preposterous thing to say. Markin just stared at him, incredulous, then muttered, "You're full of shit, Alex."

Vysovski started speaking in Russian, blubbering and stuttering, trying to get across an urgent point. Markin understood neither the words nor the urgency. He was more drunk than he wanted to be; the day was tragic and ridiculous and somehow completely ordinary all at once.

Eddie was shaking his head sadly, part of the conversation again. Markin turned to him, seeking sanity, a rock to cling to. "Eddie," he said, "Billy's just a kid. He used to play stickball with us."

"Times change, Leo," Eddie said, and Markin was stung by the note of condescension. "I worked at the Leopard for a while. Quit when I found out who owned it. Cesemen brothers. Mob."

Vysovski looked on victoriously.

"But that doesn't mean —"

"Ollanno took a dope rap for them, went to Deer Island for a few months, kept his mout' shut. That's how come he has that job now. That job pays six bills a week."

Two young Oriental men took the stools to Markin's left and Vysovski moved quickly to serve them.

"A place you hafta come back to," Eddie said.

Markin's thoughts were whirling in a sodden spin; his stomach had gone sour. He had never felt much of anything for Billy Ollanno — pity perhaps, the link of common history — but what he had just heard was more than he could bear. The noise and smoke around him suddenly seemed sinister, the whole city seemed infatuated with violence, the worst kind of power. If he didn't get away now he would twist down into the black swamp he'd inhabited years ago, a place where right and wrong got lost in the muck of loyalty.

Eddie put a hand on his arm and Markin looked up. "I have to get out of here, Eddie."

Eddie nodded. "I'll walk ya down to the door." Eddie took his white envelope and they started unsteadily across the open area behind the seats. The floor was littered with discarded tickets, crowded with knots of bettors laughing and sipping beer. Downstairs, at the mouth of the entrance tunnel, Eddie turned to face Markin and they exchanged a handshake. "I hafta tell you, Leo," Eddie said. "Me and every guy in the city wishes he done what you done. Every one of us is jealous."

The rain had ended, leaving the air of the city cool and sweet, sidewalks damp, parked cars pimpled with droplets. Markin felt young, too small for his clothes. Drunk, thoughtless, he walked west as far as Broadway, then north on Edison Street past the stone library and Averill Beach's new, flat-roofed high school, through a part of town called the Farms. He remembered when, as boys, he and his friends had hunted snakes here, roaming the fields, turning over rocks and planks, carrying their writhing brown and green treasures home in mayonnaise jars. Now the fields and sparse woods had been replaced by rows of tract houses, death itself. He walked on, mile after mile, covering all of Averill Beach's northern border on foot, forcing sobriety step by step. On West End Road he stopped in a corner drugstore and bought a ballpoint pen, a postcard of Boston's skyline at night, and a *Picture Book of America's Cities* for Elias. He walked beneath the stone arch of Holy Trinity Cemetery and followed its peaceful avenues, passing block upon block of neat burial plots before stopping at a granite headstone that read MARKIN. Inscribed below in smaller letters was the short list that had once been a family.

> Teresina A.    1915–1956
> Anton A.       1907–
> Leo S.         1949–

Markin squatted, Micronesian style, in front of the grave and called his mother to mind. His memory of her was composed of a dozen or so brief skits, staccato glimpses from seven years when he'd seen and touched her and heard her voice every day, precious fragments rescued from a rubble of forgotten hours. He saw her in the back yard, at the beach, placing a dish of ice cream and peach slices in front of him one day after school. One day! Among one hundred lost weeks.

He tried to imagine her being courted by his father, a man eight years her senior, in the crowded streets of Boston's North End. He pictured her marrying, giving birth, leaving the house on her last morning, a rainy, ordinary October Tuesday, thinking she was only going to Broadway to buy groceries. He wondered if she'd been preoccupied with God's breathing when she stepped onto the trolley tracks that morning, and he thought of the string of coincidences that had brought her to that place at that moment when it might have happened a million different ways.

The Losapans believed in a spirit called Ewo, the spirit of *chapur,* circumstances. Ewo was thought to travel the world at an unimaginable speed, consulting with all the other spirits, scheduling births and deaths and marriages, bringing strangers together and separating lovers, guiding the universe in its colossal and marvelous performance. Nothing, the islanders insisted, was coincidental. To believe in coincidence was to fail to understand the structure of life. It was an offense against the greatest spirit, an invitation to confusion and regret.

He wished peace to his mother's soul, stood, and made his way back toward the cemetery gate. As far as the idea of coincidence was concerned, he would abstain from an opinion. Maybe the Losapans did have a better understanding of the way things worked. Maybe not. It didn't matter. No theory he'd ever heard could make something good of this day.

Near the stone arch he stopped and sat on a bench and wrote Ninake's name on the postcard above the Owen Town address. He paused for a long time, pen poised, trying to decide what it was he had to tell her. Maple trees shook their leaves down around him and he shivered in a cool breeze. He loved this city, but something about the way life was lived here was wrong; it had led too many good people to misery. That something was alive in him. He had traveled ten thousand miles to find out what it was and to kill it. He put the pen to paper and printed his message of hope:

> Ninake,
> I am coming back to marry you.
> Markin

He read the words over a dozen times, folded the postcard in half, pushed it into his shirt pocket, and started back toward Wilson Street.

# 20

IN THE BUSTLING, cluttered neighborhoods that surround downtown Boston the daily business of earning a living was commencing. By seven-thirty the Southeast Expressway was choked with cars, sunlight sparkling from a hundred thousand glass eyes. Commuters clogged the Tobin Bridge, Route 9, and the turnpike, and filled the Sumner Tunnel, all of them eventually spilling into the city, parking their cars, trudging up stairways or riding elevators, and installing themselves in pleasant, mildly claustrophobic, humming offices or small factories or the bright shops along Tremont and Washington and Boylston streets.

Another army of workers arrived on the subway. They swarmed out of dank tunnels and up filthy stairs, a swirling tide. Bodies filled the sidewalks and lobbies and elevators and escalators and stairwells until, one by one, they separated from the crowd and arrived at their places in the world, their small niches in the hive of activity, content to trade another day for a certain sum of money, the sense of belonging and contributing to the world outside themselves.

The same scenario was repeated, on a smaller scale, in places like Averill Beach and Revere, Malden and Medford, Quincy and Watertown; the main streets of twenty or thirty miniature capitals swelled with life.

But a second world existed in the city. Scattered everywhere across the great and small metropolises, the old and infirm and unusual were beginning the same day, only with less movement, their world circumscribed by a few streets or a few rooms, their sense of belonging and contribution long ago having been replaced by the struggle to pass time. They battled shadowy fears and persistent pains and clung to simple, familiar pleasures: a cup of coffee, a warm doorway, a few electronic images on the television screen. The world went on without them and they knew it.

Markin awoke at seven o'clock and lay in bed listening to the traffic noise on Stadium Avenue, feeling cut off from the activity there in a way that would have been impossible on Losapas, where the old and infirm and unusual could not be separated from the rest. He imagined the great being of the city awakening, its blood and breath stirring slowly at first, then shifting into a frenetic and soothing throb, the pulse of a massive body to which he no longer belonged. For a time he wondered what kind of life he might have carved out for himself here had he come home right after the war — where he might have lived, how and with whom, what he might have done for work. But after a few minutes he gave up. It did him no good to think about that now.

Beneath him in the kitchen his father was brewing coffee. The aroma floated up the stairs into his room, bringing with it the memory of a dream he'd just awakened from. He and Louis were sailing toward Losapas through typhoon seas, rising and falling with the troughs and crests of tremendous waves. They had decided to make the twelve-hour trip from the District Center in Louis' boat, the *Pirate*, because Markin had arrived from America a day late and had missed the *Micro Dawn*. As they approached the reef that surrounded Losapas and Ayao, a blurred sun dropped into the ocean behind them, taking with it most of their light, exaggerating the heaves and dips of their voyage. But they did not have far to go now. In the failing twilight they could make out a white mountain of water crashing repeatedly against the reef. At intervals of a few seconds they would rise to the crest of a wave, glimpse the frightening commotion that stood between them and the lagoon, then dive straight down into the trough again. Louis tossed two baited handlines over the stern and said in a calm voice that he would time their arrival on the reef perfectly so that the thrust of a single wave would carry them not only over the coral barrier but through the lagoon and right up onto the landing beach. "Do not worry, Mister," he kept saying. "Do not worry." From a white cupboard in the boat's cabin Markin took a can of American coffee and spooned the grounds carefully into two big mugs. He was searching for the kettle when a wave lifted them clear of the boat, carried them into the lagoon in a roaring white curl, and deposited them like pieces of driftwood on the landing beach.

Markin went into the bathroom and stood under the shower for a long time, thinking about Angie, wondering what she dreamed of, what she thought about in the morning when she first awoke, what pulled her forward into the day, what, if anything, he could do for her now to make up for what he had failed to do before.

Downstairs, his father had put some hard-boiled eggs and toast on the table for him, then gone into the living room to watch TV. Markin ate without appetite. He washed his dish, swept crumbs from the table into his hand and threw them into the sink, straightened the chairs, and realized there was nothing he wanted to do, nowhere he wanted to go. The events of the day before were not finished with him.

He poured himself a second cup of coffee and went out into the back yard. Many years earlier his father and mother had planted fruit trees along all three fences, and now, with the vegetable garden and a small grape arbor taking up most of its middle, the sixty-by-one-hundred-foot lot looked more like a botanical garden than a city back yard. From the bottom of the steps he could see two different kinds of pear trees, two plum trees, the grapevine, an old crabapple tree, a small sour cherry tree and a large bing cherry tree, in the far corner some blueberry bushes which had never produced more than a handful of fruit.

Behind the garden was a bocce court. Markin put his coffee down on the back step and walked over to it, hefting the wooden balls, remembering a time during his adolescence when he'd indulged in something he thought of now as bocce therapy. Whenever he needed to think a problem through and didn't have the time or energy to get to the beach, he'd come out here and walk back and forth in the dust, tossing out the target ball, or *pillino* as Stevie called it, lobbing the lined and unlined balls after it one by one, competing against himself and keeping score. After an hour of these simple, repetitive motions he would stop and sit under the grapevine with a glass of iced coffee. Whatever had been bothering him would have settled out from its attendant confusion. He might not always be able to solve the problem, but at least he could understand its source, see it clear against a spacious moment.

Markin found the *pillino* where his father had left it and tossed it three quarters of the way down the court. Underhand, using a measure of reverse english, he lobbed one of the lined balls after it. The ball described a high arc and fell to the ground, raising a small puff of dust, the reverse spin causing it to skid in place for a fraction of a second before it rolled slowly to a stop an inch from its target. "Now *that's* a shot," he could almost hear his father saying. "But it's only a first shot. It means nothing — the end is what counts." Running a hand through his hair, his father would take his place in the court and move a ball from his left hand to his right, caressing it, tossing it an inch or two into the air and spinning it to get the correct grip, studying the dried-out boards that lined the court, considering the advantages of a bank shot, surveying the pebbles and dust, getting the lay of the land. "Now what I have to do is *botch* it out of there," he would say. "Your first shot was too good, too close. I'll have to break them up."

Markin picked up one of the unlined balls and spun it in his palm, mimicking the small ritual he had seen his father perform a thousand times. Just before he made his shot a movement near the house caught his attention and he turned and saw a face in the kitchen window. His father nodded seriously, as if to say, "You know what you have to do."

Again using an underhand throw, but now with less arc and more english, he sent the ball flying through the air. It smacked the lined ball with a noise that took him back fifteen years in an instant, a quick *thack,* which sent the first ball skittering into the far corner and left the second ball almost exactly in its place, a sliver of light shining between it and the untouched *pillino.* In the window his father's face was creased with a proud smile. Markin waved for him to come out and play a game, but his father shook his head and moved back toward the living room. "I need a little time, Leo," Markin imagined him saying. "I need a day or two to get used to things. *Then* we'll play. *Then* I'll give you a lesson."

Markin needed the time, too, for different reasons. He spent the whole morning pacing the bocce court, studying his shots, keeping score, letting things work themselves out inside him.

By lunchtime not much was clear. The bocce therapy had helped; he could feel the possibility of an answer in the air. Still, he needed time. Outside, in the swirl of the city, things were happening too fast. Coincidences waited there; you had to be ready for whatever might happen.

After lunch he joined his father in front of the television. They sat in the living room surrounded by furniture that had not been moved in twenty years, their backs to a wall covered with fading snapshots from the short time they'd been a family. He could look in the mirror above the TV and see his mother reflected there in a dozen different poses: a pretty, modest, black-haired Italian girl standing beside a young Russian boyfriend with a felt hat on; a bride looking over her shoulder, the train of her wedding dress spread on the floor in a white satin circle; a mother in a long wool skirt holding the hand of a four-year-old boy who wore suspenders and short pants and squinted into the sun.

For over an hour Markin and his father stared at the television together, exchanging hardly a word. They let the commercials come and go, watched people win cars and money and houses full of furniture, allowed themselves to be sedated by the bright colors and clever sound effects and the exaggerated Hollywood personalities. It was just the thing to kill the pain that came from God's mistakes, from things not happening the way they were supposed to happen, again and again and again.

Just after the start of the first soap opera the phone rang. His father lifted the receiver as if it were made of iron, and shifted his knees and neck to speak into it.

"Hello," he said gruffly. "He is. Who? Of course it's me. Of course I'm fine. Why are you such a stranger all this time? What? No, never. I'm cooking for you Sunday dinner. What? What do you mean, you can't come? You have to come. I'm inviting you. I'll call your father and tell him you insulted me and my family. Absolutely."

Part of Markin's attention followed his father's voice, which softened with each phrase until he was practically laughing into the mouthpiece. Markin was astounded. He hadn't heard that tone since the days when there still seemed to be something to live for, since years before he'd announced, in the car on the way home from mass one Sunday, that he was going to enlist in the Marine Corps. He wondered if the old man had a girlfriend he was hiding. But his father handed him the receiver, stretching the cord across his lap, and there was a smile on the stone face. Markin kept one eye on the blond woman on the screen, who was also on the telephone. She was making a threatening call to her lover's ex-wife, and he wanted to see how many of the lines she would stumble over and how many she'd get right.

"Hello?" Markin said into the mouthpiece, watching the blond until he realized it was Angela's voice he was hearing.

"I'm sorry, Leo. I just wanted to talk a little more."

"It's all right," he said, and there was a long pause.

"Your father invited me to dinner Sunday but you can tell him I'm sick or something if you want, if it's bad. I just . . ."

Markin waited, looking down at the faded colors on the carpet between his bare feet. "No, it's all right," he said. "Don't worry about it. He invited you, he meant it." Out of the corner of his eye he saw his father turn his head and scowl. "He's pissed off already." He winked. "You'll offend him." His father reached out a hand and motioned for him to pass the phone but Markin shook his head.

"I can leave the kids with my mother, she won't mind. She likes to see them on Sundays anyway. So does my father." Markin nodded to himself, trying to concentrate on the meaning of the words and not just the voice. "You didn't see him, did you?"

"I couldn't do that yet."

"Okay," she said. "Sunday, then. What time, Leo?" Markin looked up. His father seemed to have anticipated the question. He was holding up one bony finger.

"One," Markin said.

"Okay, one. Bye. Sorry."

"Bye."

He handed the receiver back to his father and, before any questions could be asked, got up and went down the basement steps, turned on the light near the dusty workbench, leaned on it, and tried to think. Through the floor he could hear organ music, then commercials, muted voices. After standing like that for fifteen minutes without one clear, understandable thought, he found a length of clear fir four-by-four in a pile of scraps near the workbench and put it into the vise. There were chisels in a drawer, not sharp, but sharp enough. The hammer was still hanging in its place. Markin picked it up and started chipping away. The wood was softer than what he was used to, and at first he just took chunks out of it, thinking of nothing, until he realized that what the wood wanted to be shaped into was a female torso. He decided to add a face, featureless, just neck and hair and jaw, and he worked on it all afternoon, then surprised himself by taking it upstairs and showing it to his father, who surprised him by saying he liked it.

# 21

THURSDAY broke clear and fine, a mid-September gem. Markin was up at dawn, determined to free himself from the languorous clutches of the previous day. He sat out on the front steps in the damp morning air, watching a neighbor get into her dented Dodge and mutter off to work, listening to the early buses on Stadium Avenue and a pair of chickadees in the willow on his father's front lawn. Around him stood a whole street of miniature kingdoms, their borders guarded by straight rows of trimmed hedge, chain-link and picket fence, brick wall. He let his attention focus on the house directly opposite him — the Mastromarino kingdom — and was reminded of one Saturday afternoon when he and his friends had been playing touch football in the street and had accidentally kicked the ball into Mr. Mastromarino's yard while he was mowing his lawn. Mr. Mastromarino pushed his new gas mower over to the ball, lifted it on two wheels, and let the rotary blade slice the pigskin to ribbons. Without even stopping to turn off the machine, he tossed the remains of the football out onto the sidewalk and went on about his chore, ignoring everyone, protecting his property.

His father said Ernie Mastromarino had retired and moved to Orlando, selling his green bungalow to a middle-aged spinster who worked in Boston, someone nobody knew. The grass was still trimmed around the edges — as it had been for decades — shrubs neat. A young maple tree on the sidewalk caught the morning light like a holy vision, its leaves still and perfect in their last few days of life.

Markin watched the sky behind the house grow pale. By his calculations it was six P.M. in the District Center. It would be twenty degrees warmer there, and louder, the air full of smells. Ninake would be outside her cousins' house in Sapuk, cleaning pots or mending clothes or entertaining children, counting the days until the *Micro Dawn* came back from its trip to the southern atolls and took on passengers for the Losapas run. If he hadn't returned by then, she would take the ship back to the island alone and everyone would think she'd been abandoned again, that the American had sailed back to his home island without her. In small conversations all over Losapas, people would begin speaking of him in the past tense. Belinda or Ulua would make up some ridiculous rumor. Once more Ninake would have to bear the weight of words she would never hear spoken aloud.

His father made a breakfast of scrambled eggs and bacon, and after they'd eaten, he took Markin on a tour of the house, pointing out things he'd purchased with the yearly checks from Micronesia: the new TV, storm door, new tile in the upstairs bathroom, a carpet and lamp in the bedroom. Markin was surprised by this gesture of gratitude and by the warmth in his father's voice. But he still would not allow himself to believe in the possibility of change until his father said something that nearly knocked him over: "I need your help today, Leo, if you're not doing anything. I'm pulling up all the plants in the garden and putting grass seed there for the winter."

"It's early, isn't it?"

"I know it's early. I want to get it done."

They worked in T-shirts in the mild sun, jerking tomato stems out of the ground and tying the poles that had supported them into neat bundles. Markin observed his father closely, but aside from the fact that they were actually working together in the garden, everything seemed normal. His father's arm muscles still showed some definition, he still went about things as he always had, fiercely, as though there were enemies everywhere — in the ground, in the air — everywhere. The attitude was as familiar as the colors of the neighboring houses. As a boy Markin had assumed it was the only way for a man to relate to the outside world: Ernie Mastromarino ripped up footballs; his father growled into the telephone and chopped the earth with his hoe. That was the natural response to a life in which the boss denied you a decent wage, the doctor charged more than you could afford and talked to you as though you were ten years old, the bank weighed you down with car payments, mortgage payments. You had to watch out for criminals, heart attacks, communism, the devil, and door-to-door salesmen. You had to be constantly on your guard to hold on to what little you had, even though, in the end, you were bound to lose all of it anyway.

Over the years this attitude had imprinted itself on his father's good Slavic features, turning the handsome face hard. People were frightened by him. Some of Markin's friends from school thought his father was an old Scrooge until he fed them once, or took them to the beach and paid for every amusement ride they wanted to try. In time Markin had learned to distinguish between the different stony expressions his father's face assumed. He knew the one that said, "I'll never give in; they can't beat me," and the one that said, "This time we did it to them before they could do it to us, the bastards." The fight was ongoing and the outcome inevitable. It was only a question of who was winning or losing a given round.

Today his father was winning. Sweating and grunting, he tramped around the garden in his old clothes, tearing at everything in sight, throwing tomato and pepper plants onto the compost heap, carrying poles and fencing into the small shed to be stored until spring. After lunch they began roughing up the earth with rakes ("scarifying" it, as his father said) to prepare it for a dusting of rye seed. From time to time they'd rest together, Markin going into the house for cold bottles of Coke, the two of them leaning on their rake handles and staring off into the middle distance, victorious but wary, father and son.

At five o'clock, when the air had started to cool and all that remained was the cleanup work, he saw his father bend to pick up a strip of cloth and stop suddenly, then turn and slowly straighten. Markin thought he'd pulled a muscle in his back until he saw the dark stain spreading along the seam of his pants. Markin quickly busied himself with his hoe, turning away, but sensing every move behind him, hearing his father make the slow, disgusted trip up the back steps, hearing the screen door open and slam shut. When he was sure his father was upstairs, Markin dropped the pretense of working, gripped the hoe handle, and brought the blade down hard on an empty Coke bottle, smashing it to pieces.

His father didn't appear for the evening meal. Markin ate leftovers, washed and put away the dishes, swept the kitchen floor, carried the empty trash barrels in from the sidewalk. When he went back inside it was only a few minutes after seven. The thought of watching television was unbearable. He could not find a magazine or fresh newspaper in the house, no books, nothing but a Bible and yesterday's *Herald* for reading matter. On Losapas this was the time of day when people would come together for coffee and singing and storytelling. They would listen to the elders and tease the children, keep boredom away from the house with their laughter, blessedly ignorant of what it felt like to be a captive of loneliness in their own homes. If someone from another island had told them the story of an old man being attacked in front of his house, they would have tilted their heads in puzzlement. What kind of an island could that be? Who would want to live there? What would be done to make things right again?

When he could not bear the clamor of his thoughts any longer, Markin climbed the stairs and tapped on the bedroom door. There was no response. "Pa," he called softly, suspecting his father was awake, lying on the bed and staring up at the ceiling, recalling seventy years' bad luck. "I'm going into town for a while. I'll be home late." He waited, his forehead touching the door. "You all right, Pa?" He paused again. "I'll see you later, okay?"

"Okay, Leo." The steel in his father's voice made Markin set his face. He knew exactly what was going on in the room. He had done it himself hundreds of times, on Parris Island, in Vietnam, in the hospital on Guam, in the District Center before he moved out to Losapas. The old man was slowly turning his thoughts around, getting up off the canvas, serving notice on all comers that he would be ready to fight again in the morning.

Out on the street Markin remembered a Russian drinking toast his father had taught him and Stevie, and he smiled a hard, small smile. "To us," he said aloud, "to hell with them." It was a fitting slogan for the old hometown, the place where a man defined himself by his ability to fight, the place that could turn you into a different person in a matter of days.

Half full with the usual collection of derelicts and teenagers and a few people headed into Boston for the night shift, the train clattered along its old tracks, rushing through what had once been a salt marsh but was now just tufts of tall grass and cattails standing guard over a few polluted inlets. Across the aisle from

Markin sat a woman wearing something resembling a fireman's hat and talking out loud so that everyone in the car kept their eyes away from her. "Sure," she was saying in a pained, hoarse voice, "the governor doesn't give a shit. You don't see *him* at the track. You don't see the mayor there at the two-dollar window. What difference does it make to them? *No* difference, that's what difference."

Suffolk Downs, Orient Heights, Wood Island, Airport. At the Maverick stop, underground, the lights went off for a few seconds while the power was switched from the overhead wire to the third rail. When they came back on, two teenage boys in dungaree jackets had taken the place of the woman in the fireman's hat. The train lurched into motion and one of the boys made his left hand into a fist and punched the metal edge of the seat a few times. Markin watched, unimpressed. He had seen so much adolescent toughness — his own included — ruined on the knifepoint of war that this little display only made him sad, for the teenagers, for himself, for the neighborhoods where they'd grown up. He thought of the initiation rite for ninth-grade boys at Averill Beach High, a kind of low-grade torture called poling. Any freshmen caught on school grounds after the end of classes would be corralled by a yelling mob of upperclassmen, lifted, and held parallel to the ground, face-up. On the count of three the initiate's legs would be spread and he would be rammed balls-first into the basketball upright, then dropped to the ground like a sack of stones.

One of the boys across from Markin caught his eye and smirked. Soon they were both staring at him, puffing themselves up. He stared back, waiting, the sadness in him slowly giving way to anger. He could feel a film of perspiration forming on his hands, a familiar drumbeat in his chest. This had not changed since he'd gone away. These boys did not understand the depth of things, he thought, casually removing his hands from his coat pockets and resting them on his thighs. They didn't realize that he knew exactly where they had come from and where they thought they were going, that he had traveled farther down that road than they ever would, and that, today of all days, with his father lying in his bed contemplating an old age ruined by punks like these, he was not in the mood to take one ounce of shit from anyone.

Nearby, a middle-aged couple stood and walked to the far end of the car, but Markin stayed where he was. Violence was no cure for anything, he told himself, but it was sometimes the sedative of choice.

He could feel himself turning now, the cells inside him jumping with bad energy, and it seemed his metamorphosis was somehow, magically, being felt on the other side of the aisle. As the train slowed, brakes squealing, into a curve, one of the boys turned his head to see which station they were approaching. The other shifted his eyes and took a sudden interest in the back of a woman holding on to one of the hanging metal straps. When the car screeched to a stop he nudged his partner and they got up and swaggered to the door. They stepped out onto the platform and, after the doors were securely closed and the train in motion, offered Markin their middle fingers. He let out a breath and felt the muscles in his arms relax. The poison drained back into his depths, but did not disappear.

He got off at Government Center and, still jittery, walked toward the Common. At Beacon Street he turned right, climbed the rise to the State House, then descended, passing townhouses with wrought iron railings, antique glass, brass plates on the front doors. What a difference five miles made! Behind these walls were art collections and Persian rugs. He imagined closets filled with suits of rich cloth, furs, evening gowns, silk, pearls, cashmere. Around him on the streets he noticed young couples out strolling in the warm evening air, well-dressed, well-educated people who walked as if their lives were wrapped in a protective coating, young fathers who had never been to war and young mothers who had never witnessed anything worse than a cat killing a bluejay on their front lawn, who were never beaten or abandoned, whose parents could walk the streets of Wellesley or Dover or Weston without ever imagining someone behind them with a club. He told himself he preferred even the demons of Averill Beach to that kind of life. And so, naturally, he was drawn away from the comfort of Beacon Hill, pulled as if by instinct down Charles, then along Boylston until he was immersed in the world of rolling neon lights and sidewalk hustlers, drug peddlers and prostitutes, a universe of people who lived without hope, confined to the shivering, bitter moment.

He walked the streets there like a native, comforted by the small tingle of wariness in his hands and the smell of obvious sin. There were, he decided, two people within him. Maybe someday he'd come to terms with that, knit Losapas and Averill Beach together in himself, mix the Marine with the sculptor, find a middle path. It was not going to happen tonight.

Markin had not intended to look for the Leopard Club — he was in no mood to reminisce with Billy Ollanno — but it rose up out of the confusion, proud and sordid, a ten-foot-tall metal woman standing above its entrance, her body outlined in flashing colors, red bulbs blinking alternately at either nipple. In the shelter of the doorway stood a man in a shiny gray suit, a combination doorman, pitchman, and bouncer. Markin recognized the breed from the alleys of Agana: hair slicked straight back; eyes quick; arms, shoulders, and hands in constant, nervous motion.

"Evenin', buddy," the man said. "Girls are waitin' for ya inside." He reached out to shake hands but Markin ignored him and, almost against his own will, stepped into the strobe-lit black velour hallway that hid the dancers from the street. He waited while his eyes adjusted to the dim light, then found a place at the U-shaped bar and sat there, not letting himself think about why he might have come in here or what he might be intending to do, which half of himself was in control tonight.

The bar smelled of burning plastic and spoiled beer and reminded him, sickeningly, of the Love Cave. Scattered on the other stools were a group of ironworkers who looked like they'd been drinking there since the workday ended; a few business-men, paunchy and bespectacled, neckties loose; a junkie who could not stop shaking. Between the legs of the U were the dancers' narrow stage and terraces of liquor bottles. A naked woman in dyed blond hair and spike heels was finishing her act. As the last few bars of grainy rock-and-roll shook the speakers, she bent over and looked at Markin from between her knees, face upside down and contorted. She flung an arm up between her legs, ran a sharp red fingernail down the line of her but-tocks, up across her pubic hair, stuck the tip of the finger in her mouth, stood and turned, tossed her breasts once, then disap-peared through a door at the open end of the bar.

Markin slid off the stool and was starting for the exit, cutting his losses, when he caught sight of Billy Ollanno standing at one of the cash registers, making change. Billy flashed his sixth-grade smile and signaled he'd be right over, and something in the gesture made Markin understand immediately that what Vysovski and Eddie had told him was true. After years of hover-ing good-naturedly around the edges of the action, Billy O. was finally part of it, finally in. Markin felt compelled to stay.

A minute later Billy strutted over and stood in front of him. "Leo," he said, clasping Markin's hand in both of his, like a politician. "Glad you could make it. For my old goombahs from Averill Beach, the first drink is always on the house. What'll it be, pal?"

He asked for a beer and watched Billy move to the other end of the bar to get it. Billy, too, had turned into a different person tonight. He walked differently, talked differently, carried him-self like a quarterback, and almost pulled it off. He was wearing a sport coat with padded shoulders, and he flipped up the metal cooler door, yanked out a beer bottle, and twisted off the cap with the cool gestures of the pro at work.

As Markin watched, fascinated, a woman stepped up to the bar and took a seat beside him. She was several shades darker than the Losapans, over forty, attractive in a tired-looking way. "Hi," she said sweetly. "Buy me a drink?"

"Sure. Why not? What difference does it make?"

"No difference," she said.

Billy served him his beer and winked. "Leo, I'd like for you to meet Suzette, our most intelligent and beautiful hostess."

"Whatever Suzette's drinking," Markin said over the bar.

He watched Billy pour a glass of club soda and notch a section of lime on the rim. "Twelve dollars," Billy said loudly, and Markin saw an old apologetic expression flicker across the large eyes before Billy winked again, leaned very close to him, and said, beneath the bar noise, "Just give me a finnif, Leo, and forget about it."

The music began again, thumping like a heartbeat in the cheap speakers. Suzette sipped her drink with one hand and with the other made small circles on Markin's thigh, scribbling some kind of message there. "Get the hell out of here," he thought the message might be. "Go. Save yourself." But it was just another illusion, strictly business.

"So," she said. "Whereabouts you from?"

"Micronesia," he said. "Losapas. Ever hear of it?"

"I've heard of Micronesia," she said in a matter-of-fact voice that unnerved him. "What do you do there?"

"I fish and I hunt. Do a little sculpture on the side."

"I'm a dance teacher. Hostess on the side." She took another small sip of club soda and began stroking the outside of his thigh with the backs of her fingers. Another dancer, this one fully clothed, mounted the stage.

"What do you hunt?"

"I hunt crabs," Markin said.

Suzette broke out into real laughter. "I'm sure you're very good at it."

"No, I'm not. I don't see well enough in the dark."

She laughed again. "Don't be modest, now."

The woman above them had loosened her shoulder straps

and was holding them cross-armed over her breasts. Suzette's hand was on top of Markin's thigh now, against his hip. He took hold of it, brought it down to his knee, and interlaced their fingers. She blinked and ran her tongue along the lime on her glass. *"Esse lefil-ifil,"* he thought she was saying.

The dancer paraded up and down the walkway, then stopped in front of them and dropped her dress. Billy had come over and joined them again, and he swung his eyes from Suzette to Markin, assessing the relationship. Markin could not bear to look at him.

"I read a lot of travel books on my days off," Suzette said, apropos of nothing. "I take a lot of imaginary trips." She paused and seemed, for just a moment, like a real companion. "What I should probably do is just pack up and go, don't you think, Leo?"

"Exactly," Markin said.

"Leo here lives on an island in the South Pacific," Billy interjected.

"Central Pacific," Suzette corrected.

Markin looked at her closely. This was not a real person; it was some kind of vision, a warning. Suzette could look up into the starless Combat Zone sky on certain nights and see the future there, predict typhoons, deaths, unexpected arrivals. He thought of Woodrow, drinking from a green coconut on the front steps of his hut. The Losapans were right: the world was full of spirits.

"Near Hawaii," Billy said agreeably. "He was a hero in Vietnam."

"Oh?" Suzette said. Markin supposed she had met a great number of heroic veterans. "Did you attend college before the Army?"

"Marines."

"Were you happy in the Marines?"

"I was someone else. Are you happy here?"

"I'm someone else here."

"Leo could of went to college," Billy said proprietarily. "He was smart enough. No one could figure out why he didn't go, or why he never came home from Nam. People thought he might be a MIA. There was a rumor he was dead." Billy was leaning over the bar now, excited at this summation of a decade, grinning proudly. At some point he had poured Suzette another club soda. Markin gave him a twenty-dollar bill and watched it disappear into the cash register. Billy served the businessmen and when he returned he seemed to have forgotten about the change. Markin let him forget. Money was high on a long list of things that meant nothing to him tonight. He could not free his mind of the sound of his father's voice coming through the bedroom door.

Bare-breasted now, wearing only black lace panties, the dancer strutted over to one of the construction workers and let him stuff a bill into the elastic near her crotch. On her left thigh, partially concealed by a dash of powder, were three quarter-size bruises, a constellation of dead blood. She began peeling off the bikini bottom, gyrating her hips in time with the music. Slowly, she brought the black bit of cloth down to her knees, then her ankles, stepped free of it and, after shaking her behind at the businessmen, sashayed upstage. Billy smiled at her approvingly and went to mix another drink. Markin saw what at first appeared to be a fourth bruise, on the dancer's right hip, but as she walked past him again he realized it was a tattoo, a leaping dolphin, not unlike the mangrove sculpture he had made for Ninake. The spirits were tormenting him. He asked Suzette to dance.

"I'd love to," she said. "But it's against the rules."

"Fuck the rules." He pulled her off the stool to a small patch of stained carpet. With exaggerated formality he wrapped an arm around her waist, held their hands palm to palm, and began a clumsy waltz.

"Why didn't you go to college?" she asked, looking at him in a way that made him think of Ninake. There was the same dark-eyed distance, but in Suzette's case there seemed to be nothing mystical about it, no love in it. Markin did not know why he should have expected there to be. He had no idea why he hadn't gone to college. The walls had begun to move in a way that worried him.

"Since you don't want to talk, would you like to go sit at a table for a while?" Suzette gestured with her chin toward the umbrous edges of the room, but before Markin could answer, the slick-haired doorman appeared and pushed between them. "You know better than that, Suzette," he said, exactly as if he were speaking to a disobedient child. He turned his flat eyes on Markin. "*No* dancin' with the girls, Mac. Go siddown and buy her a drink." He made the mistake of emphasizing his words with a slight push.

Viciously, Markin grabbed the man's lapels and slammed him back against the bar. The doorman started to resist, to use his hands, but Markin was pressing two thumbs against his throat, cutting off air and blood and whatever else might be flowing toward that brain.

There was a stir at the tables nearby. The new dancer faltered in the middle of her routine and Billy flew over the bar like an insect and began slapping Markin on the shoulders. "Let him go, Leo. Jesus, will ya? Whattaya tryin' to do? Let go! Let go!"

He let go and turned away. Billy fretted over him and, with a hand on his elbow, guided him back to his seat. "Jesus, Leo, will ya?" he kept saying. "Cool it, man. Effin' A."

Markin pretended Billy was not there.

Suzette had disappeared. Billy made a round of the bar, then returned to his place in front of Markin, shoulders and head forward, fingers drumming nervously near a fresh bottle of beer. "Jesus, Leo," he said. He looked at Markin, then to either side of him, then over his shoulder. "What's goin' on, man? I mean, thanks for comin' to see me an' everything, but Jesus Christ, was you gonna kill him? What if he calls the cops now?" The muscles in Billy's face were twitching and he was sweating a row of droplets above his lip. Behind him, the dancer finished her number to desultory applause. The construction crew had left; two college students had come in and were sipping beers; the junkie nodded as if receiving instructions from his God; the businessmen called loudly for another dancer. Billy pressed his lips together and exhaled through his nose. His pupils twitched, jumping from Markin's left eye to his right, making Markin think of the illuminated metal nipples on the woman above the door and of a B-grade gangster film he'd seen on TV long ago. At this point in the film the bartender lifted a pistol from beneath the bar and shot his customer through the heart.

"I was gonna tell you this before, Leo, but now I don' know. I mean, Jesus, man." Billy looked imploringly into Markin's face and his lower lip trembled. He could not keep the information to himself. "I think I might of found out who did your father, I mean. Somebody local."

It took part of a second for the information to take root in Markin's brain. His body became perfectly still.

"Now listen," Billy said. "Now calm down, Leo." His eyes raced around the bar. "I gotta serve some customers now and I'll be right back. Don't go. Here's another beer. Don't do anything, listen . . ." He was gone and back again in what seemed like the time it took Markin to blink. "Listen, Leo. I can take care of this for ya, okay? I mean, it'll cost you a little, I can't help that. I can't do anything about that, but I know people who can take care of it for ya, whatever you want to do with it, I mean." He looked left and right. Markin had not touched the bottle of beer and had not moved.

Someone in the back room spoke into a loudspeaker: "A-a-and n-now-w, from the beautiful island of Trinidad, for your pleasure and entertainment, the gorgeous and sophisticated *Miss Suzette!*" From the shadowy tables at the edge of the room came a few hits of drunken applause and Suzette stepped onto the walkway, her eyes taking on that glazed look all the dancers seemed to have been taught to wear on stage. She was riding a train across Europe, Markin thought. She was on horse-back in Argentina.

"I got the name just this afternoon."

Markin looked at Billy. The irises were gray, pupils the size of a pencil point. Billy, he realized, thought they were friends. "I don't want the name," he said.

Billy's face jerked back as though it had been slapped. "What?" he said after a minute. "Whattaya mean? That was your *father,* Leo."

Suzette had walked the length of the stage twice and was standing directly behind Billy now, looking straight down at Markin and smiling.

"Effin' A, Leo," Billy said in a stage whisper. "You know what I hadda do ta get this, man? I mean, what's goin' on? Don't you even care?"

He cared. There was a small cold ball of metal in his belly. His mind was perfectly clear, as clear as it had been when he stepped out of the squad bay on the morning of his graduation from boot camp and saw the world of Parris Island sparkling, as clear as it got in Nam sometimes when things were going forward without him and he felt he could concentrate and maybe not be killed, or not concentrate and certainly be killed. "Who was it?" he was about to say, but the words stuck in his throat. Billy was staring at him, ready, and it occurred to him suddenly that if Billy could just once do something that went against the rules of Averill Beach, if he could act *from inside himself* one time, then he would break free of all of it, of the mold, become his own man. For one second Markin considered telling him, freeing Billy O. from his trap, but tonight he could not even free himself.

"Who," he croaked. "Who is it?"

Billy could not suppress a smile. "Well, this isn't a hundred percent, but it's good. I mean, the guy I got it from wasn't there, but he heard some talk down the beach one night, down the Coral Club." Billy gave his waiting customers an obligatory glance over his shoulder, then for once looked Markin straight in the eye. He swallowed. "I think it was Richie Mowlen did your dad," he said. "And some of the other old guys that've been gettin' beat up, too. That's what the word is."

Markin slid off his stool and made for the door, walking fast, hearing Billy shout his name twice behind him. The doorman stepped out of the shadows at his approach and for a moment seemed to consider trying to block the hallway. He went as far as taking a step in Markin's direction, but something, what he could see of Markin's eyes perhaps, caused him to change his mind. He moved aside a few inches, and without a glance or a word Markin brushed past him, went out the door, and turned left onto the sidewalk. He heard a police siren cutting the night and the tapping of his own footsteps, but the sounds were coming to him from far off. He hurried past a movie theater with a poster of a chained, leather-clad woman in its showcase, past a novelty shop offering inflatable companions and vibrators of various sizes and shapes, past a trio of hookers in high boots standing around a lamppost. When he heard the siren approach he slowed his pace instinctively, as if the police might be coming for him already, before he'd done anything, as if they could arrest him and sentence him to prison simply for what he was thinking. The others on the street reacted in a similar way, everyone stepping slowly, inconspicuously out of the light, streetwalkers ducking into doorways, peddlers turning a corner and trying to appear innocently curious. A blue and white patrol car swung onto Washington Street from Stuart and was slowed by a gold Cadillac double-parked there for exactly that purpose. When the patrol car was past him, its impatient siren searing the sidewalks and alleys — headed, he suspected, for the Leopard Club — Markin turned onto Stuart Street and picked up his pace again, going rapidly along a block of dark storefronts like a man running away from a part of himself, trying not to show he was afraid.

# 22

MARKIN HELD the heavy oak door for his father, but he tried to do it casually, passing through the door first, then holding it open behind him and releasing it early so his father could take some of its weight and not feel he was being made into an invalid before his time. Inside, by force of habit, Markin wet his fingertips in the basin of holy water and made the sign of the cross. His father did the same (though he touched the right shoulder before the left, a throwback to his early days in the Russian Orthodox faith), then in a loose parade of other worshipers, they passed quietly through the vestibule and into the smells of the enormous church — candle wax and flowers, incense, perfume — a fragrant and severe mixture that would always be linked in

Markin's mind with death and sacrifice and holiness. Above and behind them the choir sent forth the first words of the opening hymn:

> Father in heaven
> Answer your children
> Who seek to follow
> And live your command.

His father insisted on going up the middle aisle and finding a seat near the front, only a half-dozen rows from the altar. They pulled down the red cushioned kneeler and knelt, lowering their eyes and murmuring at God, then sat quietly for a few minutes, shoulders barely touching, waiting for mass to begin.

St. Lucy's had been built by donations from the first wave of Italian immigrants, and the names of these early benefactors were everywhere — cut into the brown marble behind the altar and the white marble along the side walls, written on plaques beneath the elegant stained glass windows, at each station of the cross, on the dome above the altar. Everything was exactly as Markin remembered it. Two banks of votive candles still stood at either end of the altar rail, silent calls to God, to help or remember or save, burning feebly in the Sunday morning drafts as though at any moment they might flicker a final time and disappear.

There were sixty rows of pews, most of them already filled. In the side aisles, by the confessionals, stretched two short lines of men and women seeking last-minute absolution. Markin remembered riding the bus here on Saturday afternoons, pulling open the big doors, quietly taking his place in those lines with the other sinners. Body by body the lines would shorten, each exit from the confessional marked by the *thunk* of the kneeler and the *tip tap tip* of footsteps echoing toward the altar rail. Finally his turn would come, and he would duck beneath the heavy purple curtain and kneel in the dark cubicle, a window of smoked glass in front of him, the bronze crucifix a few inches from his ear. He would hear the sounds of a murmured confession on the opposite side, then the priest's flat-toned absolution, feel a lifting in his stomach as the glass was pushed to one side and he was confronted with Monsignor Calliselli's silhouette, the dark ear of God.

There was a period early in his adolescence when, after crossing himself and asking the priest's blessing, he would suddenly forget how he'd offended God during the previous week. This became so embarrassing that he took to listing his sins on a piece of notebook paper and studying them as he stood outside the confessional awaiting his turn. During this period also — he must have been twelve or thirteen — he recalled asking his father how soldiers in World War II had been able to make an accurate confession. How could they possibly have known how many men they'd shot, how many people had suffered from the bombs they'd dropped or the ships they'd sunk — how many good people and how many bad, and did the distinction matter?

"All a soldier has to do is tell the priest he's been in the war," his father told him. "The priest knows what to say to God."

It had seemed too easy, even then. Now it seemed ridiculous. What you had done in your life was inside you, a part of you. You could no more atone for it by saying a few sentences to the priest than you could take a knife and cut out your liver or bladder or heart. The best you could hope for was the right mixture of memory and forgetfulness, and the chance to choose your penance.

They stood when the priest appeared. The sacred mystery of the mass began. His father absorbed himself in it completely: he knelt and stood and sat and prayed and even sang with great seriousness, and Markin tried as hard as he could to do the same. He looked at the Christ figure ascending above the altar and, for an hour, asked to be forgiven for what he had done and failed to do, prayed that the great Jatsos, who could make men and women and children grow from his footprints, would keep him from doing what he was thinking of doing, would help get him through this day and this night without doing it, would find for him some doorway of escape from the viciousness that had taken root inside him here and was flowering here again, would show him forgiveness instead of revenge. When it came time for Holy Communion, Markin followed his father to the altar rail and took the host onto his tongue, believing that it might be something other than bread (but even if it wasn't, that bread was enough of a miracle), hoping it would dissolve into his blood and, through some old Catholic magic, rescue him.

Touched with the priest's parting blessing and accompanied by a joyous hymn, they followed a crowd down the center aisle and emerged into the light of the morning. His father seemed rejuvenated. He stood near the front steps for a little while, shaking hands with the other retired ushers and introducing his son Leo, "home from the war." Markin didn't mind. He was happy to let his father show his friends, this one time at least, that he, too, had a child, that his son had not abandoned him. Markin was even able to convince himself that he felt cleaner, just as he'd felt fifteen years before, after a Saturday afternoon confession. For the first time since his strange hour with Billy Ollanno, he was able to consider a punishment for Richie Mowlen that was completely legal and neat and safe, something consistent with the laws of the Commonwealth, not the laws of Averill Beach. He wondered how long the mood would last.

On the way home he and his father stopped for a doughnut and coffee at the corner of Shirley Avenue. Markin insisted on paying, and they sat near the window of the doughnut shop in their good clothes in the thin September light and looked at each other. It was the first time they'd been away from the house together since he'd been back, and to Markin it felt like they were finally seeing each other as others saw them, as whole people. Sitting there among the smells of fresh doughnuts and coffee, surrounded by talk of football and local politics, stacks of Sunday *Globe*s and *Herald*s, and a few small-time Southeast Asian businessmen, they had the kind of moment he had never dared hope for during all his years of absence. For those few seconds, he almost came to believe that the present could change the past.

"I never asked you," his father said, breaking his plain doughnut into three pieces on his plate and dipping the first piece into his coffee, "how you live."

It was true. The short letters his father sent him every five or six months — near his birthday, before Christmas — were composed of local news ("Julia DeFrancese's mother died last week, Leo, and I went to the wake at Rizzo's. They say she had cancer of the lung. Julia said to tell you hello." "They're tearing up the street in front of the house to fix a water pipe. I can't take a bath for two days now and I stink.") and, always, his father's idea of a profession of love ("You're still my son." "If you need anything, tell me."). Never were there questions about Losapas or his life there; the old man never asked why he didn't come home. In return, Markin sent back longer letters, slightly more frequently, in which he'd ask after Stevie or one of his father's old cousins, say something about the weather ("We had a typhoon here last month, Pa. Just like the hurricanes we used to get at home but worse because there's water all around and it gets blown up into the air and soaks everything and brings down the weaker trees."), inquire about his father's health, and close with "Love, Leo." It had never seemed strange to him that his father didn't want to know about Losapas, and he didn't particularly want to tell him. They had always orbited each other at a great distance. As a child, he'd sometimes felt, guiltily, that Stevie was more of a father to him. Stevie would ask about school, and sports, and his girlfriends; his father would tell him to do his homework, come to all his football games, be polite when Markin brought his friends by the house. But it was always at arm's length, as though he were trying too hard not to assume any of what he thought might be a mother's duties. Markin had kept his distance, too, never venturing too close, into the territory that might be a wife's. His father went to work every morning at the General Electric plant in Lynn, came home every night and made his lunch for the next day, and Markin never asked him about work, if he liked or hated his life, whether he ever thought about getting married again. The language they spoke with each other was composed of syllables of silence, but they both understood it perfectly. To a fault, they let each other be.

"Do you have your own house out there?"

"A small one."

"Any snapshots?"

"No."

"What do you do out there, for work?"

"I fish a lot. And I make sculptures, like the one I showed you."

"You're a fisherman?"

"Yes."

"You have a boat?"

"We have a boat but we fish mostly underwater, with spears." With his tanned, calloused hands Markin tried to mimic the movements of spearfishing: he fit the forked end of the spear into the loop of surgical tubing, drew it back, sighted over a knuckle on his clumsy left hand, and fired at a *nilanil* lurking near the coffee machine, but the gestures meant nothing to his father. The old man was staring into him, trying to see his life there, deep in his eyes. "And people buy the sculptures?"

They give me fish and bananas for them, Pa, Markin wanted to say, but he only nodded.

"That's a good living. That's better than welding. Welders get old when they're still young. Almost everyone I worked with at GE is dead, did you know that? Eddie Stefanowich is still alive but he's in a nursing home in Lynn. He has to be connected to a machine every day to breathe. Seventy-six." His father sighed, looked out the window, then back at his son. "So you're happy out there?"

"I'm pretty happy, Pa. I felt bad for not coming back."

How trivial it sounded, he thought. I felt bad. How impossible it was to capture your inner life in words.

His father waved an arm. "That's nothing," he said magnanimously. "Your mother isn't here to see you anyway. I can take care of myself."

"Are you happy, Pa?"

Markin got an angry look for the question. What followed did not surprise him. "I haven't been happy since the last time your mother made me breakfast," his father said. "The day she died."

Markin sipped his coffee. He'd understood long ago that for his father, happiness was forbidden. Being happy would mean, by the strange standards of the old man's life, that he hadn't loved his wife enough; it would be a kind of sin in retrospect. And Markin knew he was not so different. Being happy would somehow mean, by the strange standards of his own life, that what he'd done in Vietnam, and what he'd failed to do afterward, could be forgotten, that it didn't count anymore because a certain amount of time had passed. He watched his father finish his coffee and felt a mysterious kinship with him that had nothing to do with biology. They were Catholics; they had their rules, their strict and distant God, bleeding on his cross forever.

"What would make me happy now," his father said, "is if God called me."

"Don't talk like that, Pa, will you?"

"Why not?"

"You're only seventy. You could live another fifteen or twenty good years."

"But I don't want to, Leo," his father said, and Markin saw that once again the mask had slipped. This was not his father he was talking to now, but another whole person; not even another person, but, almost, himself. He would have reached across the table and hugged the old body there, if either of them liked being hugged.

"You're home now. I've done what I had to do in this life. Except for Stevie and Cammy Panechieso, all my friends are dead. Your mother's gone. Tell me why I shouldn't say I'm ready to see God. Tell me what's left."

"What's left is you're supposed to cook dinner for me and Angie this afternoon."

His father laughed then, a real laugh, a sentence of happiness, something Markin couldn't remember ever hearing from him.

At twenty-five minutes to one Markin was out in the back yard, pacing, trying to cling to the clean feeling of the morning, trying not to think about who Angie was married to or how much she knew or didn't know about what her husband did in his spare time. Stevie had called at noontime, excited as a child, and invited them down to the bar after dinner. Markin couldn't think about that now.

At one-fifteen he heard a car come to a stop in front of the house and his stomach froze. Heading for the back door, he saw the car pull away up the street, and he caught a glimpse of the driver: Marilyn Panechieso, Angie's brother's wife.

He met Angie at the door, his father half an inch behind him. She was wearing new jeans and a cream-colored blouse that looked expensive (a gift from her parents, he told himself). She'd put on a touch of makeup and had brought a small box of chocolates as a gift. It wasn't hard to believe she was the same young woman who had stood in this doorway so many times in the past, and it wasn't so hard for him to welcome her in, make an attempt at an awkward kiss on the cheek. As soon as she walked into the house, his father took over with a real hug. Markin took a step back and Angie stared at him over his father's shoulder, her eyes blue and uncertain, searching his face for his feelings.

In some mysterious way, the interior of the old house absorbed part of the discomfort between them. It had something to do with the smells coming from the kitchen, the pictures on the walls, the backdrop of the parlor rug and chairs. It had something to do with the way his father said her name, "Aahngela," and the way Angie looked, sitting there on the old imitation leather sofa, as if she knew it and it knew her and was trying to help her out here. Markin could feel the human history of the house, which had witnessed its share of troubled moments. It seemed to offer the possibility of peace, a bloom of hope at the end of a hopeless week. Even the hut on Losapas, which he loved, could not do this for him.

For the time being, at least, Markin's father seemed to have put the recent past in its place, made it subservient to an older and better time. He was wearing a suit for the occasion of Angela's visit, and now he smoothed the sleeves and straightened the lapels, as if preparing to be photographed. When they were all seated he stared at Angela for a long moment, until she shifted her weight uncomfortably and let her eyes move around the room — pictures, voiceless images on the TV screen, anywhere but into the old eyes.

"Leo," his father said in his best fake-gruff voice, "get us something to drink, will you?"

Markin took a bottle of anisette from a cupboard below the television and poured three large shots. "*Na zdorovye,*" the old man said. They raised their glasses and drank.

"She's beautiful, isn't she, Leo?" His father beamed. "Just like always."

And she was, Markin thought. In spite of everything, she was still beautiful. Even Richie couldn't take that gift away from her.

"Mr. M., you look exactly the same."

His father drew back his shoulders and tugged at his cuffs. "*Starost nye radost,* the Russians say. It's not fun to get old." He sighed, wrinkled his forehead, smoothed back his white hair with one palm. "You heard what they did to me, Angela, didn't you?"

Angie looked down at the carpet. Markin watched her face and could tell nothing. It was half a minute before she spoke. "I'm sorry, Mr. M. I . . ." She faltered, touched the rim of her glass with one finger, then went on. "You look good, though. You bounced back all right, didn't you?" She shot Markin a one-second look.

"As good as before," his father said, and the strain of the lie seemed to take something out of him. His posture changed slightly, the shoulders sagging, and for a moment he drifted away from them, off into the quiet provinces of age. A metal lid began to tap and rattle in the kitchen, intermittently at first, then with an irregular clamor. Markin heard water splash onto the stove top and hiss. "Are you boiling water, Pa?"

His father frowned and stood up quickly.

"Do you want some help?" Angie asked, placing her glass on the coffee table and getting ready to stand.

"No. Sit here and talk to Leo."

When they were alone Markin studied the sofa just to the left of her right knee and listened to the noises coming from the kitchen: hard pasta sliding from its box into the water and hitting the bottom of the metal pot, the soft bump of a cupboard closing, click of the stove knob. He imagined his father tasting from the worn wooden ladles, stirring, sniffing, stooping to adjust the gas flame. He recalled their Thanksgivings together — it was usually just the two of them, Stevie Palermo, and a twenty-four-pound turkey — his father saying grace, then pausing for a few seconds before picking up his fork. "Look at all the colors," he would say, marveling at his full plate. "Look at all the different colors and shapes." A meal moved him the way a great painting or symphony moved others. Food spoke to his soul.

"My father thinks he's Italian," he said to Angela, to keep the silence from engulfing them.

She smiled someone else's smile. "He cooks like one."

Mr. Markin reappeared once, to hand his son a bottle of Chianti and a corkscrew, then, mercifully soon, he called them to the table and spoke a prayer over the food: "Bless us, O Lord, and these your gifts, which we are about to receive from your bounty, through Christ our Lord, amen."

"It's a feast," Angela said gaily. "It's a beautiful meal, Mr. M."

The old man shook his head and stared at her again. "Angela, you're grown now, you don't have to call me that. You can call me Anton, like Leo does."

This was news to Markin. In almost thirty years, he had not addressed his father by his first name once.

"I don't know if I can get used to that, Mr. M., after all these years —" She stopped and Markin saw her eyes start to fill. This was what he had hoped would not happen. He'd hoped they'd be able to keep away from this. But there was no getting away from it, just as there was no getting away from doing something with the information Billy Ollanno had given him. He was sitting to his father's right, and as the old hands passed him the ziti and bracciole and sauce and stuffed peppers and Italian bread soft as cotton, Markin felt himself wanting to believe in a past that was safe from this kind of pain and these kinds of decisions. He clung to the Sundays of his childhood, the ritual meals here and at the Panechiesos. He recalled tables covered with food, a harmony that reminded him of Losapas, all of it nothing more than an attempt to say, "I know you. I love you. I would sacrifice for you." And now, it seemed to him, they could no longer really say that. The best they could manage was an imitation of those times, a hollow reproduction. He felt his father's hand on his arm. "Eat, Leo. The tomatoes for the sauce are from our garden."

*Our* garden. At the top edge of his vision, Markin could see Angela eating. He tried to picture Richie hitting her, kicking Richie Junior in the balls, striking an old man, *this* old man, in the back of the head. The clearer his imagination drew those scenes, the better Markin understood what it was that he had to do. These were not the Sundays of his childhood. And this was a long way from Losapas.

"My mother says she wants to have you over for dinner some Sunday, Mr. M.," Angie said, and his father nodded. "She says they invited you up twenty times and you always found an excuse."

"I'll go. I'll go next time she asks. I haven't been feeling good lately."

"Since the accident?"

His father pretended not to hear. "Leo can come, too."

"My father wants him to," Angela said, looking across at him. Markin concentrated on swallowing and did not meet her eyes. He and Richie at the dinner table together with her parents, his father, and the kids? They were all playing the game now, making up a better world. It was not the right way.

Angie turned back to his father. "You and Papa used to be best friends," she said. "He was saying that the other day."

"The *best*. We were like this." His father held up two fingers of one hand and pressed them together, and now *his* eyes filled. Markin watched in disbelief. "When he had the sciatica that time, I walked up the hill after work to visit him every day for a month."

"He was just telling me about that. He said you always brought something, cookies or cake or something to drink."

"I did."

"He said he gained thirty pounds that month."

"He was always big anyway." The old man stopped eating for a moment and looked at Angela as if she'd been sitting there beside him for eight years and he hadn't noticed her until this minute. "What happened?" he said.

Markin could not stand it. Thoughts were in the air; he felt compelled to speak them out loud. "I left and I didn't come back. That's what happened."

They both looked at Markin as though they hadn't thought of that. "But you're back now," his father said.

"It's too late now."

Angie lowered her head, and Markin could see the tears dripping onto her blouse. After a minute she stood, touched his father's arm to excuse herself, and went into the bathroom. Markin heard the door close and listened to the water running. His throat was full of food. His father had stopped eating and was holding the wine glass up near his face but not drinking.

"She's married now, Pa," he said when he was able to swallow.

His father didn't look in his direction. "I know that, Leo," he said. "She invited me to the wedding." He kept staring off at the wall, lost in a vision. "That girl," he said finally in a slow, dreamy voice, "is class."

They sank into silence for several minutes, waiting for Angie to come back to the table. Markin's mind was on fire.

"Who did she marry?" his father said abruptly. "I never heard of him."

"Richie Mowlen," Markin said, and he could feel the rest of the words coming out of the hate in his heart, rising up through his chest and throat, rolling along his tongue and stopping just behind his front teeth. He bit down hard and managed to keep himself from saying them. HE WAS THE ONE WHO HIT YOU, PA. I'M GOING TO RUIN HIM.

His father looked at him blankly and said, "What kind of name is that? Irish?"

Markin shrugged. When his father stood and began clearing the table, Markin went to the bathroom door and tapped on it with the tip of one finger. "Ang," he said quietly.

Angela opened the door and came out, and he put his arms around her and pulled her very hard against him, feeling her all along the front of his body, touching the back of her hair with one hand.

"I'm all right, Leo. I'm sorry. I didn't want to . . ." She took a deep breath and stepped back from him. "I'm okay."

Okay or not, it didn't matter now, he wanted to tell her. It was too late. Richie's pathetic little reign of terror was over.

They returned to the table and started in on the green salad, eating more deliberately now, sponging up oil and vinegar with halves of bread slices, sneaking glances at each other.

After the salad course his father set a pot of coffee on the stove, pulled a plate of chocolate eclairs from the refrigerator, and placed them and the box of chocolates in the middle of the table. "I can't, Mr. M.," Angela said. "I'm so full my pants will burst if I eat any more."

"That's all right," his father said. He placed one hand on her forearm. "It's all right, Aahngela. You and Leo go down and visit with Stevie like you were going to, and you come back later on with him and we'll have meatball sandwiches and eclairs and watch TV."

She nodded.

"You think I don't mean it?" he said. "You think I'm just a crazy old man?"

"No," she said. "I just wish I hadn't cried. I just wanted it to be different. You made a special meal, you got eclairs and everything."

"It's all right," Mr. Markin told her again, and he looked at his son to let him know he was telling him, too. "It's better than the worst it could be. We're here today, anyway. That's something. We're eating good food. Some people don't have that."

They sat in his father's car for a few minutes without saying anything. Markin played with the key ring but didn't turn the key. "Do you still want to go?"

"I don't care, Leo," she said. "I'll go if you want to go. I haven't seen Stevie in a long time."

"What about Richie?"

"It doesn't matter. He goes out all day Sunday and comes home late. He won't know the difference."

"What if he shows up at Stevie's?"

She thought about that for a minute, and he imagined she was picturing the scene in different variations, with different endings, designing something she liked. "He'll come and put his hand on my ass," she said, "and you'll knock his other tooth out."

## 23

THEY HADN'T TAKEN two steps beyond the threshold of Stevie's Place before the owner of the establishment was upon them, wrapping Markin in a 260-pound bear hug and twirling him in a clumsy, joyous dance right there between two tables of diners. Stevie couldn't speak. He held Markin's shoulders in his stovepipe biceps and turned him around and around, pressing him against his belly, practically lifting him off the floor. Squeezed against his godfather, arms partway around him, Markin opened his eyes and caught a glimpse of Angela spinning slowly past, her face showing traces of a light he'd seen there long ago, the forgotten shine of happiness.

After a minute Stevie released him, kissed and hugged Angela, then escorted them to the bar. "It's unbelievable to see you two together again," he said, finding his voice. He was beaming. He kept a hand on each of their arms, as if to prevent them from ever separating again. "Everything's on the house. Name your pleasure."

"My father just cooked us one of his dinners," Markin told him. "No way we could eat another bite of anything."

"Then we'll have an after-dinner liqueur to help you digest, and when you've digested I'll make pizza. You have to let me make pizza after all this time, don't you, Leo? You can't come in here and not have pizza."

Stevie's face seemed unable to contain his happiness; his cheeks bunched up, squeezing his eyes to slits and stretching the skin of his jaw and huge neck. The shot glasses looked like thimbles in his hands. Markin wanted to reach across the bar and hug him again, just look at him for an hour or two to make up for lost time.

"This okay?" Stevie said, pointing to a bottle of peppermint schnapps, words spilling out of him. "I called Lisa Friday to see how things were going and she told me you came by. I would have come back right away but I was at a funeral. I called your father this morning from Logan. He tell you?"

"He told me."

"I said if you didn't get your ass down here this afternoon I was going to write your name and telephone all over the men's room wall." Stevie grinned, showing a set of neat false teeth.

"You should have come to the house for dinner."

"He invited me." Stevie shrugged and winked. "I wanted you three to have a little time alone." He turned to Angie. "All these years and you still look like that, Angie," he said. "You still have that sad look in your eyes that makes everyone go crazy for you."

The look in her eyes, Markin thought, went beyond sad. It contained everything a person could feel, misery and joy and hope all held in one moment.

"You really full?" Stevie said, and she nodded. "The old guy can really cook Italian, can't he?" He laughed and patted his belly. "How you think I got like this?" He poured out three shots and raised his glass. "To us!"

There was a loud cheer from the far end of the room. A knot of young men sat in front of the wide-screen TV there, its volume turned up so high Markin could hear the quarterback's signals. In the raucous, beer-drinking group he recognized two or three faces, no one he cared to greet. They saw him, too, saw who he was with. He knew the word would be all over the city by the end of the day and he suspected Angie knew it, too, and had wanted it that way. They would both have to pay a price later on, but this was worth it: just to sit with her and Stevie in this place again was payment enough for whatever might happen.

But then, just as he had with his father an hour earlier, Markin began to feel a pretense clouding the moment. He was barely able to restrain himself from asking Stevie to serve them draft beer in coffee mugs. Stevie would do it. Angie would go along. For two or three hours they would have nothing but smiles for one another, smiles and happy stories before they hugged and kissed goodbye and retreated from the pleasant lie of one another's company.

Once, long ago, Stevie had told Markin the story of how he came to quit boxing. He was old for a boxer, thirty-four, and had been granted a shot at the tenth- or eleventh-ranked heavyweight, a Canadian named Chuvaski, and had beaten him after ten bloody rounds. Not boxing, Stevie had made a point of saying. Fighting. Hand-to-hand combat. A real war. His family and friends threw a party for him at the old dance hall that stood out on the end of Averill Bay pier. For hours people came up to congratulate him. He signed autographs, shook hands, posed for pictures. His manager, Philly Texeira, said they'd get a shot at the title after one more fight. Exhausted, Stevie had left early and walked home along the beach, stopping every quarter of a mile or so to sit on a bench and think. At some point in that slow walk he'd come to the realization that neither he nor anyone else really believed he had a chance of winning the title. It was all a game they were playing, a show. They thought Stevie wanted to hear them say he'd be champ. And he thought they wanted him to go on fighting, for them. A house of cards, he called it, the wrong breed of kindness.

"You're thin, Marine," Stevie said. "Let me see your head. Where was the wound?" Markin pointed to the scar above his ear, and Stevie examined it like a ring physician. "A quarter inch this way and we lost you," he said. "Hear okay?"

"What?"

Stevie laughed and grabbed both Markin's shoulders. "You didn't lose your sense of humor over there anyway."

"Not all of it."

"How's the place look?"

"It looks perfect. I get a good feeling just walking in the door."

The cheeks bunched up again. There was an explosion of groaning and cursing from the crowd near the TV screen, and Markin tried unsuccessfully to keep from turning his eyes in that direction. "Rough bunch," Stevie said. "Two of them are on probation in here. One more incident and out they go. Air freight."

Markin saw Angie's face tighten, felt the present drawing close around them. "What's been happening in AB?" he said to Stevie, knowing the answer but needing to talk, wanting to believe that if he and Angie could just sit here like this and make smalltalk with Stevie for an hour or two the hatred inside him would slowly burn itself out. Maybe afterward they could sit on the hurricane wall if it wasn't too cold, or in the car, and talk about Richie. Maybe, between them, they could come up with some kind of sensible solution: they could go to the state police, or pay someone to break Richie's legs.

Stevie wiped a dishcloth across the bar with an automatic sweep of his arm. "It's changed, Leo," he said, and the sudden bitterness in his voice caught Markin off guard. "It's changed more since you went in the service than in the forty years before. The old-timers are dyin' off, the young kids are movin' out. The best ones don't want to live here now, and I can't blame them."

But Markin saw that he did blame them. To Stevie, moving

away from Averill Beach was a defection worse than any treachery that might have been committed on any other field of battle. A wild shout burst from the end of the room. The circle of men there celebrated the Patriots' touchdown by thumping each other on the back and shouting, "Fuck New York."

"The beach is being taken over by this element." Stevie jerked his thumb in the direction of the screen. "It used to be you could walk the Boulevard on a Friday or Saturday night and the place would be jam-packed with tourists — kids on the amusements, line a mile long in front of Joe and Nemo's. Now all you see is Cambodians digging for polluted clams. And this element. We have our own arsonist down here now — they torched the High Tide last summer, you know, the Escapade about a month ago. The city has its problems."

"Business bad?"

Stevie shrugged and tossed the dishcloth into a sink below the bar. "Not so bad. And I don't care that much anymore, Leo, to tell you the truth. I've already put in my eighty-hour weeks, that's a thing of the past now. I just work enough to keep the place going, not let it run down like the rest of the strip. I've even thought of selling it, to tell you the truth, if I could find the right person." He paused a moment, looked at Markin as if he might be the right person, then went on. "I spend most of my time with my nieces' and nephews' kids, take them to the circus, a ball game, Ice Capades. Once in a while, if there's a good fight in town, I go."

"I saw Eddie."

"Eddie's a good boy. Drinks a little, but a good boy. Still puts flowers on his mother's grave every week. He'll be here any minute." Stevie raised his eyes to the front window and in them, for just a second before the famous smile returned, Markin detected a scar of disappointment. Some unspoken promise, something Stevie had been led to expect from life, seemed not to have been fulfilled.

"Well, Miss Panechieso, you ready for that pizza?"

Angie smiled her sad smile again and Markin could see she

was distracted. Thinking about her children, he guessed, or what was going to happen when Richie found out she was down here with her ex-boyfriend, reliving old times. He wanted to put his hand on her leg but was afraid it might spoil any chance for a real talk later on.

"I could squeeze in maybe half a piece," she said.

Stevie rested two of his scarred, enormous fingers on her arm and brought his face close. "When you smell that smell coming out of the kitchen," he told her, "you'll change your mind. You'll be asking me to make another one."

"I don't know, Stevie."

"You'll be asking me to make the Special." He looked at Markin. "And don't think either of you is leaving here till closing. You're here all night."

"My father invited you back for coffee later on."

"Absolutely, Leo."

"I don't know if I can," Angie said, but Stevie had already turned and gone into the kitchen.

"Ang," Markin said, finding the courage to touch her lightly on the shoulder. "When you have to go, tell me, okay? When you have to get back."

She thought a moment. "We have to go alone someplace and talk, Leo."

"I know."

While Stevie was still in the kitchen, Eddie and Lisa came through the front door. Markin saw them in the large mirror behind the bar and they saw him. Lisa ducked into the coat room. Eddie came to the bar, shook Markin's hand, and kissed Angela on the lips. "Good to see you, Leo M.," he said. "Angie. Good to see you sittin' there together like that. It makes my day. Really. You both awright? You need anythin'?"

"We're okay. Stevie's making us a pizza. We just left my father's."

Eddie searched Markin's face for a moment, then squeezed his arm. "How's he doin'?"

"He had a good day."

"You tell him Eddie O'Malley said we're gonna find the moth-erfucker, Leo. You tell him just like that, okay?" Eddie looked at Angela and smiled. "Gotta go to work," he said. "Stay until closing and we'll talk. We'll drink all night."

Angie tried to smile back at him. Her face was white.

"And don't worry about that guy who's your husband," Eddie said, trying hard to make it sound like a joke, but it was the wrong joke, not a joke at all, and all three of them knew it. "I'll take care of him, don't you worry."

All the smiles were forced now. Eddie was patting Markin on the back, squeezing his arm. "I'm here if you need me," he said.

There was another burst of cheering and swearing from the group watching the game. Someone stood up and stomped his foot. Eddie walked over, said a few quiet words, then took up his position behind them, watching the screen as intently as if he were in uniform and on the field. Stevie returned to the bar while the pizza was baking. He babbled on and on, trying to cram eight years of news into an hour. To Markin, he seemed obsessed with the deterioration of Averill Beach. Even his box-ing anecdotes, which were famous all over the North Shore, took a back seat to stories of boardwalk fires, a notorious drug dealer, prostitutes, botched arrests.

Eventually, as Markin knew they would, when the ice had been broken by talking about things that hurt them, but hurt them less, they got around to the attack on his father.

"I'll tell you," Stevie said, looking at them in turn, "when I heard about it I ran out of here, got in my car, and went eighty over the Mystic Bridge, right through the toll booth. I parked in the red zone at Mass. General. They rushed him to the Mass. General, you knew that, right Leo?"

He nodded, ashamed for not knowing it.

"I went in there and the nurse didn't want to let me see him. She wanted to know if I was family, can you imagine? 'Are *you* family?' I said. 'No,' she said. 'Then I'm going in there,' I told her. 'I'm his boy's godfather. I've known him all my fucking life' — excuse me, Angie. 'You try and stop me,' I said. She called the head doctor, and when he came I told him to go fuck himself — excuse me — and when I saw your old man was gonna make it I promised him right there that I was gonna find the sonsabitches and I was gonna break their arms and legs. I swore it to him." The blood was flowing up into Stevie's cheeks. Markin could feel Stevie's pulse pounding from across the bar; he could feel the words in his own stomach. The name Richie Mowlen rose up into his mouth again, like bile, and it was all he could do to keep himself from puking it onto the bar. What Stevie was saying sounded like what Eddie had said, which sounded like the half-empty threats he'd grown up on. Big talk, they called it then. There was big talk about the commies, about the punks in East Boston or Everett or Chelsea. It was big talk that had sent him to Parris Island, and there had been more big talk there, which had sent him to Da Nang, where the big talk had come from the generals and colonels, and, after a while, only from them. The two punks on the subway were big talk in the flesh. The sad thing about it, he wanted to tell Stevie, was that not enough people ever found out what it led to, or how much worse it was for their sons and daughters than saying "fuck" or "shit" in front of them.

But Markin couldn't hold anything against the man looking at him from the other side of the bar. His godfather had defined courage and love for himself as best he could, had led a life rich in both. The fact that those definitions had turned out to be different from his own was nobody's fault. It was just sad. He represented the old Averill Beach to Stevie, just as Stevie had always represented it to him. They looked at each other and at Angie, they spoke of his father and could not help remembering an older time, which — at least in their lives — had been a better time, and which was now as dead as it could be.

"Pa's doing better now," he told Stevie, masking his thoughts. "We were at church this morning and he was doing okay."

"He looked fine," Angie added. "He looked just like he always looked." She had moved her arm on the bar so that her elbow was touching Markin's.

They were all lying like ex-cons, Markin thought. A house of cards.

"Yeah," Stevie said. "Okay. But nobody his age should have to go through that. Right in front of his own house! What kind of scum would do something like that, tell me, huh? What kind of human being is that?"

Neither of them offered an answer.

Markin found himself thinking about the twelve spirits, a concept that seemed completely out of place in this room. And yet, from another angle, it put everything into perspective. The twelve spirits created circumstances in the world, and the circumstances were there to be learned from. Richard Mowlen was simply the embodiment of a certain kind of evil in his life, a spirit in human form, a question he had to learn to answer. Markin wondered what Mahalis would do with such a spirit, and what he would make of this island.

Proudly, Stevie served his special pizza and each of them started in on a slice. The room grew more restive as dinnertime approached. By five o'clock half the tables were occupied, and Stevie was having to excuse himself every few minutes to check on things in the kitchen. Markin chewed absent-mindedly, feeling torn apart by forces pulling in opposite directions, his attention drawn simultaneously to Angie, the noisy crowd watching the screen, the interrupted conversation with Stevie, the question of Richie Mowlen. In the mirror he watched one unfamiliar face after another come through the door. The men swaggered, holding their arms away from their sides as if cordoning off a bit more territory for their bodies; the women trailed behind, wearing tight jeans, smoking, trying too hard to look tough. The room seethed with tense laughter, and when Lisa accidentally dropped and broke a pitcher, everyone started, then muttered and let out a breath.

When Stevie returned to the bar Markin remembered that he

had been meaning to talk to him about Woodrow's visit. It was Woodrow, after all, who had started all this — at Stevie's urging. Without Woodrow, he never would have thought of coming home. That option had been killed; Woodrow had brought it back to life.

It seemed so strange now, the whole sequence of events. Losapas seemed like a product of his imagination, something unreal, a place he had never lived.

"Your friend found me," Markin said across the bar.

Stevie gave him a strange look.

"Gene Woodrow. He came to the island. We went fishing together. He gave me the message from you."

There was something in Stevie's eyes Markin could not make sense of.

"I wondered if he got out there," Stevie said.

"Didn't he call you?"

Stevie took a dishcloth from the sink and began running it across the edge of the bar. "That was his funeral I just came back from, Leo."

"But Lisa said you were in Wisconsin. My father said Canada."

"Minnesota," Stevie said. "St. Paul. They don't know the difference, Leo." He looked at Angie, folded the dishcloth in half, and smoothed the wrinkles with one scarred hand. "He used to call me and talk about Vietnam. It drove both of us crazy, Vietnam."

Markin did not want to hear this now. His mind was bursting with questions that had no answers. He moved his eyes from Stevie's face to the mirror and saw Richie Mowlen and two of his friends come through the door.

"Every night I had the TV going in here," Stevie said, "and when the news came on I turned it way up so I could see. I kept looking for you over there, Leo. I kept hoping one night I'd see your face on the screen and know you were all right. I still have every letter you wrote. Want to see 'em?"

Markin lost Richie in the mirror, then picked him up again

out of the corner of his right eye. Richie had gone over to the TV screen. It was all very real now, a matter of time. He'd take it second by second.

"And Angie was doing the same thing, weren't you, Ang? Every night on the TV. When I saw the hippies start demonstrating I could've choked them. I wanted to Shanghai all of 'em and send *them* over there. Peace," he said disgustedly. "Peace, my ass. With peace like that . . ."

Markin was nodding, paying no attention. He could feel the blood carrying bad energy to his hands and arms, and he concentrated on trying to control it, to breathe with it. Across his thoughts flashed a picture of his father bending over and stopping, the stain, the slow, defeated walk toward the back steps. He clenched one hand beneath the bar and tried to think of church, of Mahalis. He made himself consider the possibility that Billy Ollanno was full of shit. He was shaking.

"I waited all this time to ask you, Leo. You think God wanted us to do it different over there? I mean —" Stevie stopped in mid-sentence, realizing that Markin was no longer listening. Angela turned to see what was wrong and saw her husband coming across the room. Markin kept his eyes straight ahead.

"Well, hello Angie," Richie said venomously.

It was an evil voice, Markin thought, the voice of a person who hated his life. The sound made his face twitch.

Richie stopped behind him and Angie, facing Stevie across the bar the way Eddie had a few minutes earlier. Stevie fixed him with a look that would have been warning enough for anyone who cared whether he lived or died. In the mirror, Markin could see one side of Richie's body, his shoulder and one arm, held slightly away from the hip like a gunslinger's.

"That's funny, Ang, seein' you down here on a Sunday afternoon after all those times I asked you to come down here with *me*."

"Not once —"

"I thought we were takin' the kids to our mother's for the

afternoon, and here we are." Richie shifted his weight back and forth for a moment. "Ain't that funny."

"Listen —" Stevie said, but he was cut off by another eruption from the crowd in front of the TV screen.

Out of the side of his vision, Markin saw Eddie turn and look at them, and noticed two men break off from the crowd and move toward the bar. He felt as though someone were running a hairbrush along the skin of his back. He made himself wait.

"And who's this you're with? Who don't even turn around to say hi."

Markin counted to three very deliberately, then spoke into the mirror. "I was waiting for you to smack Angie in the back of the head, Richie," he said, low and cool now, all the bad energy running in a neat pipe in his throat so that the words came out as clean as ice. He turned around very slowly and drilled his eyes into Richie's. "That's what you're known for, isn't it?" He waited. Richie widened his eyes in a great, exaggerated gesture of affront. The angry little beads shifted once, to Angie's face, turned mean there for a second, then jumped back to Markin. He raised his arms, palms up, away from his sides. In the cold clear room of his mind, Markin was aware of one voice: Say something, Richie. Just say anything now.

"The war hero finally comes —"

The war hero moved off his stool like a snake striking. In the first second the punch squashed Richie's nose against his face and drew a rush of blood. There were screams from the people seated nearby. Several of them scrambled out of the way. Chairs toppled. Richie bent forward, covering his face in his hands, blood dripping between his fingers, and in second number two the war hero brought one knee up, snapping the square head back, dropping Richie to the floor. Second three and the war hero was on top of him, thumbs in his neck, totally and completely lost to himself, hearing and seeing nothing but the roar of his own upbringing, which could not be strangled silent. Instantly he was knocked flat on the floor beside Richie and covered by layers of bodies, a crushing weight of men. He could not move his arms or legs; he couldn't breathe. Someone was trying to bite him through his sweater and someone else was twisting his left ankle as if to snap it off. Markin jerked his head to one side to take a breath and saw Richie's face, not a foot away, the eyes already swelling, half closed, blood on his cheeks and chin, the nose hideously flattened and bent, and half of one broken tooth embedded in a bloody, shredded lower lip. As the weight above them slowly lessened in a song of grunts and curses, Markin's head was pushed even closer to Richie's, but he made himself keep looking.

Richie was breathing but ruined, and so, Markin thought, was he.

Stevie and Eddie were lifting bodies from the pile and pushing them toward, then through, the open front door. Soon Markin could move his hands a few inches in either direction, but he did nothing with them. Stevie encircled his waist and in one motion picked him up and swung him gently toward the bar. Markin looked for Angela. She was standing in a corner with Lisa, hands over her face. Two men he didn't know were wrestling near the TV screen and someone was shouting, "You fucker. You little prick." Customers were leaving. Eddie stood at the door, making sure none of the ones who'd been fighting got back inside, watching the sidewalk where a couple of minor scuffles continued like aftershocks. The area around the bar looked as though it had been the target of a small bomb. Two of the heavy, marble-topped tables had been tipped over. There was blood and glass and beer and the scattered remains of several pizzas on the floor. Stevie knelt over Richie Mowlen and yelled for Lisa to bring him ice.

Markin made it to the bathroom and vomited into the toilet. He stood at the sink in the cramped room, splashing water on his face over and over and over again, not wanting to have to stop. Finally, his legs would no longer support him. He slid to the floor, crawled to the toilet, and threw up the rest of his father's meal there, then fell back against the door.

He watched his left hand slowly puff up into a grotesque parody of itself. The triangular scar near the wrist, a shrapnel tattoo, went white. He turned the hand over and studied the thinner scar on his palm and a flood of images from Losapas swept over him, unconnected visions: Elias scrambling up a palm tree with his father's machete dangling from his belt; Olapwuch, stoop-shouldered, carrying a string of fish along the beach; Louis's broken smile; Mahalis flashing him some incomprehensible signal, the breadfruit club raised beside his head; Ninake's face turned to him in the darkness of the hut. It seemed then that the world's ordinary dimensions had shifted, tearing him free of perspective and limit. Everything was both perfectly real and pure mirage, a face with faces behind it, a living dream. It seemed at least possible that everything, including what he had just done, was exactly, excruciatingly correct.

His stomach heaved violently, wanting to rid itself of the last drops of the day's poison. After a minute someone knocked on the wooden panel just above his head. "Leo. You all right?"

"I'm okay, Stevie. I need a minute."

"Take two minutes. Someone called the cops. Stay in here till we get rid of them."

"Fuck the cops," he said.

# 24

Stevie had served him two shots of brandy after the police left, so the pain in Markin's hand seemed dull and insignificant. His ear and lips and ankle hurt. Angie said there were two deep fingernail scratches on his forehead, but he refused to look in the rearview mirror, or think at all about the pain, or allow his mind to play back any of the scenes of the afternoon. That was the kind of thing he had to put a stop to immediately or it would go on for years: he'd see the piece of broken tooth in Richie's bloody lip for the rest of his life if he didn't leave it alone now.

Markin glanced across the seat at Angie but she could not face him yet so he turned forward again and stared through the windshield. Darkness was sliding up over the pallid ocean. He watched the color drain out of the world beyond the hurricane wall, his body restless, his mind an empty room with a cold, vicious wind screaming outside the walls, rattling the windows.

After a long time, when darkness had settled in over the Boulevard, Angie spoke. "Now he's really going to do something. Now he's either going to kidnap the kids and run away or try to kill you, or me."

"No he isn't."

"I know him better than you do, Leo."

"He isn't, though. I talked to Eddie on the way out." Markin recounted it without pleasure; it was a matter of fact. "I told him Richie was hitting the kids. I told him to tell Stevie."

Angie sucked in a sharp breath. "What's going to happen?"

"Eddie will go have a talk with him."

"A talk?"

"That's what he told me. 'A little talk.' "

Angie was quiet. She shifted her weight so she was an inch closer to him on the seat and sighed, almost inaudibly. "He was doing other things, you know."

Markin did not look at her or say anything. He'd hoped she would be the one to bring it up, and now that she'd brought it up, he didn't want anything else from her — neither explanations nor apologies.

"You knew it, didn't you, Leo?"

"Yes."

"I was going to tell you when I called your house that day, but when I heard your father's voice I just couldn't." She turned her head and looked out the side window. A car was angle-parked against the wall there, fifty feet away, its windows pale with condensation in the streetlight. The submarine races were on that night. "Do you believe me?"

"Yes."

Thinking about it, Markin felt something stir in the bottom of his stomach, but it was nothing, not anger, only the shadow of anger, a remnant. He put his right arm on the back of the seat and let his fingers dangle near her neck. "I didn't mention that to Eddie," he said, understanding, in that instant, that part of him had been cured. He hated Richie, but he could forgive him, which had to mean that he himself could be forgiven.

"It's funny," Angie said, as if she hadn't heard. "You can go for such a long time doing things and not knowing why you do them."

"Your whole life," he said, and she nodded.

"Then one thing happens that seems to have nothing to do with anything else, and you understand."

More because he needed to be doing something with his hand than because it was cold in the car, Markin turned the key one notch and pushed the heater button to low.

"You make a mistake," he said, "and then you convince yourself it wasn't. You start to think wrong."

He stared at the back of her hair and saw her nod several times, a series of small, carbon-black understandings falling into place one after the other, like dominoes. He let his fingers rest on the top of her shoulder but she didn't turn around. "You have someone over there, don't you, Leo," she said after a time.

"Yes."

Her shoulder muscles sagged. "And you're going back?" She turned finally, holding his arm so that his hand stayed against her neck and looking at him in a way he knew he would never be able to forget. If he could have cut himself in half and answered yes and no, both truthfully, he would have.

"I don't know, Angie. Right now I just don't."

"All right." She thought a moment without taking her eyes off him. "Your father was right. It's better than the worst it could be."

The brandy was beginning to wear off; every time Markin's heart beat he could feel a throbbing pain in his hand and ankle. "He's waiting for us, you know. He has the coffee on and the eclairs and everything. Stevie's coming."

Angie shook her head. "I want to get to my parents' house and tell them before they hear it from somebody else."

"You could call."

"I can't visit now, Leo."

He started the car and, though it meant a delay of ten minutes or so getting her home, drove to the end of the beach, made a U-turn at the traffic circle there, and headed back down the strip, passing the blackened remains of the High Tide Club, then the Coral Club, the Virginia Reel, the row of white clapboard shacks, boarded up now, where in summertime a few people still came to play for stuffed animals and cheap TVs; the Tropics Motel with the concrete palm tree growing out of its roof; places selling pizza and submarine sandwiches, fried dough and stuffed quahogs; the old bowling alley with the sagging roof, where his father and mother had gone on their first date.

Light was pouring from the front windows of Stevie's Place and there were still a few cars out front. Angie looked away as they passed. Tomorrow Markin would call Stevie and ask to meet him at the bar for lunch — perhaps even his father and Eddie would join them. They'd talk about the strange way things happened. He'd offer to pay for the damaged tables and chairs. Stevie would refuse. They'd sit there, eating and drinking and going over the whole sad story of the past ten years, replaying it, altering history until it made perfect sense. It would be understood that Leo had not turned out like them, but that wouldn't matter so much anymore. After a few bourbons, Stevie would tell them about the night he got up off the canvas, his face a slab of raw meat, and beat Chuvaski in the tenth round. From the wreckage of the past they'd build something new and fragile and slightly better.

The Boulevard ended in a dark stretch of three-story brick apartment buildings and a vacant lot where Markin could see white sheets of paper floating in the east wind like the hands of ghosts. A stocky man in an old-fashioned felt hat and running shoes was making a diagonal crossing of the dirt lot there, headed for Ocean Avenue, stepping cautiously through the litter as though it might be booby-trapped. A white Cadillac Seville was parked at the curb with its motor running; a woman in a tight skirt was standing on the sidewalk next to it, leaning in the front window.

Mountain Avenue, where Angela's parents lived, was quiet, even for a Sunday night. Both curbstones were lined with cars, bumper to bumper, and the picture windows were all bright with the light from living room lamps. Family life in Averill Beach, Markin thought as he drove past, a thing he had never really known and never would know.

As they approached the Panechiesos' house, Angie sidled over to him on the seat, and when he stopped the car she put her hand on his arm and they kissed like teenagers, as if there were nothing beyond that they were allowed to do. Her tongue tasted of smoke. "You made my father happy," he told her.

"You owe me in that department."

"I'm sorry about Richie," he said, just to be saying something, to keep her there another minute.

"No you're not," she said. "And neither am I."

Getting out of the car, she smiled at him and he tried to smile back.

He parked the Pontiac in the driveway and sat for a few seconds, watching the light from the television screen flicker on the curtains of the living room windows, deciding what, if anything, he was going to say to his father.

He got out, opened the gate, limped along the flagstone walk and up the back steps. Just as he'd imagined, sat a coffeepot on the stove, low heat, and the table had been set. If he opened the refrigerator, he'd see a plate of chocolate-covered eclairs and more meatball sandwiches than four people could eat in a week.

From the living room came the sound of the Sunday evening wildlife show his father had always loved. Judging by the voice, the commentator was the same thin, white-haired man whose name Markin could never remember, the same one who'd been doing the show for twenty years. He walked toward the voice, calling, "Hi, Pa," as he went, preparing himself for the questions about the cuts on his face and the hand, which was almost twice its normal size now and hurt the way it had hurt all those months on Guam. He still didn't know what he was going to say.

His father failed to answer, and Markin thought he was asleep until he saw the open mouth and the clouded eyes. For a very small part of one second he stood there refusing to believe it. For that instant, every fiber of him tried to take what was and change it into what he wanted it to be. He felt his father's wrist — still slightly warm — then the throat and lips, then he knelt and rested his forehead on his father's thigh and cried the way he hadn't cried in twenty years, sobbing quietly against the thin leg, which would turn harder now with every second, the life that had been in it floating off somewhere no one knew about. Everything happened for a reason, he told himself, but the reason was not something you could ever know. It was like a note being sung just beyond the range of the human ear, a sad and magical tune, beyond goodness, beyond thought, implying but not promising forgiveness, requiring the most brutal, stubborn kind of faith. He made himself raise his head and look into his father's face, not as stern now as it had had to be in life. There would be no enemies now. Markin took his good hand and ran it along the stiff, wrinkled cheek.

# 25

HE WAS NOT going to hide any part of himself from anyone anymore. Whoever came through the door he would face, talk to. He'd watch them to see whether they'd heard about the trouble at Stevie's, whether they judged him for leaving his father alone all those years, for not marrying Angela, but it wouldn't matter in the same way it had mattered before. For reasons he did not understand, he was free of that now. He was what he was.

Stevie stood with him near the casket so he wouldn't have to stand there alone. From time to time he'd feel a big hand on his shoulder, or Stevie would step into the lobby and return with a cup of water for him, or they'd exchange a word or two about one of the visitors. But for the most part they were quiet with each other. He'd called Stevie even before he'd called the undertaker. While the body was being carried out of the house, they'd accompanied the stretcher down the steps, each with a hand on one of his father's arms, each making his own private farewell.

Rizzo's Funeral Parlor had been remodeled since the last time Markin had been there, for the wake of his uncle Leo. A plush maroon carpet covered the floor. The woodwork shone. But in spite of the changes the room remained eerily familiar to him, a dreamscape. There was a bank of floral arrangements behind him, rows of gray metal folding chairs in front, the polished casket with his father's body to his right. Almost continuously during the two-hour evening session, people stepped through the door into the hushed room, approached the coffin, and knelt there, heads bowed, hands folded. Some of them reached out to touch his father's arm or forehead before they made the sign of the cross and stood and came over to Markin and told him they'd known his father all their life, or worked with him, or were related to him through marriage; they said what a good welder he'd been, what a good friend, what a generous person. What a shock, they all said. What a shock. Markin listened carefully to all of it, letting it fill in some of the empty space he felt inside him, knowing that nothing could ever again fill it entirely. Part of his life was lying there in the coffin, hard as stone, and would be buried in the ground tomorrow. What he would have in its place were these kind words, memories, the house, the photos, a plot of land in Holy Trinity. He would have the fact that he had come home — late perhaps, but he had come back.

Just after eight o'clock Angela arrived. She had Richie Junior with her, the boy dressed up in his first-day-of-school outfit, looking angry when he didn't intend to. They knelt at the coffin for a minute, then came over to him. Angie's eyes were full of tears. She kissed and hugged him and introduced her boy, Richard Mowlen Junior. Markin could not help but think of the day he and his father had knelt at his mother's coffin in this same room; he could not look at Richie Junior, uncomfortable in his new clothes, without wondering what would become of him, what dreams would sleep in his memory for twenty years, then come back to haunt him. Angie smiled down at her son and smoothed the hair away from his eyes, and Markin hoped that that frail love would be enough to carry the boy through. "My mother and Marilyn and I cooked some things in case people come by the house later," Angie said, looking at him just the way she had looked at him over his father's shoulder three days before, searching his face for his feelings. "We'll bring them down about nine or a little after. Will you be back by then?"

He nodded, reached out and took her hand, and stood there for several minutes, unable to get any words to come out of his mouth, not caring at all that people were waiting to express their condolences, or that Richie Junior was staring at him, wondering about this stranger holding his mother's hand and looking into her eyes, squeezing her fingers.

After a while Angela hugged him again, kissed Stevie, then went to sit with some friends. Markin lost sight of her among a rush of mourners waiting to shake his hand and say a few more words about his father. Eddie appeared at the end of the short line, head and shoulders above everyone else, his neck pinched in the white shirt collar so that his face was pink. He knelt at the casket for a long time and Markin saw that he was crying. A minute passed and Eddie was hugging him, breathing whiskey on him, then standing next to Stevie and looking out into the room, silent as a mountain. Billy Ollanno made an appearance, too, dressed in a black silk suit, a lavender shirt, and no tie, his eyes bouncing around the room, taking in all the faces, a chamber of mirrors. He stood before the coffin with his hands crossed in front of him, staring, then genuflected twice and approached Markin, Stevie, and Eddie. "Jesus, Leo," he said. "Jesus Christ, man, I'm sorry. I really am." And Markin saw that he was. Even Eddie saw it; he shook Billy's hand as though they were friends.

Markin asked Billy to stand with them near the floral arrangements, and Billy tightened his lips, trying to look the way he was supposed to look, then took his place beside Eddie, lost in his shadow, shoulders back, chin up, red eyes more or less steady.

Markin was exhausted by the consolation. He hadn't slept at all the night before. He'd paced the house and the back yard and walked up and down the dark streets of the neighborhood. Every few minutes now he'd glance over at his father's face, trying to fix it in his memory, trying to take in, for the hundredth time in his life, the mystery of it. On Sunday his father had been here; now he was not. It was as simple as the sun rising and setting every day. It was as ordinary and as magical as breathing. All you could do was make yourself pay attention and try not to be afraid.

At a quarter to nine, when the stream of visitors had slowed to a trickle and Rizzo's employees were visible in the entryway, going about the business of closing shop for the night, Markin saw Carmine Panechieso step in off the street. He, too, like Eddie and Stevie, was dressed in a suit that seemed unable to contain him. It stifled something in him, made his hands and neck look big and red, made his walk the walk of a timid man, something he had never been. He knelt at the coffin and stared into Anton Markin's face as if seeing himself there, and Markin could tell he was saying something under his breath, his eyebrows and lips twitching with the effort. For what seemed like ten minutes he remained by the casket, carrying on his quiet conversation, an elderly couple waiting behind him at a respectful distance, the funeral home manager watching from the foyer. Finally, he leaned over and planted a kiss on the frozen forehead.

"Leo."

Markin took his hand and looked straight into his eyes, but he could not make his voice work. Beside him, Eddie, Stevie, and Billy turned away slightly, moved half a step toward the wall, and shifted one shoulder to give him a private moment.

"I'm sorry, Leo. I'm sorry about everything."

"Cammy" was all he could manage to say.

"Angie told me everything and I just wanted you to know

she's leaving him. She's living with us now for the time being and it's all gonna be for the best. Everything but your father. Everything but him." Mr. Panechieso's face twitched again and he stopped for a moment, swallowed, glanced at Stevie and then back at Markin, hoping he wouldn't have to look for more words.

"Cammy," Markin said, then stopped. It wasn't a question of not knowing what he wanted to say. At some point during the sleepless night he'd sat in the dark living room, in the chair where his father had died, and gone over everything a thousand times to make sure he had it right. There was really only one path to take now, only one way that finished things instead of starting them all over again. Once he'd understood that, the rest fell into place almost as if it had all been planned out long before he'd ever left home. All the coincidences suddenly seemed meaningful; Mahalis' perplexing hints took on the tone of the voice of fate; even the pain seemed to be worth something, to hold in it some reason, at least the possibility of logic. He looked at Carmine Panechieso's face and saw the years etched plainly there around the mouth and eyes. There was the past and there was the future, obvious to anyone who wanted to look. "My father left me the house," he said in someone else's voice.

"Of course, Leo."

"I'm giving it to Angie."

# PART FOUR

# 26

IT WAS DUSK in Owen Town, the hour when a cool breeze rose up over the ocean like God's tired hand and came ashore, chasing off the flies and mosquitoes, bathing the island with a lush peace that could not be found in the pounding heat of midday. Downtown, shop owners were closing their doors. A small fleet of government cars abandoned the parking lot behind the municipal office building, and children walked barefoot in the dusty roads, swinging strings of fish and breaking out in dance steps that followed a song no one else could hear.

At the southern end of the island, far from the civilization of the city, the families of Sapuk gathered around cookfires or sat in doorways, eating with their fingers and telling stories in a quiet evening voice. Just before the sky lost the last of its color, their meal was interrupted by a muffled roar. They looked up. There, over Etal already, went the *chet,* a silvery toy that meant little to them and changed their lives by the day.

A few minutes after the 727 lifted off from the dusty runway, the airport was shrouded in a sweet darkness. Those passengers who remained near the chain-link fence soon vanished into taxis and were carried off down somnolent streets. A coconut rat scuttled out from beneath the customs shed and sniffed in quick circles on the coral. Along the road to Sapuk a car engine backfired, stirring in Markin what seemed now an ancient memory.

A taxi driver called to him, but he chose to walk. Seven years earlier he had walked this same dark road, seabag on his shoulder, a scared and skinny visitor pushing himself forward through the dark alleys of doubt. Now he was not searching. He knew where he was going; it was just a question of how he would get there.

Beyond the Harbor View restaurant, at the end of a littered dirt path lit by a far-off streetlight, a series of four wooden piers jutted out into the filthy harbor. It was an unofficial marina. At some point after World War II, the poorer local fishermen had simply laid claim to the area, built piers, and tied up a few dozen boats there. Markin stopped at the foot of the first pier and put his seabag down. In spite of the sea breeze, the air around him was unbelievably foul, a mix of raw sewage, rotting fish, and mudflat, a stench like death. He walked through the thick air and, after a brief search, located Louis' *Pirate.* The outrigger canoe was lashed to the stern and looked like it had been washed aboard by a rogue wave. Except for the straining of ropes and a quiet slapping of waves Markin heard nothing, saw no one. He tossed his seabag aboard the *Pirate* and set off in search of its captain.

The Wharf Bar and Lounge was already half filled, some of the men shirtless, a few already drunk on yeast liquor or Philippine beer. From the kitchen came the smell of frying fish.

Markin ordered a bottle of beer and a plate of tuna and made his inquiries. Yes, the girl from Losapas had taken the ship. The ship had left on time, in spite of the approaching typhoon. The radio said the typhoon was twisting through the Westerns, headed northeast. Smell that wind?

Louis, he was told, was definitely on the island. He had been seen in town just that afternoon. He might appear at the bar tonight or he might not; he might be sleeping at his own house or at Samwen's house or at one of his ex-wives' houses; he could be at the movie . . . Within an hour every seat in the room was occupied, but there was no sign of Louis. People jostled Markin as they came and went with their drinks. Someone in the corner was shouting out an open window, warning about the typhoon, then laughing hysterically. The island men could not hold their liquor. From what Louis had said, there were bad fights in town almost every night, sometimes a machete murder — once in a while, rarely, a rape.

None of that mattered to Markin now. He ignored the noise around him — shouts, chairs scraping the floor, a scuffle near the door, the Japanese pop tunes on the radio, a bottle breaking. He was thinking of Stevie standing out in front of Rizzo's Funeral Parlor in the middle of the night with a question stamped on his big face: why? Markin had wanted to tell him not to ask.

He paid for his meal, pushed his way out the door, and stood on the edge of the road for a minute, listening to the wind moving through the trees near the shoreline and someone pissing against the metal wall of the building. He flagged down one of the pickup-truck taxis cruising the strip and offered the driver five dollars — ten times the normal fare — to take him down the treacherous road to Sapuk. The driver took off before anyone else could climb in, and Markin stood alone in the truck bed, holding on to the roof as the taxi bounced away from the city.

There were streetlights for the first mile, as far as Monoluk, then the road turned completely dark and wound like a snake along the shoreline, slithering between metal boat shacks and outhouses and small bays on his left, and the steep, black, tree-covered hillside on his right. Where he could — where he knew the road to be reasonably straight and solid — the driver sped along as though he expected bandits to leap out of the jungle and steal his five dollars. But most of the time he had to slow to five miles an hour, ford huge puddles, swerve around stones and tree branches. Markin was tired from the long flight, and the fish dinner was not sitting well in his stomach. Somewhere near Tunnuk it occurred to him that sailing to Losapas in a boat the size of the *Pirate,* with a typhoon threatening from the west, was a journey no sane person would attempt.

At the edge of Sapuk village, the driver stopped to let him jump out, then spun around in the dirt and raced back toward town. Markin began walking, tripped on an invisible stone, and fell on his hands. He got up and started forward again, stumbled, caught himself before he fell, cursed. Somewhere in the darkness ahead of him a dog started howling. The sound lofted into the hills behind the village, a place where no one lived, where men went only to harvest their breadfruit and banana trees. More dogs joined in. Markin thought he could smell them. He could smell *apwut* fermenting, wet foliage rotting, drying copra, the shoreline *benjos.* It was the aroma of Micronesia, and the richness of it penetrated his tiredness deep, like welcome.

At last he came upon a house set into the hillside, completely surrounded by trees. In the starlight he could make out the corrugated iron roof, the rusting fifty-five-gallon water barrel out front, plywood sheets covering the window holes to keep out mosquitoes and Sapuk's huge flying beetles. A soft, steady wind moved the treetops. From the house came a woman's voice, and then the laugh that was famous all over the district.

As quietly as he could, Markin stepped across the front yard and lay down in a pile of green palm fronds that had been cut and left to dry. Above him clouds slipped across the sky, covering and revealing a field of flickering stars. A vision came to him.

He was lying on the pandanus mat in his typhoon hut. Ninake came into the room and lay beside him, and in a moment they started making love, very slowly, very gently, with the unspoken intention that this time they were creating a child. He could feel the texture of her skin. He could smell her. She was whispering something in his ear, and her words and the pressing and twisting of her body soothed him in a way he needed to be soothed right now. He needed to hear that language.

Sapuk seemed full of a wonderful mystery at that hour. Markin could sense it in the darkness near the house, a fragrant swelling and chirring, as though the jungle were breathing peacefully in sleep. For a little while, before exhaustion overcame him, he lay in the living starlight and tried to think of names for his children.

## *Epilogue*

LONG AFTER the other men had stopped working and gone home, Mahalis was still at the taro bog, painstakingly fortifying an earthen wall the men had built in case the lagoon rose high enough to flood mid-island. Late into the afternoon he worked, barefoot, driving his hoe into the thick, mucky soil, carving out a series of drainage trenches, packing the levee as high as he could in the time he had. Only a very bad typhoon would bring the sea this far inland, and a very bad typhoon would mean the ruin of boats and houses and coconut trees; it would strip the island of half its foliage, spoil Ayao's fruit crop, change the shape of the landing beach and some of the fishing grounds, foul the wells. The radio was typically vague. Ida, the reports said, would make landfall somewhere in the Westerns or Northerns sometime between six P.M. and midnight — unless the wind shifted unexpectedly, in which case she would move west toward Yap and touch Losapas only with a few breaths of high wind.

All day the men had been asking Mahalis what would happen, and all day he had been unable to tell them.

He stopped working now and looked once again for signs. The papaya tree was an angry woman shaking her hair, its fruit swaying side to side, its leaves flying up in anxious fits. Losapas' coconut palms appeared to be making welcoming nods at the storm, receiving it as a guest, the way the islanders had received the Japanese soldiers that first morning, before they knew better. From time to time the banana leaves would shiver violently, then settle back, nervous and tattered, into place.

Mahalis shook his head, said a short prayer to Jatsos, a few words to Alali, the wind spirit, made a final inspection of the levee, and started down the path toward home.

The excited air made him think of the day Markin's uncle Gene had visited. He took the red knife — a gift from a Merikan starman — out of his pocket and spent a moment toying with the various accessories and examining the odd insignia before he continued along the path, sniffing the air for rain, wondering if Markin would ever return and take up residence again in the empty hut. Ninake had been home three days and could not eat or sleep. Elias hardly spoke.

At the end of the path, just as he came in sight of the water tank and the trembling thatched shelter, Mahalis stopped abruptly and looked around him. He examined the writhing sky and the excited surface of the lagoon. He listened. He ran his eyes back and forth across the horizon where a faint gray light was fading. He checked the inlet, the big breadfruit tree on Ayao. The spirits were discussing something, almost arguing.

Suddenly he understood it. He dropped his hoe and made for his house as fast as he could go. Autei, Elias' friend, was playing alone in the clearing near Markin's hut. "Where are you going, Mahalis?" the boy cried out, startled at seeing a grown man run.